"I want *you*..." Kate chal...

W9-CBE-714

"But *why*, Katherine, *why* do you suddenly want me so much?" Edmund asked.

"Because…" She almost let something betraying slip out, but stopped herself just in time, just as she always had when it came to her feelings for him.

"Because I'm irresistible? Because I make your world shift and brighten whenever I come into the room? Or is it just because I'm the first man to get past your ice-queen defenses and make you feel the possibilities of being a real woman?" he pressed.

"I really can't imagine," she said with a superb attempt at frosty dignity.

"Oh, I think you can, Kate," he murmured.

"So you can prove to me I'm just a foolish woman like any other you might care to kiss in the dark? I think you just did that," she said quietly.

"If that was all I wanted, I could have done it perfectly well three years ago and got it out of the way," he said flatly.

"Arrogant, boasting braggart that you are?"

"Adult, realistic man that I am now," he corrected.

* * *

One Final Season
Harlequin® Historical #311—July 2011

ELIZABETH BEACON

lives in the beautiful English west country, and is finally putting her insatiable curiosity about the past to good use. Over the years Elizabeth has worked in her family's horticultural business, become a mature student, qualified as an English teacher, worked as a secretary and, briefly, tried to be a civil servant. She is now happily ensconced behind her computer, when not trying to exhaust her bouncy rescue dog with as many walks as the inexhaustible lurcher can finagle. Elizabeth can't bring herself to call researching the wonderfully diverse, scandalous Regency period and creating charismatic heroes and feisty heroines work, and she is waiting for someone to find out how much fun she is having and tell her to stop it.

One Final Season

ELIZABETH BEACON

TORONTO NEW YORK LONDON
AMSTERDAM PARIS SYDNEY HAMBURG
STOCKHOLM ATHENS TOKYO MILAN MADRID
PRAGUE WARSAW BUDAPEST AUCKLAND

If you purchased this book without a cover you should be aware that this book is stolen property. It was reported as "unsold and destroyed" to the publisher, and neither the author nor the publisher has received any payment for this "stripped book."

Recycling programs
for this product may
not exist in your area.

ISBN-13: 978-0-373-30620-6

ONE FINAL SEASON

Copyright © 2011 by Elizabeth Beacon

All rights reserved. Except for use in any review, the reproduction or utilization of this work in whole or in part in any form by any electronic, mechanical or other means, now known or hereafter invented, including xerography, photocopying and recording, or in any information storage or retrieval system, is forbidden without the written permission of the publisher, Harlequin Enterprises Limited, 225 Duncan Mill Road, Don Mills, Ontario, Canada M3B 3K9.

This is a work of fiction. Names, characters, places and incidents are either the product of the author's imagination or are used fictitiously, and any resemblance to actual persons, living or dead, business establishments, events or locales is entirely coincidental.

This edition published by arrangement with Harlequin Books S.A.

For questions and comments about the quality of this book please contact us at Customer_eCare@Harlequin.ca.

® and TM are trademarks of the publisher. Trademarks indicated with ® are registered in the United States Patent and Trademark Office, the Canadian Trade Marks Office and in other countries.

www.Harlequin.com

Printed in U.S.A.

Did you know that some of these novels are also available as ebooks? Visit www.Harlequin.com

Author Note

Welcome to *One Final Season*, the story of Miss Katherine Alstone and handsome, disillusioned Viscount Shuttleworth, in London to find a suitable wife as unlike the heartless beauty who carelessly dismissed him three years ago as she can be. While Kate's story stands alone, her elder sister was featured in *A Less Than Perfect Lady*, and Kate also appeared in *Rebellious Rake, Innocent Governess*. By the end of that book, I knew Kate must have her own story one day.

The passionate, argumentative Alstone family have been special to me from the moment they sprang to life on the page, so I hope you like reading prickly, loyal Kate's love story as much as I did writing it. And, as for Edmund, Lord Shuttleworth, I'll leave you to judge if he's worth enduring one final season for!

Chapter One

'Lord Shuttleworth!' Eiliane, the Marchioness of Pemberley and formerly Lady Rhys, exclaimed as she recognised with unaffected delight the vigorous young gentleman strolling towards them across Lady Finchley's ballroom. 'What a pleasure to see you again; it seems such an age since I saw you that I hardly recognised you.'

'I would have known you anywhere, my lady, and must offer my belated congratulations on your remarriage,' the most desirable viscount currently on the marriage mart replied easily, whilst briefly eyeing the lady at Eiliane Pemberley's side as if trying to place her. 'Miss Alstone, I trust you are well?'

'Very well indeed, I thank you, my lord,' Kate Alstone replied coolly, for if he hoped to fluster her by watching her with frost and mockery in his grey-green eyes he was doomed to disappointment.

'Nonsense,' Eiliane swept on, as if she had no idea

Kate and Lord Shuttleworth had the least reason to be awkward together and were being over-polite out of sheer perversity. 'You sent a very proper letter and a handsome present, one I didn't have to consign to the back parlour for my own peace of mind, either, in case it gave me nightmares. You should see the epergne my new sister-in-law chose, probably for that purpose! Kate saw it—isn't it a horror, my dear?'

'Indeed it is, but perhaps we'd better not let her know we said so.'

'Shuttleworth won't tell her, and he's sure to agree with me when he finally sees it anyway; such a pity you couldn't attend our wedding, my boy, although it was a very quiet affair as Pemberley and I were both married before.'

'Aye, a very quiet affair for about two hundred of your closest friends,' Kate muttered darkly, casting her far-too-innocent-looking friend and mentor a sharp look as she realised she'd invited Lord Shuttleworth to her wedding last summer and not told her chief bridesmaid.

Not that he'd condescended to accept, she added to her silent displeasure with both of them, because he doubtless knew she would be included in Eiliane's vast adoptive family and obviously had no desire to meet or converse with her. That much had become very clear when she'd glimpsed him exiting the first evening party she'd attended this Season very shortly after she had arrived with a group of friends. Then there had been a trip to the theatre when he'd chosen to visit a box no lady could dream of drifting into by design or accident and she wasn't fool enough to think he hadn't noticed her sitting in the one opposite. Watching him enjoy the company of one of the highest steppers of the *demi-monde* and her current keeper had, Kate told herself, been almost amusing. If his lordship wanted it to make it perfectly plain he hadn't been wearing the willow for Kate these last three years, he was quite welcome to do so. At the very least it would provide an antidote to the ennui yet another Season might have held for her without his antics enlivening it.

'And you know perfectly well that keeping it to even that number took the wisdom of Solomon and the tact of a whole diplomatic corps,' Eiliane reminded her friend, with a reminiscent shudder at the very thought of arranging her own wedding to her and her new lord's satisfaction.

'Oh, I do,' Kate agreed fervently, since she'd been caught up in trying to defuse far too many arguments once the Marquis's relatives realised their twenty or thirty closest friends would not be added to the guest list so they could boast of attending the most exclusive and fiercely anticipated society wedding of the year.

'Still, it's done now,' Eiliane said of her triumphant second marriage to a man who adored her as fervently as she did him.

Kate wondered how anyone could begrudge them such happiness and was secretly pleased that Edmund Worth obviously did not, at least if the warmth of his smile as he eyed her rather smug-looking friend was anything to go by.

'Again, I congratulate you on that fact very sincerely,'

he said as a prelude to moving on, but Eiliane wasn't going to let him escape so lightly.

'We will see you later, no doubt, as nobody could describe this affair as a crush and it'll be impossible to avoid bumping into one's friends all night, don't you think?' she said artlessly.

'I do my best to avoid anything so unfashionable,' he returned blandly, but Kate could see the tension about his firm mouth and the hunted expression in those silvery-green eyes even if her most partisan supporter wouldn't.

Eiliane deployed her most unexpected weapon, an awkward silence she quite failed to fill in her usual easy manner.

'I think I see Julia Deben over there, Eiliane; perhaps we should join her before someone else annexes the best seats in the room and you're left with a mere rout chair,' Kate managed in the hope of filling that horrible quietness and giving his lordship an excuse to go.

'Will you do me the honour of promising me a dance tonight, Miss Alstone?' The wretched man seemed to take perverse pleasure in asking her after all.

She silently handed over her dance card, refusing to gush or let him know the idea of dancing with him filled her with far more dismay than he could ever be allowed to know. Once they'd danced together so easily, their steps so harmonious there was no need to think about it. It had been the one thing they agreed on without any effort at all, and now even that would be blighted by his profound dislike of her. He handed the card back and she saw he'd put his initials beside two dances with a sinking feeling in the pit of her stomach. Now she must endure two cold and indifferent waltzes with him—the very prospect made her shiver.

'Until later then, Miss Alstone, Lady Pemberley,' he said with an elegant bow and a social smile that made Kate's heart ache for some odd reason.

She managed to curtsy with equal elegance and flash just as bland and indifferent a smile. 'Later, Lord Shuttleworth,' she managed to agree airily and kept that mere upturn of her lips in place for several moments after he walked away, lest anyone see her flinch at how her formerly impassioned suitor had grown so cold and distant towards her.

'Are you actually going to find yourself a husband this Season or not, Katherine Alstone?' Eiliane demanded with would-be carelessness that didn't deceive Kate one iota about which particular one she had in mind, despite Viscount Shuttleworth's obvious antipathy to the very idea.

They strolled across the room to greet friends and acquaintances, whilst Kate considered her answer and tried to tease Edmund Worth out of her errant thoughts. How very like Eiliane to ask the question nobody else dared, just when she didn't want to be asked most.

'Maybe,' Kate replied cautiously as Eiliane plumped down on an elegant sofa. She fervently hoped nobody else would be able to hear the conversation she'd been trying not to have for a week or more against the babel of noise caused by musicians tuning up and the general hum of greetings and gossip.

'Well, if you're not sure, I might as well make a

superb match for your sister Isabella while you make up your mind if you want marriage and a family of your own, or would prefer a lifetime of dull spinsterhood and worthy causes. Miranda and I have wasted three years of effort on you between us already, and I'm not inclined to seek out a man you won't turn your nose up at if you have no intention of marrying him when I finally manage to find him,' Eiliane continued relentlessly, just as if the most eligible gentleman Kate had ever refused to marry hadn't just crossed their path again mere minutes ago to remind them what a fool she was.

'How kind of you to point out that I'm one and twenty and almost on the shelf, Eiliane, but you'll have to wait for Izzie to recover from the mumps first.'

Her so-called friend waved the exquisitely painted fan her besotted husband of nearly a year had presented her with before he'd left her alone in London for a whole week—barring his entire London staff, Kate herself and Eiliane's legion of friends, of course.

'The Season's hardly begun yet, so if your sister is a week or two late in arriving it will only add to the sensation she'll cause when she does get here. I feel I can safely predict that dearest Isabella will be proclaimed a diamond of the first water the instant the gentlemen of the *ton* set eyes on her.'

'Of course she will be,' Kate agreed equably, 'but I still don't intend to snap up any available bachelor who crosses your path before she arrives to eclipse me.'

'Sometimes, Kate Alstone, you make me completely furious,' Eiliane accused contrarily. 'You just *will* not realise your looks are out of the common run and none the worse for being unusual. You'd have been the toast of St James's ever since you came out if you'd just hold your tongue and simper winningly for once. The gentlemen quake in their shoes when they're rash enough to pay you a compliment and receive one of your waspish disclaimers instead of a polite smile for their pains.'

'And I suppose you always held your tongue and smiled until *your* cheeks ached when you were a débutante, your ladyship?'

'I was different,' her ladyship admitted with a reminiscent smile that made Kate wonder just how different her chaperon had been and envy her a little.

'You still are,' she replied with her real smile that always showed the warmth of her affection for the recipient and this time made Eiliane chuckle, despite the apparent urgency of her quest to marry Kate off.

'Well, if you say so, my love, although I never had any looks to speak of, and only got dear Sir Ned Rhys and then my darling Pemberley to look at me twice by being good company, instead of twittering at them endlessly as the mercenary females who flocked round like a pack of vultures insisted on doing.'

'And you're always so outstandingly modest with it.'

'Any woman who is wilfully ignorant of her own advantages constitutes a danger to herself and every sentient male who has the misfortune to set eyes on her,' Eiliane announced with queenly dignity and a significant look in her direction Kate managed to pretend she hadn't seen.

'Izzie hasn't the smallest chance of being unaware of her looks when most of the unattached gentlemen of the *ton* will line up to tell her what she can easily see in her own mirror,' she said cheerfully, for she'd never envied either of her sisters their spectacular looks. 'Not that she'll relish the sort of nonsense the silliest will pour over her at every turn when she does finally arrive. So the answer to your very rude question, Lady Pemberley, is that, yes, I must marry if I don't want to become an antidote, and finding me a suitable gentleman to wed will prevent you foisting some handsome idiot on my little sister out of sheer ennui,' Kate said, eyeing one such gentleman who'd proposed once, all too certain he'd succeed where others had failed.

'You've kept too many of his ilk at a distance for too long, Kate my love.'

'I'd certainly never encourage such a straw man,' Kate replied, but the prospect of her fourth London Season had made her think very hard about what she wanted out of life before she'd come to town this year.

Over the long winter months she'd decided mutual interests and a sincere friendship with her future husband would last longer than an uncomfortable heat and irrational passion disguised as love. Of course, she was too cool and sceptical a lady now to feel that sort of midsummer madness for a gentleman anyway and, imagining how that sensible decision would be applauded by most noble families, she gave vent to a long-suffering sigh.

Her own family didn't even seem to realise how tedious it could be to be watched with misty-eyed speculation whenever she met a new gentleman. 'Would this be The One?' they seemed to ask themselves constantly and Kate had even detected signs of such mawkishness in her brother-in-law, Christopher Alstone, Earl of Carnwood, of late. She'd always thought him far too hard-headed and cynical to think that because he'd made a love match, she must necessarily want to do the same.

His marriage to her elder sister Miranda demonstrated that passionate love *existed*, of course, and then her one-time governess had tumbled headlong into love with Kit's best friend and business partner, Ben Shaw, to prove it beyond all doubt. Ben and Charlotte clearly adored each other, for all they sparred constantly, and now even Ben's natural father and dear Eiliane Rhys had joined in the conspiracy and wed each other at last. Yes, love obviously wasn't a myth, but she'd seen the damage it could do as well and had no intention of succumbing to such an unreliable emotion herself.

'Any woman in search of an amenable husband should discount that one immediately,' she added distractedly, considering the idiotic man striking a pose nearby and wishing she could recall his name. Meeting Shuttleworth seemed to have interfered with her memory as well as her ability to think rationally. 'I want a gentleman good-natured and polite enough to make me an amiable husband, not one with too high an opinion of himself to treat me with any consideration.'

'Advantages we have wasted our breath pointing out to you in various gentlemen until we're nigh hoarse for the last three years and in all that time you've proved as indifferent as a marble statue. If you don't mean to fall in love, at least banish the thought of such a wicked travesty of marriage from your mind this instant, Katherine Alstone. You possess completely the wrong temperament for a cold and businesslike alliance and would be wretched within a month if you made one,' Eiliane Pemberley pronounced in a fierce whisper that spoke volumes of her disapproval and her new position, for she'd never harm her husband's public dignity, even if she had little concern for her own. 'Besides which, I couldn't bear to watch you belittle yourself and whomever you chose to make miserable for the rest of your lives. Most men deserve better than that from a wife, Kate, even if you don't seem to think you do from a husband for some odd reason.'

'Most of our kind think it perfectly normal to feel no more than friendship and a polite affection for their spouse,' Kate muttered mulishly, 'and all those deluded gentlemen must actually *want* to marry me, since they keep begging me to say yes.'

'Which is precisely why they're so unsuited to make a so-called convenient husband, although, given the way you treat them, I can't but wish the lot of them would come to their senses and teach you a lesson or two in humility.'

'I'm always perfectly civil,' Kate said defensively.

'When you don't happen to be busy, or would like a personable gentleman to squire you about a ballroom while you flirt and gossip with no fear of comeback. That's not civility; it's cynical exploitation.'

A strong sense of justice forced Kate to reluctantly

agree that she took her admirers for granted. Only one of them had ever tempted her to yield to his urgent wooing and marry him and she'd treated Edmund Worth, Lord Shuttleworth, so abominably in order to fend off his increasingly passionate demands that he'd left London before the end of her first Season and not indulged in another until now. Let Eiliane know that particular dark secret and she'd throw Kate at the unfortunate man's head and embarrass both of them beyond bearing.

Not that he fitted any description of an unfortunate man she'd ever come across. He was noble, wealthy and an unusually intelligent gentleman of wit and character. Three years ago his youthful intensity and fiery devotion had frightened Kate into insulting brusqueness, borne of an irrational fear that he could too easily steal her heart, just as her elder sister's treacherous first husband had cynically taken hers and then trampled on it ruthlessly and even gleefully, before callously deserting her in the most appalling circumstances.

Now she was one and twenty and still unwed, even if that was by her own choice. With the added disadvantage of flaming red hair she still found annoying after twenty-one years of living with it, even possessed as she was of the famous dark blue Alstone eyes and just enough height to render her graceful, Kate thought of herself as an oddity. She formed part of a close circle of family and friends who only wanted her to be happy, yet perhaps she just didn't deserve to be so after breaking a young man's heart so callously once upon a time?

Watching Shuttleworth avoid a matchmaking mama with a preoccupied nod, she wondered where her wits had gone wandering off to three years ago. If she'd only seen a hasty, impulsively passionate and rather callow youth in the man he'd been then, didn't that make her almost as headstrong and foolish as her sister Miranda had been at seventeen when she'd fallen in 'love' with a man so unworthy of her he wasn't fit to kiss the hem of her gown after a muddy walk? If she had been wilfully blind in her determination not to follow Miranda's example, could that mean Lord Shuttleworth might have been the love of her life and her ideal husband, if only she'd had the courage to say yes to him three years ago? Indeed, had the passionate sincerity of his youthful determination to wed her been the real reason her suitors ever since had seemed so colourless and interchangeable that she felt not a single qualm about refusing any of them?

His lordship had clearly got over any lingering infatuation he'd ever felt for her while he was away, since it had taken him two evening parties and a night at the play to find time to reintroduce himself to her after three years of absence. Tonight it would have been rude beyond anything his gentlemanly instincts could endure to ignore her in Eiliane's company, but all the time they'd been together he'd watched her with cynical grey eyes, their irises rayed with a silvery jade green that she couldn't recall studying quite so diligently in the past. Her heart had actually fluttered under his steely scrutiny; she'd felt it and cursed it for being so susceptible as she curtsied and observed his elegant bow and finely tuned indifference to whatever she might feel upon meeting him again.

'Perhaps I became useful to some of the eligible bachelors somewhere along the way,' she mused absently to Eiliane now. 'A safe habit we have fallen into on either side without noting it. They know I shall turn down their suit, so they feel safe declaring themselves my slaves and proposing to me in the certainty I'll refuse.'

'And you truly think that sort of habit would make a suitable basis for a lifetime commitment to love and honour a man if you broke it and shocked and perhaps horrified him by accepting him at last, Kate? It sounds a nightmare to me when you're young and full of promise and would do so much better if you'd only look for happiness within this theoretical marriage you're contemplating so coolly,' Eiliane retorted.

'Love can't always be a bolt of lightning.' Kate defended herself rather uncomfortably, because all of a sudden it seemed rather a sterile scheme to marry for less even to her. 'Sometimes I dare say it needs time to grow into something much more comfortable and this year I might meet a man I can respect for his integrity and honour as well as his sense of duty. Mama and Papa made a marriage of convenience, don't forget, and they seemed happy enough together.'

'They made the best they could of second-best, my girl, being people of wit and character. It was their love for their children that gradually bound them together, rather than any great passion for each other, and I know for a fact that your mother loved a man her family deemed unsuitable for her until the end of her days.'

'Oh, so it's all her fault then, is it?' Kate asked impetuously, finding someone to blame for the streak of passionate recklessness that ran through the Alstone sisters like a fault line in a mining seam, then she realised what she'd given away and could have kicked herself. Give Eiliane such a promising bone to worry at and she wouldn't rest until it was stripped bare of all sorts of possibilities.

'I knew it!' Eiliane exclaimed, as Kate winced. But at least her so-called friend's shrewd gaze had slewed away from Lord Shuttleworth, which was some consolation, for it now being centred so mercilessly on her instead, she supposed ruefully. 'You're terrified of falling in love with a handsome face, then bitterly regretting it, just as your sister did so disastrously, aren't you?' Lady Pemberley accused her triumphantly, as if she'd won a significant battle and Kate must now admit love was vital to a happy marriage after all.

'Of course not,' she lied hotly, but felt her cheeks flush and cursed her telltale redhead's complexion.

'You are, my girl, and you wouldn't be prattling to me about marriages of so-called sense if you were not cravenly terrified of letting your heart rule your head. What you should do if you possess even a sliver of good sense is use this Season to find the man you'll love and respect for the rest of your days together, before it's too late. If you meet that man after you've contracted some hollow alliance with another, you'll condemn both him and your unfortunate lover to a lifetime of suspicion and misery, as well as putting your very soul in jeopardy into the bargain!'

'Stop overdramatising everything. I possess a much colder nature than my mother or either of my sisters,'

Kate insisted and Eiliane just raised her darkened eyebrows sceptically and refused to be drawn. 'Because I was born with this unfortunate-coloured hair, everyone thinks I've got fiery passions to go with it, and you're all quite mistaken!' Kate told her crossly, wishing even her nearest and dearest would stop falling back on the ridiculous cliché that redheads always had temperaments to match their fiery colouring.

'Having watched you grow from a babe in arms into an intelligent, beautiful and often exasperating young woman, Katherine Alstone, I do believe I know your true nature far better than you do yourself,' Eiliane said slowly, as if she'd just discovered the key to a conundrum that had long been puzzling her.

'Then you'll also know how much I don't *want* to be engulfed by a grand passion, or become pale and interesting as I pine uselessly for a man who might well pass me by without a second glance,' Kate defended herself uncomfortably.

'I suppose we *might* find a gentleman who's either too preoccupied with another woman, or too blind or daft to be knocked all of a heap by your youth, beauty and usually shining intelligence and wit, if we searched the whole kingdom for him diligently enough, my love, but very few men will ever pass you by without a glance, I can assure you,' Eiliane said with a knowing smile. 'And love won't kill you, you know, Kate. I've endured it twice now and found it quite breathtakingly wonderful both times. Indeed, I consider myself exceptionally blessed to find it twice, even if I am rather a superannuated wife for poor Pemberley to lay claim to.'

'Nonsense, he was lucky indeed to win you and well he knows it,' Kate responded hotly, ready to argue black was white in order to see someone she loved as much as Eiliane happy again. 'It's just that I can't bear the idea of depending on someone else for my happiness, Eiliane, not that I don't believe in the possibility of love for anyone else.'

'Which is ridiculous if you'll only think about it a little harder, Kate. Indeed, it's totally illogical if we're going to go about this in the cool way you seem to favour.'

'I know, but I can't seem to change my mind, even with so many examples of wedded bliss in front of me to form a corrective,' she told Eiliane ruefully.

'I blame myself,' her friend replied gloomily, 'I should have insisted on wrenching the two of you from your grandfather's custody as soon as your sister Miranda turned up on my doorstep one morning with such woe and misery in her poor sad eyes that I knew he wasn't fit to look after a couple of kittens, let alone three vulnerable and lively young girls.'

'Don't do that to yourself, love, for none of it was your fault and how could you have removed us from Wychwood without kidnapping us? Once someone eventually noticed we were gone there would have been a fearsome uproar and my aunt would have insisted we return to even less freedom than we had to start with. Don't ever blame yourself for any of what happened when we were children, dearest Eiliane. And if not for you, we would never have been sent to school, so just think what we would have missed in dear Charlotte Wells, as we all thought she was then.'

'Aye, that's true, Charlotte is a darling girl and exactly the right wife for my new son, for all Ben wouldn't thank me for naming him so, since he's far too big and self-sufficient to stand in the least need of even an unofficial stepmother, but Charlotte couldn't make up for the neglect of your entire family, Kate. You have such a vast capacity for love, my dear, it seems an appalling waste that it might be lost or misplaced in some insipid and bloodless marriage when you could have so much more if you let yourself believe you could safely fall in love.'

If all three Alstone sisters had been born plain as porridge and wall-eyed, they'd still be beautiful to the Marchioness of Pemberley, and only the finest gentlemen in the land good enough for any one of them, Kate thought, affection overcoming exasperation as she acknowledged to herself how lucky they all were to have her. Eiliane was wrong, though, and if Kate wasn't to die an old maid, then she'd have to find a man she could respect in order to have the children she longed for, and what point was there in regretting what might have been?

Chapter Two

Her bridges could fairly be considered irrevocably burnt so far as Edmund, Viscount Shuttleworth, was concerned and Kate would have to look elsewhere for a convenient husband. Which was just as well, she reassured herself, considering she'd always sensed a huge capacity for passion and melodrama in herself and curbed it as sternly as she could, lest it lead her into some terrible tangle of love and fury and wanting that would damage all concerned beyond mending.

'I intend to make a list and, when I'm sure my choice of husband is quite suitable, I'll just have to find some way of making sure that gentleman agrees with me,' she asserted stalwartly, not quite able to meet Eiliane's eyes as her scheme sounded cold and rather depressing even to her when she said it out loud.

'Why wait?' Eiliane prompted sardonically, obviously at the end of her patience with such an implacably self-deluded idiot. 'If you're so very determined to go against your very nature, and God help the poor man you settle upon if you are, then why not begin straight away? Tonight's entertainment should make an ideal opportunity for you to start such a search—considering that most of the débutantes haven't yet arrived and those who have are still too overawed to offer you much competition. Why, you will almost have the field to yourself, my dear, apart from all the other not-so-young ladies who've been out too long and are desperate to catch a suitable husband, of course.'

'I'm only one and twenty,' Kate protested feebly, unable to keep a still tongue in her head in the face of what she knew perfectly well was deliberate provocation.

Eiliane gave an airy wave of her exquisite fan. 'No longer a sparkling young débutante, nor yet quite a faded quiz at her last prayers. How some of those vibrant young girls just out of their schoolrooms will pity you,' she went on relentlessly, seeming determined to provoke Kate into an argument that would disprove her claim to be chilly and passionless. 'To be so sought after initially, then left unwed three years on argues either that you're ridiculously finicky and far too high in the instep, or that the gentlemen have stopped asking you.'

'Then why do they still do so in such numbers, I wonder?' Kate defended herself absently, her eyes once again on Lord Shuttleworth as he seemed almost as if he'd felt her gaze on him and decided to allow her a closer look.

'Because the unattainable is always so very alluring,' Lady Pemberley replied, a little too seriously for

Kate's taste, 'and I don't want you to become a target for the less scrupulous rakes of the *ton*, my love. Better if only you'd accepted Shuttleworth years ago rather than take that primrose path to misery, I suppose. At least marriage to him would put the predators off until you presented him with a couple of heirs. Not that he'd make anyone a complacent husband,' she ended with a warning nod at the fascinating masculine figure they'd both been watching.

'Please don't turn all intense and Celtic on me just now, Eiliane dear,' Kate said absently, most of her attention on the nobleman forging a path towards them. She wondered fleetingly if he still felt more for her than he'd have her and the rest of the world believe—which only went to show what happened when she listened to her friend's ridiculous ideas about love.

'No, my love,' Lady Pemberley replied meekly and Kate shot her a rueful, exasperated glance, before going back to surreptitiously watching his lordship.

If only Shuttleworth had still been inclined to fall at her feet and beg her to marry him, they could be wed by the end of the Season and then nobody would be able to lecture her on the subject of love matches ever again. Except this older, grimmer Edmund Worth looked very unlikely to agree to an affectionate alliance with her, based as it would have to be on mutual interests and polite friendship instead of the flash and burn of love he'd once promised her. It seemed impossible to picture living at his side in such a temperate style, but was she capable of offering more even to him?

'Lord Shuttleworth,' she greeted him, oddly chagrined

when his expression became more guarded rather than less so.

She smiled awkwardly in the hope of establishing a polite sort of acquaintance between them, since nothing else seemed likely, and he eyed her cautiously, as if she might launch into a mad jig at any moment and embarrass him in front of the assembled company.

'Is it time for our waltz already then, my lord?' she asked clumsily and groaned inwardly at her own ineptitude. Obviously she wasn't very good at actually *encouraging* gentlemen, even if it was only to be a little more civil.

'And if only this next dance were to be one, how delightful that would make my evening,' he replied with an unforgivable glint of amusement in his grey-green eyes. He pointed helpfully to her dance card, which stated unambiguously that she was to honour another gentleman with the quadrille. Lord Shuttleworth must have been merely passing when she had made it impossible for him to do so without snubbing her even more crushingly than even he seemed prepared to do.

There was no point in stuttering and apologising, so she sent him a weak parody of a smile and stood silent and embarrassed, wishing she could think of a way to banish the suggestion of mockery playing about his mouth. It wasn't quite a sneer or altogether a smile and she found it flustered her ridiculously in a man who had once been her devoted cavalier. Anyway, she really didn't want him to kiss her—well, not that much—and, even if she did, it was probably out of sheer, perverse curiosity. He'd grown into a much more formidable man than she'd ever dreamt he would. What a shame if he'd cooled toward her just when her interest in him had sharpened, she decided, with an odd jar of panic in her stomach. And where had that ridiculous idea come from in the first place? Why on earth would she want this man-icicle to kiss her, ever? She must have run mad without anyone noticing if she thought being kissed by Edmund Worth would bring her anything but confusion and distaste, swiftly followed by their mutual embarrassment and an even chillier estrangement between them than there was now.

If only she hadn't had to leave him enjoying the company of her devious duenna far more than he did that of her charge, Kate might have found her dance perfectly agreeable. Her partner was an excellent dancer in direct defiance of the air of world-weary cynicism he seemed to think marked him out as a pink of the *ton*. Instead, she missed steps in her attempts to watch Eiliane and Lord Shuttleworth having a comfortable coze and silently dreaded what that unconventional lady might be saying to his lordship.

'Come now, Miss Alstone,' the gentleman beside her chided, finally losing patience with such an inattentive partner, 'either dance with me or pretend to be overcome by the heat, so we may be quit of each other and this dance without causing a scandal.'

'I beg your pardon, sir; I must be a little distracted by all this noise and bustle after so many months in the country, but I shall do better from now on,' she excused herself rather feebly.

'Good, for it does nothing for a fellow's good opinion of himself to dance with a lady whose attention is so patently on another man,' he told her with a frankness she found surprising in one she'd always thought dandified and affected.

Kate was very careful to mind her steps for the rest of the dance while she wondered if she had truly seen *any* of the gentlemen who had habitually sought her out at the balls and parties of the London Season. Until tonight she'd been able to flatter herself she was a reasonably intelligent and well-educated female who was also independently wealthy and up to snuff. So what hope was there of her finding that perfect husband for herself when she'd clearly misjudged herself so very badly?

'Thank you, Miss Alstone,' her partner said as the music faded and he bowed to her with jaded grace, 'you know how to depress a gentleman's pretensions most effectively,' he told her quietly and calmly. 'I shall not be troubling you with them again after tonight.'

'Sir, I have no idea of your meaning,' she protested rather faintly as that sense of nothing being quite what it seemed tonight haunted her again.

Was she asleep and in the grip of a nightmare where everything seemed normal, but in truth nothing was quite as it should be? Unfortunately not, for her dance partner was continuing and she doubted she'd allow him such an air of disillusioned cynicism in her dreams.

'Not your fault, Miss Alstone. I should have had the sense to listen to fair warnings when they were given me. Had I done so, doubtless I wouldn't feel so disenchanted now I've discovered they were correct.'

As they'd reached the sofa Lady Pemberley had annexed by the end of that crushing speech, the disillusioned gentleman bowed and took himself off to the card room to join his cronies, no doubt to confirm that Miss Alstone was a shameless flirt who lacked the courtesy to keep her attention on her conquests once she'd made them in order to eye up her next one. Kate's mind reeled. How odd that she'd got up this morning believing that she was a pleasant enough person to be with.

'Now *this* is our dance, is it not, Miss Alstone?' the cause of it all informed her suavely, getting to his feet as she approached and looking as if exchanging Eiliane's lively company for her own was a sacrifice he was most unwilling to make.

How did this confounded man ever delude himself he wanted to marry me so desperately when he's clearly revolted by the idea of spending half an hour in my company nowadays? Kate asked herself wordlessly as they joined the couples on the dance floor for a waltz that seemed more in the nature of a penance to him rather than a pleasure. 'So why *did* you keep asking me?' she finally questioned aloud, startling herself and shocking him into actually looking at her. His arm went across her back to take her other hand and a cool shiver of something untamed with an edge of warning ran through her like wildfire.

For an instant she felt strangely shaken by the intimacy of their locked gaze and the fluid, familiar movements of their bodies as his warmth engulfed her, taking the sense of chill and alienation out of her evening for a blissful moment as their bodies at least recalled how well they'd always danced together. She was strongly tempted to lean into his arms and let him guide her expertly around the floor without making much effort on her own part. Instead she made herself whirl and turn and glide as actively as he did himself, partly because he was a superb dancer and it seemed a waste not to, and partly because it gave each of them time to think of all the changes three years had made in the other whilst he considered that appallingly crass question she couldn't believe she'd actually asked him out loud.

'Maybe because you dance superbly,' he finally said with a faintly mocking smile, taking her remark at its lightest value and lobbing it back at her with a neatness that made her heart skip a beat in what felt oddly like panic.

Not because he'd once wanted to be with her above any other female then, or had dreamt of holding her in his arms from one waltz to the next, one ball to another? Not because he'd missed her sadly through all the long weary summers and winters since the last time he'd held her so close and danced with her, so superbly matched to every step as they had been so very long ago and ironically still seemed to be now when everything else was different between them?

'Thank you, my lord,' she replied a little stiffly. 'Luckily I can return your compliment without the least risk of flattery. Lord Shuttleworth has always been rated one of the finest dancers to grace the *ton*.'

'Now *isn't* that fortunate for him?' he parried sardonically, but his only response to her implied challenge was to make their dance even more energetic, perhaps to stop her finding breath to ask him any more inconvenient questions.

'Very,' she gasped and decided to wait for anything more until they stopped spinning about the room in this dizzying whirl.

He moved with a poise and latent strength she couldn't recall noticing before and a tingle of awareness shot through her when he tightened his grip on her to guide her past a dab of candle wax on the highly polished floor. Kate had to remind herself she was looking for a courteous and undemanding husband, not a disdainful and probably very demanding lover, and that Shuttleworth clearly didn't want to occupy either position in her life anyway. Her body remained unconvinced by such logic and troubled her with the most outrageous fantasies which her mind shied away from while they waltzed in apparent harmony. Kate did her best to ignore her own baser instincts and Shuttleworth's unspoken disdain while she smiled at nothing in particular as if her life depended on it.

Edmund George Francis St Erith Standon-Worth, keep your head, that gentleman silently demanded of himself as he held the ravishingly lovely Miss Katherine Alstone in the crook of his arm and tried not to think her being naked and passionately willing as she danced in his arms to an even more intimate tune, preferably without the interested gaze of the cream of fashionable society upon them, of course.

What on earth did the copper-haired torment mean by staring at him across the ballroom as if she'd never set eyes on him before, as if he'd finally come to her attention as something more than a dancing, talking marionette and she was intent on beckoning him to her side by sheer force of will? Could anything good be flying about her busy brain? he wondered, as he tried his best to pretend she was merely a polite acquaintance, despite the fact that his disobliging body and most of society knew he'd been besotted with her from the first moment he'd laid eyes on her three years ago. Unfortunately she knew it as well and, try as he might, he couldn't relax and just enjoy this dance with a graceful and accomplished partner who should now mean absolutely nothing to him.

He'd been far too boyish and silly to hide his infatuation with her three years ago. When she'd carelessly turned him down that last time as if she was waving away an annoying fly or a brash young puppy pestering her with unwanted adoration, he'd told himself his stupid obsession with her had been a youthful folly he would very soon grow out of, and that one day he'd look back on it with astonishment that he'd ever been so young and gullible. Well, he'd made it so at last by cutting her and all the dreams he'd had of her painfully and painstakingly out of his heart so he could come here again to find the woman he could marry and live with for the rest of his days, and that woman was *not* Katherine Alstone.

This spring, he'd assured himself as he travelled from his very substantial estates in Herefordshire to his impressive house in Grosvenor Square, he'd look about him for a quiet and biddable female to become his viscountess. Marrying the too-clever, tricky and far-from-biddable beauty his heart had once been set on so uselessly would have been a disaster on both sides. He'd told himself blithely that he was grateful to her for saving them both from such a fate and he should thank her on his knees for refusing him again and again.

It had seemed such a sensible plan when he was still at Cravenhill Park, where Miss Alstone had refused an invitation to stay for the summer and get to know him better with a sweet, distracted smile and a brief assurance that they were too young and probably wouldn't suit anyway.

How would she know? he silently quizzed himself as he struggled with a strong urge to shake the slender, curvaceous, infinitely desirable and utterly contrary female until her perfect white teeth rattled even now, when both of them were three years older and supposedly wiser.

He shifted uncomfortably to avoid making yet closer contact with her and inflaming himself even further and caught surprise in her blue, blue eyes as she turned to look up at him questioningly. Turning the movement into a demand that she spin fluidly past a less sure couple, he fought a whole pack of demons at the feel of her body so close to his, moving so gracefully to the steps of the dance and reminding him, as if he needed reminding, exactly who he held in his arms at last, warm and desirable and all too real.

No, he ordered himself as his body responded instinctively to hers and he fought the magic fiercely, he was done with self-inflicted torture. He'd wrung Kate Alstone from his thoughts and routed her from his heart and never again would he spend restless nights tossing and turning as he was driven distracted by a bitter yearning for her in his bed, at his board and for ever by his side. Knowing, for the simple reason of having tried it in the throes of youthful desperation, that making love with a *demi-mondaine* he'd fooled himself looked just like her would never satisfy his ridiculous fantasies of Kate, warm and shameless in his bed, with every inch of her velvety skin and stubborn will in tune with his desires at last, he utterly refused to become the besotted, driven idiot she'd once made of him ever again.

Once he'd let himself see the gaping chasm between heated dream and chilly reality, he'd contented himself with his estates and the odd trip to Bath to see his elderly aunt, until the blessed day when he had finally got himself under strict enough control to be indifferent to Kate Alstone. By some benign fluke, it was in that elegant and usually middle-aged spa town that he'd met Therese, a lush and lovely widow ten years his senior, who took him to her bed and taught him there were other women in the world besides Kate, however little his heart wanted to admit it at the time. Then, after what he'd thought was a mutually satisfying association, Therese decided to marry again. So she'd wed a man ten years *her* senior after declaring herself quite ineligible as the next Viscountess Shuttleworth when he offered to make her so.

'You are too young, my love, too idealistic and intense to be happy in such a lukewarm arrangement,' she'd told him that last time they were together. 'We have been happy, but it's time for us to part. I shall wed my colonel and make him an excellent wife, but I'm not the woman you dream of when you cry out her name in your sleep. Either convince that one to marry you, dearest Edmund, or tear her out of your heart before you wed some poor girl who'll be for ever second-best.'

He'd protested, of course. Assured her that if she married him she and the family they could make together would always come first. But Therese had chided him for offering what he couldn't deliver and he'd hesitated too long before she gave him a sad smile and left to plan her wedding to her still handsome and rather rich colonel and to settle three counties away, which was probably just as well for all three of them. Therese was a fine woman with a quick wit and a kind heart and she now had a settled life with a man who adored her. Edmund liked and admired her, but he didn't adore her. Though nor, he told himself sternly, did he adore the redheaded beauty who'd once driven him half-mad with headlong, youthful love and longing for her.

So this year he'd quit Cravenhill for London, determined to find himself a wife who wouldn't drive him to the brink of insanity every time she smiled at another man. With her he would retire to his acres, where they'd live a life of quiet contentment and usefulness, spiced by an occasional visit to the capital to catch up with old friends. Such a pity that it all sounded so deadly dull just now.

No, it wasn't dull, it was sensible. He wanted to be at peace in his own skin and he wanted children, not just to inherit his title and lands, but because he'd been a lone, noble and therefore very privileged orphan ever since he learnt to walk. And he wanted sanity and routine and a sense of rightness about his life, not insanity, uncertainty and a mess of passion, frustration and exasperation that Kate Alstone would offer her long-suffering husband, when she finally condescended to admit one to her bed, if not her heart.

Easy enough to weigh his hopeless passion for Kate against that yet-to-be-born tribe of children and the face-less, sweet and loving Lady Shuttleworth, who would give them to him and love every single one as much as she adored him, and be quite certain he was cured. Now none of it was quite so clear-cut and he felt thoroughly out of sorts and nearly as deeply exasperated with Kate as he was with himself.

Curse the contrary female for looking at him tonight as if she liked the man he'd become far more than the foolish boy he'd once been. Trust her to reawaken the slumberous, wanton siren he'd once made of her in his obsessed, Kate-tortured dreams and remind him how lifeless his sweet wife sounded by the side of the rich and passionate promise Kate could offer a potential husband. If, of course, the lucky devil succeeded in awakening the sensuality she managed to hide so well from herself. For he doubted she had any idea with what heady promise her delightfully curved lips and very pleasing form tantalised an idiot like him.

'She—is—not—what—she—seems,' he intoned under his breath, enduring the feel of her delightfully formed body brushing his tension-tightened muscles as he shifted her for the final turn and prayed for a rapid end to this torture. *She is everything she seems and more*, the faint waft of her rose-perfumed skin in his oversensitive nostrils taunted him back, the soft shift of woman-warmed silk tantalising his guiding fingers even through his supple evening gloves, as if every sense he had was uniquely attuned just to her. But she's not for you; she's not part of your domestic idyll. She doesn't *want* to love you, the argument began again in his head and he was relieved when the music finally wound down and he could let his hand drop with what might seem unflattering haste to someone who couldn't read his mind.

Three years on he was more mature, cynical and tried and tested by life than he had once been, but she was three years lovelier, three years away from the eighteen-year-old débutante she'd been then. Then she'd been a girl close to being unformed compared with the gorgeous creature she was now, all rich curves and slender, elegant limbs that carried the usual Alstone height with a panache all her own. He forced himself to remember she was also haughty and cold as he finally made himself step away from the unattainable siren she really was.

What she really was just now, he observed rather ruefully, was an offended goddess who considered herself slighted by some mere mortal who'd dared turn his back on her extraordinary beauty. He caught the hint of suppressed fury in her indigo gaze, the tightening of her lush lips into a line and then a brief pout that warned him his danger wasn't over, as if he didn't already know it from his dratted body's reaction to her proximity. He so desperately wanted to kiss those rosy, lushly discontented lips of hers that he had to clear away an imaginary frog from his throat to manufacture an excuse not to offer her his crooked elbow for a precious moment of respite from her touch.

It was either that or stalk off and abandon her to the giggles of the avidly watching gossips and seek less incendiary company. Even to avenge himself for all those broken nights and wasted days, he couldn't do it to her. She still had no idea what she did to a man, he decided. High time she wed some unfortunate idiot, who could then spend his time rescuing her from her own folly and leave Edmund to find his sweet, nebulous viscountess and an easier life. The sooner the better, he assured himself and finally decided he was cool enough to offer Miss Alstone that arm and escort her into the supper room after all.

What a fool he'd been to be so full of misplaced confidence she meant nothing to him any more that he'd written his initials on the supper dance to prove he was cured. Evidently something about her called to him on a deeper level than he'd realised, but there was still time left this Season to effect a complete cure. Legions of débutantes would soon arrive and might even be lovely and amenable enough to put Kate Alstone out of his head entirely. He frowned as an inner voice informed him that rumours of such a fabulous paragon would have reached him by now, if such a creature existed outside the covers of a highly coloured novel.

Such an impossibly ideal girl would cause riots if she

so much as set foot in the capital, but instinct informed him lugubriously that he'd still prefer the woman at his side to such an exquisite creature. No, he told himself doggedly, he'd choose his kind, pleasingly pretty and so far purely mythical wife, and just managed not to pull his arm away before Kate could settle her hand gingerly into the crook of his elbow, as if he might bite her if she didn't keep a strict eye on him.

Suddenly Edmund's sense of the ridiculous reawakened and he made up his mind to distract himself with the heady task of confusing the lovely Miss Alstone, whilst searching for his true quarry. It would do the redhaired witch good, he assured the doubter within. He wouldn't be cruel, heaven forbid, but someone should make her realise she existed in the same world as the rest of faulty humanity, not on a higher plane where everything was ordered to her convenience.

Chapter Three

'How is everyone at Wychwood, Miss Alstone?'
he asked in a tone even he knew was insufferably
indifferent to her answer, although he liked the Earl of
Carnwood and his spectacularly lovely wife. Now he
came to think of it, if Miss Kate Alstone resembled her
fiery sister as strongly in character as she did in outward
beauty, he couldn't walk away from her to wed a less
unique woman. Thank you for not being made in your
elder sister's extraordinary image, he silently praised
the beauty at his side, but even he wasn't yet a bitter
enough man to say it out loud.

'All very well,' she replied stiffly, as if she could
read his thoughts, and he made himself look into her
intriguing indigo eyes to make sure he was mistaken.

No, he informed himself sternly, he refused to cave
at the hint of wistfulness in her gaze, the faint droop of
discontent and perhaps a hint of longing in the curve of
her rosy-lipped mouth. It was an illusion, he reminded

himself. She might look as if she longed for a tithe of her sister's passionate and mutually loving marriage for herself, but she didn't have the least intention of following Miranda Alstone's stormy path through life. After enduring her chilly lack of attention for a whole Season, he'd concluded Kate had no heart to lose. Trust her to decide to feel piqued that she'd finally lost his adoration tonight, just when he was starting his hunt for a very different female.

'My sister is expecting to present Lord Carnwood with another pledge of her affection very shortly,' she added to her terse assessment, again with that hint of wistful longing in her voice he wished she'd learn to conceal a little better.

To anyone else he supposed it might seem a tone of rueful irony, a discreet nod towards the fact that her sister and brother-in-law were deeply in love and therefore made insufferable company for a rational human being. Too many months spent learning her moods and interests from avid observation, he thought crossly. What an irony if she so longed to carry brats of her own that she was prepared to take him as her husband after all, just when he'd realised he couldn't tolerate such a marriage to a wife he'd once longed to adore until his dying day. Compassion threatened as he wondered why she thought it safe to love her children and not her husband, who could be her equal and her passion. No, Carnwood and his countess were unique and he was done with dreams; Kate was not the wife for him.

'Ah, well,' he replied carelessly, 'your brother-in-law is sadly in need of an heir.'

'Kit will feel the need for whomever my sister presents him with, my lord. Not even the most cynical and uncaring spectator could deny that.'

Now he'd really offended her, just as he'd intended to. What a shame, then, that the fleeting vulnerability of hurt he glimpsed in her eyes, the not-quite-hidden wince as he pretended indifference to two people he liked and envied, pained him as well. Better this way, he reminded himself and smiled encouragingly at a certain Miss Transome he'd been introduced to earlier and her hovering swain. With any luck, they would join them at supper and break up any suggestion of a tête-à-tête between himself and the beauty at his side before too many people recalled that he'd once been mad, deluded and desperate for her.

'La, my dear Miss Alstone,' Miss Transome spouted so fulsomely so that Edmund almost regretted encouraging her, even to save himself an intimate supper with a woman he couldn't have and didn't want. 'How finely you two do dance together. It quite put us off our own feeble attempts, did it not, Mr Cromer?'

'Yes, quite,' poor Cromer replied as if his throat was parched after all the monosyllabic replies he'd made this evening to his voluble companion. 'Get supper for the ladies, eh, Shuttleworth?' he managed in a magnificent feat of oratory.

'Quite,' he replied, apeing his old school friend's sparse conversational style and they resorted to the groaning supper table to procure enough refreshments to silence even Miss Transome for a few idyllic moments.

Edmund decided both he and his taciturn friend had been rash to attend a party so obviously organised for the benefit of single ladies who'd survived too many Seasons unwed, before fresh débutantes arrived to outdo and outflank them. It was perhaps the last chance for such ladies to catch the eye of a potential husband before open season was declared on them. One glance at their hostess for the evening and her superannuated eldest daughter should have any sane bachelor saying a hasty farewell and dashing off to his club in order to survive and fight another day. He, of course, had a reason to attend any party where he might meet his elusive future viscountess, but what on earth had led Cromer to risk it?

'She's m'aunt,' Cromer explained obscurely and Edmund must have looked almost as puzzled as he felt, because his friend added a brief explanation. 'Lady Finchley, she's m'aunt.'

'That accounts for it then,' he conceded.

'Your excuse?' Cromer asked morosely.

'Idiocy,' Edmund replied, borrowing some of his friend's abruptness.

'Must be,' Cromer commiserated as they turned back with their booty. 'Though the Alstone icicle's a beauty,' he conceded generously.

'Aye, but is she worth enduring the frostbite for, I wonder?' Edmund asked in a thoughtful undertone as he watched her nod regally to an acquaintance.

'M'father wants me to wed. Always liked Amelia Transome, but the thing is that she *will* talk. Much better tempered than my cousin Finchley, though,' Cromer risked waxing lyrical.

Scanning the room and finally spotting Miss Finchley seated at a flimsy table with a widower of at least five and forty, who still looked hunted and not very willing, Edmund sympathised. Miss Transome was open and amiable, but the thought of being fluttered at over the breakfast table for the rest of his life must make the strongest man hesitate. Neither female bore the slightest resemblance to his dream wife, so he turned his attention back to Kate Alstone with a sneaking feeling of relief that he didn't stand in Cromer's shoes and could at least please himself whom he brought to supper, so long as she wasn't the woman who pleased him all the way to the altar.

'Oh, how perfectly lovely,' Miss Transome gushed at the loaded plates.

'Quite,' Kate said with much less enthusiasm, and Edmund wondered if she'd been talked into a headache by Miss Transome's busy tongue and dreaded carrying the burden of conversation with her on his own.

Kate nibbled unenthusiastically at her supper, despite poor Lady Finchley having pushed out every boat she could launch in the hope of netting her daughter a husband at long last by hiring an excellent chef. To be fair, the headache she felt tightening her hairpins and nagging at her temples had nothing to do with Miss Transome's prattle, so the blame for that must lie at Lord Shuttleworth's door. Wretched man, she decided, as she surreptitiously surveyed him with a disillusioned gaze.

Once upon a time he would have fallen at her daintily shod feet given the slightest hint of encouragement, but now that she'd finally steeled herself to accept a husband, he certainly wouldn't be one of her suitors.

She hoped she was too proud to wilfully mistake his indifference to her tonight for a fleeting headache or a black mood on *his* part. There was too much distance about him to lay his behaviour at such a random and socially convenient cause and gaily expect tomorrow to bring amendment. He no longer desired her, now she finally wanted to become a wife and mother, and it was the frustration of it all that had caused her headache. It wasn't as if she cared for him, other than as she might for any man she'd once known and come to value for his integrity and the dry sense of humour that had once lurked under his youthful enthusiasm.

Now it was gone, she decided guiltily that she'd always secretly revelled in Edmund's apparent obsession with her and the certainty that he'd always long for her, even if he couldn't have her. Had it been a guilty pleasure she knew she ought not to feel to know one person on this earth probably still thought of her as uniquely desirable? She really hoped not, since that would make her a tease or a shrew, then and now. And he certainly didn't want her now, so why did it feel as if someone had taken away the most promising treat she'd ever pretended she didn't really want in the first place?

So all in all it was little wonder that she was nursing the beginnings of a fine headache and an inexcusable grievance against Edmund Worth, just because he no longer felt inclined to make a fool of himself over the

Honourable Katherine Alstone. Now that there was no chance of him offering for her ever again, she supposed she could acknowledge in her own head that it would have been wrong to accept him anyway, when he so obviously wanted to love his wife and she certainly didn't want to love her husband. However, she wondered uneasily if she would have found it so wrong to accept him on such terms if he hadn't made it so very clear they were no longer on offer.

Kate surreptitiously scanned the room under cover of Miss Transome's interminable prattle for any likely bachelors, now the most promising one of all was struck off her list. Not one of those present made the idea of sharing the intimacy required to bring her children into the world seem anything other than a nightmare. There would be other balls and routs, of course; ones where the gentlemen were both more plentiful and a little more willing to be charmed, although the other ladies would also be both more sparkling and more innocent, if also more tongue-tied.

Most eligible gentlemen had spurned Lady Finchley's rout for their clubs, which severely limited her choices. Sensible gentlemen, she decided, as she noted her fellow quizzes dotted about the supper room, trying their best to be all the things their desperate mamas bade them be. Miss Transome was projecting vivacity with such determination Kate wondered if she might sprout wings and fly up to the ceiling and circle about them all, still twittering frantically as she did so. Nearby, Miss Wetherby had cornered the market in pale and interesting and was reclining gracefully on a fragile chair that looked to

be her only support in a failing world. And just what was
Miss Alstone doing? Wilting too, Kate decided crossly;
she was drooping like a wallflower and refusing to even
try to be civil to those about her, just because she'd been
disappointed in hope, if not in love.

'Do you attend Mrs Flamington's ridotto, sir?' Miss
Transome asked Mr Cromer with apparently artless curi-
osity, and Kate could have told her just from reading Mr
Cromer's hunted expression that it was unlikely.

'No,' he managed reluctantly, before courting even
more silence by popping a bite of lobster patty into his
mouth and consuming it very slowly as if to stop his
reckless tongue committing him to something the rest
of him didn't agree with.

'Are *you* planning to be there, Lord Shuttleworth?'
the lady asked earnestly.

Yes, how about you? Kate asked him with silent
malice as she watched him swallow his chicken puff
with gallant determination and even manage not to cough
while he did so. Seeming to read her very thoughts, he
cast her a repressive look and Miss Transome a warm
smile that probably gave her far more encouragement
than he ever dreamt it would, if the flush of sudden
colour in her cheeks and the pleased sparkle in her eyes
was anything to go by.

Kate sympathised with the foolishly romantic nature
concealed under all the fluff and froth, even as she had
to fight a primitive urge to ruthlessly crush any hopes of
capturing Shuttleworth's interest that might be stirring
in Miss Transome's receptive breast. He wasn't hers to
be possessive about, and had made that abundantly clear

tonight. If he wanted to land himself with a wife who'd foolishly long for his love and affection for the rest of their days together, then that was his problem. Except that some annoying part of her argued it was hers as well, however hard Kate tried to ignore it.

'I fear I'm otherwise engaged that day,' he said with apparent regret.

'Yes,' Kate said with a hint of malice, 'Lady Tedinton has a waltzing party, has she not?'

When she'd heard rumours that a lady with a French-ified name, who might or might not be Selene, Lady Tedinton, had shared a lot more than a mere friendship with young Lord Shuttleworth while they were both in Bath one spring, Kate had dismissed them as mere gossip, even if the thought of him sharing that exotically beautiful lady's bed had pained her with surprising sharpness while she did so. An honourable young gentleman like Shuttleworth wouldn't cuckold a man of Tedinton's venerable years and genial temper, she'd assured herself, even if her ladyship was twenty or thirty years younger than her lord and reported to hold to a conveniently elastic interpretation of her marriage vows. Since neither had confirmed or denied the rumour, it had flourished on and off and Lady Tedinton was even said to preen to her friends for having fascinated such a potent young lord.

Now Kate was nowhere near so certain Edmund would refuse the invitation in the lovely Lady Tedinton's somnolently knowing sloe eyes and could see how his leanly handsome face and fine form would appeal to a jaded wife of her ladyship's sybaritic nature. In that

lady's position, with a much older husband preoccupied
with affairs of state and his estates, as well as his children from his first marriage, would she be tempted to
dally with a vigorous young gentleman who'd be sure to
make her a passionate and considerate lover? She hoped
not, but eyeing Viscount Shuttleworth surreptitiously
now, Kate knew she'd find him nigh irresistible if she
stood in Lady Tedinton's expensive Parisian shoes, even
if she wouldn't much like the fit of them.

Anyway, it certainly wasn't jealousy that pricked at
her as Edmund explained himself to Miss Transome far
more warmly than he'd spoken to her all evening. It was
merely pique that one who had once seemed to adore her
had returned to town looking as if he couldn't imagine
what madness had come over him to have ever thought
her the centre of his universe.

'I am engaged on business that day, Miss Transome,
but most of my acquaintance seem set on going to the
ridotto, so you certainly won't lack for companionship
if you intend to go yourself.'

If only because Mrs Flamington was rumoured to
possess a very pretty daughter it would abound in eager
young gentlemen, Kate thought cynically, then ordered
herself not to be such a sharp-nosed nag and to sym-
pathise a little more with her new friend when she was
only intent on the same outcome as herself. In fact, she
informed herself ruefully, she and Miss Transome were
sisters in adversity.

'And you, Miss Alstone,' Lord Shuttleworth asked at
last, as if she were only a polite afterthought, 'are you
bound for Hill Street or Cavendish Square that day?'

'Neither, Lord Shuttleworth,' she replied uninformatively.

'How unfortunate for your admirers.'

'I dare say they will endure it.'

'Ah, but endurance and enjoyment are so distant, Miss Alstone, that I wonder you don't at least try to pity your disappointed admirers a little more,' he taunted her, and drew Miss Transome's attention by doing so, which felt far worse to Kate than enduring his contempt unnoticed.

'I intend to enjoy my visit to an old friend who is currently bereaved and therefore does not seek out such bright company, but I wish both hostesses and their guests well in my absence of course, my lord,' Kate managed coolly.

'Beautifully put,' he acknowledged with a fencer's bow and Kate felt tears prick her eyes at the thought that where once upon a time they'd almost been friends, now they were very much more like bitter enemies.

The air of chilly politeness between herself and Lord Shuttleworth hadn't escaped the notice of the gossipmongers and Kate felt every speculative gaze and insincere enquiry after her health like little darts. Longing to be securely among family and friends once again, Kate realised how privileged she was to have escaped the attention of the more vicious gossips until now.

'I knew you were feeling low for all you denied it, my love,' Eiliane scolded gently as they rode home in the carriage at long last. 'So why on earth did you insist on staying so late at that very dull party?'

'Because to leave early would have provided even more food for the gossips,' Kate admitted wearily and silently thanked her friend for not rubbing her nose in tonight's many humiliations, especially after their earlier discussion. A conversation that now seemed so arrogant and misguided on her side she could hardly bear to recall it with hindsight and squirmed in her comfortable seat. If he'd managed nothing else tonight, Lord Shuttleworth had taught her how little she mattered in the great scheme of things and most especially how little she meant to him.

'Oh, don't concern yourself about them,' Lady Pemberley said cheerfully, 'they're so hungry for something juicy to chew over after so many months away from the capital that if they can't find a real scandal they'll make one up out of nothing. Give them a few days for a real one to erupt and they will soon be distracted from trying to make trouble where it doesn't already exist.'

'And it's not exactly a scandal if a gentleman who once admired me no longer does so,' Kate replied rather hollowly, not sure if she was reassuring Eiliane or herself.

'Of course not, but don't forget most of the younger ladies present tonight have been found wanting in comparison to you over the last few Seasons, my dear, and feel a little pity for their plight. Many of them will never climb off the shelf fate has left them on so pitilessly, the poor dears.'

'I'm not sure I will now and I do feel for them, even if I can't admit they were ever measured by my low standard and found wanting. I never intended to set myself A1 at Lloyd's and everyone else at nought, Eiliane.'

'Ah, but that's the problem. Not only are you beautiful, graceful, well born and surrounded by people who love you, but you're also astonishingly unaware of how unique and lovely you are. No wonder half the ladies of the *ton* secretly envy you and the other half want you to fall flat on your very pretty nose, Kate dear. If I didn't love you so much, I might dislike you myself for being so unreasonably beautiful.'

'How can anyone possibly be so appallingly mistaken, let alone you, Eiliane? I'm the least perfect person you'll ever encounter, even if you live to be a hundred, and I'm certainly *not* beautiful.'

'I know none of us are perfect this side of heaven, but you really are fortune's favourite, my love, even if it doesn't feel like it just now,' Eiliane replied with that depth of understanding that always floored Kate at unexpected moments. As Lady Rhys and now the Marchioness of Pemberley, her friend had set up so many humane schemes for rescuing the poor, the unfortunate and even the plain criminal, that Kate could only wonder at her energy and try to respect her judgement.

'It certainly doesn't,' she admitted as she stepped out of the carriage, glad of the comfort Eiliane had managed to bring into her husband's lofty town mansion as they were welcomed home after a trying evening. 'Although I do feel blessed to exchange Lady Finchley's ballroom for your fine residence, Madam Marchioness,' she managed to tease her friend and hostess lightly.

'It's nice enough now, I suppose,' Lady Pemberley

conceded rather absently as she set eyes on her new lord, gracefully sauntering out of his library as if he hadn't galloped his poor horse back to his London home almost mercilessly, then waited with restless impatience for his lady's return once he finally got here.

'I thought you were meant to be away for a whole week,' Eiliane chided, eyeing her tall, upright and still very handsome lord as if checking him for any sign of damage.

'I soon got my business over and done, so there seemed no point lingering to me when I could be more comfortable at home,' he replied, gazing at his lady as if he'd not set eyes on her for a month.

Watching them with exasperated affection and faintly amused by their refusal to admit they were happy as larks together, Kate left them to it and went up to bed, allowing her maid to fuss over her with such unusual docility that the girl finally asked if her mistress was sickening for something.

'No, it's just the headache,' she explained as patiently as she could.

'Oh, then you're not in love, Miss Kate?'

'Certainly not. I can imagine nothing worse,' she replied with such revulsion even Eiliane might have believed her, if she wasn't otherwise occupied.

'I can, and I think it would be wonderful,' came the dreamy reply.

'Bah! For heaven's sake, take yourself off to bed and stop bothering me with such absurd notions, before I feel compelled to scream.'

'You'll see,' her maid informed her with sharp nod

and, deciding there was no more to be done to change her young mistress's mind, took herself off to bed, presumably to dream of a nebulous lover who'd take her for granted and father ridiculous numbers of babes on her before neglecting her for someone less careworn, Kate decided, with a cynicism that seemed excessive even to her.

Maybe it would be better to have the illusion of loving someone to look forward to though, at least until cold reality broke through and spoilt it all, she thought wistfully while she climbed into bed and extinguished her candle. Before she succumbed to exhaustion, she thought that for as long as the enchantment lasted, a person might be deliriously happy with the one they thought they loved, before real life proved what a fairytale it all was and that so-called love faded away as if it had never been.

Chapter Four

Hofwever much she wanted to, it somehow seemed impossible to make her excuses and stay home when Kate received an invitation to the ball Lord and Lady Tedinton were holding to launch his lordship's daughter into society. Of course, it wasn't jealousy of lovely Lady Tedinton and whichever gentleman she might or might not have taken as her lover in the last couple of years that had made her so reluctant to come, but Kate couldn't help wishing the evening over and done with before it had scarcely begun now she was here. Her ladyship was looking exotic and sensuous and strikingly beautiful, and Kate supposed it was no surprise that Lord Tedinton had succumbed to her youth and voluptuous figure and seductive smile, even if he clearly should have known better at his age.

Either others didn't share her reluctance to be here, or were so curious to see how her ladyship would behave towards a stepdaughter barely seven years younger than she was herself that they couldn't bring themselves to stay away, because it seemed to take for ever for the parade of coaches drawn up at the Tedinton town house to reach the front door. Kate wondered why this particular party was so popular, when Lady Tedinton made so little effort to court her own sex and the patronesses of Almack's and one or two other *grande dames* could make or break any social event. Obviously his lordship's good character and generous opinions commanded loyalty from his peers, but Kate thought many of those present were here in expectation of hearing or seeing something scandalous and would be acutely disappointed if Lady Tedinton failed to provide it.

Kate took one look at Miss Tedinton and decided the poor girl knew exactly what was in the minds of many of those who were so effusively wishing her well. As Eiliane had pointed out, the gossips were eager and primed for mischief after a dull winter and Kate heartily wished she didn't have to be here to witness the poor girl's obvious embarrassment. Yet if she'd stayed away it would probably cause even more speculation about Shuttleworth's defection from the ranks of her admirers and her reaction to his coolness toward her. Too many people knew, or thought they knew, that Lady Tedinton might have captured Lord Shuttleworth's very close attention if the rumour mill was to be believed. How gleefully they'd all have talked tonight if Kate had played the coward and not come when they also knew Shuttleworth had once been her most devoted cavalier. As she waited with Eiliane to be announced and greeted as effusively as a marchioness and her protégée must be, even if the words must stick in Lady Tedinton's elegant throat, Kate wished someone would wave a magic wand and telescope time so she could be at the other end of this evening in the time it took to snap her fingers.

'You look splendidly,' Eiliane murmured reassuringly and Kate was cross with herself for betraying any hint of her feelings. 'That new gown is a triumph and you'll cast all the débutantes into the shade in it tonight because, although it's white and perfectly proper, none of them could carry it off with such *élan*.'

'Thank you. It seems there may be something to be said for being one and twenty after all, then,' Kate managed to reply as she smiled ruefully at her chaperon and wondered yet again why she was still feeling so nervous about tonight.

It was true that her white silk gown with its corded and looped trim and belled-out skirt was considerably more sophisticated than anything a débutante would dare wear and she felt a little better at the sight of her looking elegant and surprisingly assured in one of the long mirrors probably placed to throw more light on to the stairs. The style was a little fussier than she liked, but as the dressmaker had informed her, when she'd tried to order it made up in a plainer style, that was the mode and it was unthinkable for Miss Alstone to be thought dowdy and behind the times. The belled skirt and very high waist undoubtedly suited her figure and one of the few advantages of red hair was that even the most severe critics could never accuse her of being insipid. Being one and twenty, she could also wear her mother's pearl-and-diamond set without being informed she was fast and the fact of them at her neck and wrists and ears felt both reassuring and right.

Funnily enough, it wasn't the débutantes she was most concerned about, but Kate smiled brightly and tried to look eager for the delights ahead of her when they finally reached the head of the receiving line and she met Lady Tedinton's apparently sleepy-eyed gaze. Her ladyship's dark gaze chilled and Kate was tempted to seek out another of those well-placed mirrors to check there wasn't a knife plunged between her shoulder blades she was, as yet, too frostbitten to feel.

'How lovely that you could both attend our humble little entertainment,' her ladyship cooed as if utterly delighted they'd come.

'Oh, we wouldn't have missed it for the world,' Eiliane responded just as insincerely and Kate wondered once more at the polite lengths the great ladies of the *ton* would go to in order to best their enemies. 'Such an interesting use of flowers and drapery to accentuate the colouring of such an angelically fair girl,' Eiliane added with a pointed glance at his lordship, who suddenly looked thoughtful about the unsuitable cerise-silk swags that festooned the ballroom at such an innocent affair as a débutante ball.

'Dear Philippa is such a passionate lover of this particular shade of dusky rose silk that nothing I could say would change her mind about ordering yards of it to drape the ballroom with. Wise heads are so seldom found on young shoulders, don't you agree, Lady Pemberley?' their hostess parried sleepily.

Kate saw 'dear Philippa' conceal a frown and shoot

a helpless, hunted glance at her papa behind a fan that was also dark rose to match the silk draped behind her and quite the wrong colour for any débutante to carry, let alone a blonde and blue-eyed girl like Miss Tedinton. The expensive and elaborate fan looked distinctly odd against the stark white simplicity of the ball gown even her ladyship hadn't been able to argue against buying for such a young girl, as if she'd been given it to hold while someone far more sophisticated was busy. After all, Kate thought cynically, why spend a penny more on her stepdaughter than necessary, when her ladyship could pass on her cast-offs to her and spend it on herself?

Lord Tedinton looked pitifully relieved at his wife's implausible explanation and was obviously too blinded by his beautiful countess to see beyond the end of his own nose. Kate ardently pitied the children of his first marriage and smiled encouragingly at the unlucky Philippa while Eiliane exchanged insincerities with their hostess. Receiving a shy smile in return, Kate made a mental note to bully the more pleasant youths of her acquaintance into demanding Philippa Tedinton's dance card, before her stepmama pushed her into more venial hands in the hope of getting her off her hands more swiftly, and cheaply.

'Dreadful woman,' Eiliane whispered as they walked down into the ballroom and paused to take a discreet survey of the company.

'I doubt most of the gentlemen present would agree with you,' Kate murmured, watching a few of the fascinated males and searching for one in particular, although she chided herself for being such an idiot all the time she did so.

'Some have sense enough to see through the obvious,' Eiliane said, sounding as if she was trying to reassure her protégée that Edmund was one of the wise who'd already done so, although why she should when he meant nothing at all to Kate was quite beyond her.

'And some do not,' Kate said bleakly, her eyes briefly pausing on Edmund's golden-brown head. He was bending over one of the prettiest of the current crop of débutantes to initial her dance card. Then he gave her a gallant bow and an altogether too charming smile of farewell, until later.

'Not that you care what he thinks,' Eiliane continued blandly and Kate stopped pretending not to watch Lord Shuttleworth long enough to give her so-called friend a long cool look instead.

'No, not that I have so little sense as to do that,' she agreed silkily.

'Liar,' Eiliane murmured softly, then spying out the best seat in the house, again managed to procure it with a polite, ruthless smile that suddenly made it hers by right. 'I'm far too old to stand about like an exhibit at a fair and too young to sit on a chaperon's bench,' she said placidly when Kate raised her eyebrows at her tactics.

'And you only ever lay claim to whatever age you're admitting to at the time when it suits you to make use of it.'

'One of the few gifts middle age offers is the opportunity to exploit it at regular intervals.'

'And your rank?'

'Oh, yes, that, too, of course. A sensible person must make use of any unfair advantages the good Lord gifted them in support of a good cause, don't you agree, Shuttleworth?' Eiliane asked the one man Kate didn't want to see until she'd got over watching him either court an overgrown schoolgirl, or be eyed by their hostess as if she were a hungry cat intent on catching the finest prey she could spot.

Kate told herself she was merely disappointed not to be given the chance to avoid him all evening and greeted him with the brusque nod he deserved for all the self-doubts and turmoil he was putting her through. She then could have cheerfully hit him—if she weren't such a rational person—when he returned it with a distant bow.

'That depends on the circumstance, your ladyship,' he replied with an easy smile Kate envied her friend as she felt her own face stiffen into a chilly mask so she'd be ready for the contrast when he finally deigned to meet her eyes.

'Always so cautious, Shuttleworth?' Eiliane teased.

'Not always,' he parried rather dourly and Kate would have been a fool to read his cool glance as approving of her in any way. 'But I always agree with *you*, your ladyship, as it saves me so much energy,' he said with a lazy smile that did such unfair things to Kate's breathing she wondered if she was coming down with more than just bruised pride and dented self-esteem. A severe cold? Influenza, perhaps?

'The rest of us have to live with the consequences when she becomes more certain of her own omnipotence than Madame Marchioness here has any right to be though, my lord,' she reproached him lightly, wondering why she was bothering to speak to him at all when he didn't seem to welcome either her presence or her conversation.

'Neither of us will ever attain such a happy state whilst we have the corrective of your abrasive tongue available to put us right, Miss Alstone, isn't that so, Lady Pemberley?' he parried.

'It is,' Eiliane said with such heartfelt sincerity that Kate felt her confidence in her own judgement falter once again.

'Am I really so brusque and disagreeable?' she asked unguardedly.

'Only when you're not being right all the time. It really is most annoying in you,' he said, openly taunting her now and Kate told herself she was a fool to feel shaken and deeply unsure of what she'd built on the wreckage she and Izzie had been left with after the collapse of their once-safe little world.

'Just because you happen to think it's your divine right to be correct instead?' she asked him smoothly enough, refusing to even try to meet his eyes this time.

'Of course,' he said with the hint of a frown between his dark brows, so perhaps her avoidance of his eyes had given away her uncertainty and, yes, just a touch of hurt that he seemed to think her so arrogant and self-satisfied.

'I won't allow masculine superiority as a defence, just because the rest of the world suffers from the delusion it actually exists, your lordship. To claim it, you'll have to prove you possess it,' she challenged him and finally managed to meet his silver-green gaze as if it cost her nothing but a coolly ironic smile.

'I'd be delighted to do so, when you finally manage to screw up sufficient courage to risk defeat at my hands, Miss Alstone,' he replied, making no attempt to mask a heat in his look that echoed the wolfish, challenging smile on his suddenly very tempting masculine mouth.

Feeling as if she'd already suffered a loss when her wildest fantasies centred on his lips as if they could unlock the secrets of the universe, Kate clenched her fists resolutely at her sides. Seeing the threat of an easy victory in his intent and suddenly very green gaze, she made herself hold it steadily, as if doing so cost her no effort at all. Hopefully only she knew her fingernails were threatening to bite through her kid gloves and into her soft palms as she clamped down on her more primitive instincts in the hope they might give up in the face of bleak reality.

'Don't flatter yourself, my lord,' she warned him softly.

'No need, when you've done it for me by refusing to pick up any of the challenges I cared to throw out in the past.'

'I am not a coward, and you're the one who retreated from the fight.'

Suddenly the air was crackling with something more than the slightly bitter teasing of two people who'd once had such promise of linking and entwining their lives, yet failed to take that vital step together. Kate's mouth felt inexplicably dry and her pulse was racing, but she made herself meet him glare for dare. Half-conscious they were in all too public a space for such a contest of wills and wishes, she still couldn't let her eyes fall modestly and step away from him. Giving an involuntary sigh as she continued to hold his jade-and-steel gaze without flinching, she allowed herself the small concession of licking her lips to slick their inexplicable dryness and marvelled at the feral heat that flared in his eyes as he changed from confident, taunting challenger to offer a darker and deeper world of sensual threat instead.

'I think you're going to miss the first waltz if you don't hurry, my dears.' Eiliane intruded a little too brightly on their silent, too-significant struggle for some victory Kate didn't even understand wanting to achieve so desperately in the first place.

'And what a shame that would be,' she managed to say as acerbically as everyone seemed to expect her to, even if her lips felt numb and her tongue oddly stiff in her parched mouth.

'Have you already promised yourself to someone else, Miss Alstone?' Edmund asked relentlessly, for some reason best known to him refusing to do what she fully expected him to and walk away to find the pretty little miss he'd been talking to earlier.

'No, but I dare say you have.'

'You'd be wrong and not for the first time then, so perhaps you'd best hurry up and join me for it, before we attract even more attention to ourselves,' he replied.

'I never dance with noblemen who order me to do so, attention or otherwise.'

'Then pray do us both the favour of joining me on the dance floor, before the tabbies make all sorts of mistaken assumptions about our tardiness, Miss Alstone,' he demanded more than asked.

Seeing that he was right and they were attracting far too much notice for comfort, she took his offered hand and let him lead her onto the floor, as if she could imagine nothing more pleasant than to dance with the rude, contradictory, disturbing man. Instead it felt as if he'd just snapped the tethers of the polite pretence that should have held them both in check and left them perilously adrift in a world where she had no bearings or familiar landmarks to chart it by.

'Why do you suddenly seem to hate me, my lord?' she heard herself ask as soon as they were launched into the dance. She was silently cursing herself for agreeing to be held so close to him, so curiously in sympathy considering their new antipathy and the odd fact that he'd never affected her like this in the past, when he'd just been a skilful partner who didn't tread on her toes.

'I don't hate you, Kate, would that I could,' he answered her with no hint of a smile to soften his hard-eyed scrutiny of her upturned face.

'Perhaps it would be easier,' she agreed rather wistfully.

'For you or for me?'

'For both of us.'

'Then you *are* a coward,' he murmured, but still he held her as if she was precious and their steps harmonised with such ease it felt as if they'd been born to dance together.

'How so?' she managed to murmur, fighting a stupid urge to lay her head on his shoulder and dream her way through this waltz, as if all that mattered was being held so close to him nothing could come between them. At least imagining how that shocking spectacle would appear was enough to stiffen her spine and make her set a little distance between them.

'If you ever find the courage to really look into that guarded heart of yours, Miss Alstone, you might find your answer to that question and a few others as well,' he informed her even as he twirled and confused her in time with the dance.

'I don't know what you mean,' she said, wishing she was in a position to cross her fingers against that uneasy lie, for she was beginning to wonder herself.

'I know, that's the pity of it all,' he responded rather grimly and they spent the rest of the dance in uneasy silence.

Their waltz was over too soon and not soon enough, so they could step away from each other at last with more than just physical space yawning between them. Kate marvelled at herself for being such a fool as to have refused to marry him so often in the past, even as the guarded part of her drew back and whispered he'd always ask too much of her, however many times he asked and she said no. She told herself to be grateful he'd had the sense to slash through whatever bonds bound them to each other three years ago. Yet it didn't feel right that they should now go their separate ways as if they'd never once mattered to each other. She hesitated ridiculously when he offered her his arm so distantly at the end of their dance, as though he were about to conduct someone he barely knew and didn't much like back to her chaperon.

She laid her fingers on his immaculately tailored coat sleeve and did her best to look undaunted and serene while a flash of hot and confusing warmth shot through her at the feel of such latent power beneath her fingertips. It was utterly ridiculous to feel intrigued by even so light a touch on his muscular arm, when she'd been more or less immune to his physical allure on first acquaintanceship. She was still struggling with this odd twist to their relationship that now left her more conscious of him than he was of her when they were rudely interrupted.

'What a delightful display that was, don't you agree, my love?' Lady Tedinton greeted them with apparent laziness as Kate and Edmund unwarily stepped off the dance floor and straight into her path.

'Oh, they'll need to practise for a few more years yet before they're even half as good at it as you are, my dear,' her husband replied and Kate could see how little her ladyship relished being lumped in with those who were accomplished and experienced, but no longer young, even if her husband seemed oblivious to her quick frown of displeasure.

'Practice makes perfect, don't you agree, Lord Shuttleworth?' the lady responded, avid hunger brazenly obvious in her heavy-lidded eyes as she ran them over him, as if testing his power as a lover and liking the idea of taking him as her current one a little too well, whatever their past relationship might be.

'Only until that perfection is achieved, my lady,' he said with a supremely elegant bow Kate thought was more an attempt to distance himself from the woman than offering her even a hint of encouragement.

'But if it's not properly maintained, even perfection can fade away from lack of application,' the lady murmured and Kate wondered at her daring, at the same time as she marvelled at her husband's wilful blindness to her true nature as she tried to joust with a potential lover under his very nose.

'A little imperfection always seems so much more human to me,' Edmund replied with a surprisingly warm look in Kate's direction that she decided was his way of subtly informing Lady Tedinton she was much less to him than she thought herself to be, since he'd just put Kate ahead of her and everyone knew they were no longer even friends.

'Yet no doubt surprisingly tedious after a while. A person of taste and refinement, not to mention experience, cannot find it easy to be burdened with a bungling amateur forced to strive for mastery of a set of skills that comes to others with almost instinctive ease. It must be tedious indeed to endure such gauche fumbling at such times,' her ladyship responded.

How so much malice could be directed at her with one heavy-eyed, apparently amused glance was almost beyond Kate. She was tempted to shrug her shoulders and make a polite excuse before drifting away with an absent farewell, but she owed Edmund more than that,

even if he was confounding and confusing her more
than she'd dreamt he could when she was three years
younger and even more foolish.

'If one takes lessons from a fine teacher, they can be
enormously stimulating for both pupil and educator in
my experience,' she managed to defend herself as coolly
as if she had no idea their three-way battle concealed a
nasty set of double meanings that were all going straight
over Lord Tedinton's head.

'Since I hear that your former governess used her
position in a noble household to gain a rich and powerful
husband, one can only suppose the less wary gentlemen
among the *ton* need to be very careful indeed of those
lessons, Miss Alstone,' her ladyship said with a faux
smile only her husband would ever trust.

'Would it be her position as my governess, or that of
the only grandchild and sole heiress to the Duke and
Duchess of Devingham you intend to cite, my lady?'
Kate said with such apparent pleasantness she was
sure she heard her adversary's perfect white teeth snap
together with impotent fury.

'Since the odd creature foolishly renounced the
latter, then it must be the former, and what a very fine
scheme it turned out to be,' Lady Tedinton said, letting
temper flash out recklessly, as if she sensed her most
coveted lover slipping out of her grasping fingers when
Edmund's eyes iced over in obvious contempt.

'Sometimes,' he said with such chilly calm even Kate
shivered, 'it takes an inveterate schemer to spot a careful
plan where none ever existed, my lady.'

Since he also bowed to the apparently noble couple

with ceremonious elegance and an empty social smile, Lord Tedinton laughed and seemed as unaware of his lady's fury as he was that she was being subtly accused of being devious and spiteful.

'Indeed it does—now, are you going to honour me with that dance or not, my dear?' he said as brightly as if they were all getting along famously. 'After all, you lured me away from our duty of greeting belated guests on the promise of one, so we'd best join the next set and let them see exactly why we deserted them, eh?' he urged his wife indulgently.

Kate smothered a chuckle at her ladyship's barely masked impatience with his doglike devotion. The obnoxious female was already watching them with ill-concealed fury; presumably she wanted Edmund to share that devotion and hated Kate for being there to rescue him from her witchy wiles. If only the deluded female knew how little Edmund actually wanted Kate herself now, the awful woman would probably triumph and crow unbearably over her, she decided, sincerely hoping she could escape such an unpleasant encounter when Edmund's engagement to some dewy-eyed débutante was finally announced.

'What did you ever see in her?' she asked unwarily once their host and hostess had taken to the dance floor and the music was loud enough to mask her voice from an interested listener.

'Since you refused to become my wife more times than either of us care to be reminded, you have renounced all right to ask me that impertinent question, Miss Alstone. So I suggest you keep your arrogant opinions and any

other ill-informed and ill-natured gossip you have gar-
nered about me to yourself in the future,' he told her as
icily as he'd just set down her ladyship and Kate knew
she'd be on the verge of tears if she let herself risk such
a public loss of control.

Biting her lower lip to keep it from wobbling, she
nodded to him regally as words deserted her, but she
refused to let her steps falter under his icy silver-green
gaze, or show any sign that she was even conscious of
Lady Tedinton's darts of dark-eyed resentment, as that
lady barely even bothered to pretend her attention was
centred on her husband or the dance.

'I wish you a good evening, my lord,' she managed
to say expressionlessly enough as they neared Eiliane,
who was gossiping happily with one of her cronies on
the dark rose-coloured sofa that now reminded Kate
almost insupportably of their hostess for the night.

She curtsied to him with formal grace, he bowed with
almost as distant a hauteur as he'd used to depress her
ladyship's pretensions and they parted before Eiliane
had even spotted them returning together and been able
to come up with a pretext for keeping them so.

'This must be one of the most tedious parties either
of us ever had the poor judgement to attend, Kate,' her
mentor greeted her cheerfully, once the friend she'd been
so absorbed in pumping for the more interesting secrets
of the *haut ton* had departed to bully some hesitant
youth into dancing with her débutante daughter.

'Indeed,' Kate managed as she resorted to the small
amount of cover allowed by her fan to conceal some of
her confusion.

'You're overset, my love,' Eiliane exclaimed, even more concerned when the hectic colour in Kate's cheeks ebbed as she recalled Edmund's cold fury with her at even the mention of his rumoured *amour* with their hostess.

'I'll do well enough once I've got my breath back,' she managed to say calmly enough as she wondered why on earth she'd let her tongue run away with her in such an appalling fashion just because the very idea of Edmund making love to that vixen had made her feel ill.

'Nonsense, we'll call for our carriage and go home. I'll be glad of an early night and you look as if you could do with a week of them all of a sudden.'

'No!' Kate thought of how insufferably Lady Tedinton would triumph and smirk if she was weak enough to turn tail and go home like a whipped dog after that obnoxious encounter. 'I would rather stay a little longer and perhaps go on to Mrs Farnborough's as we had planned. That last dance was quite a vigorous one and I shall be perfectly fine in just a moment.'

'Will you, my love?' Eiliane asked shrewdly and Kate wished her a little less acute for once, but hoped her friend had no idea of the real reason why she was feeling so out of sorts and low spirited.

'Yes, I shall feel quite restored once I've had a rest. It would never do if I gained a reputation for giving myself die-away airs after all, for you'd never get me off your hands then,' she joked weakly. She refused to even consider the fact that it felt as if she'd never look at another man for the rest of her life and feel the least desire to marry him, or even stand up with him for a waltz after her bittersweet ones with Edmund had spoilt her expectations of any other partner.

She certainly refused all invitations to waltz for the rest of the evening, but brazened out the remainder of the pantomime it rapidly became to her. Seeing the daughter of the house dance with the suitable young gentleman she and Eiliane managed to throw into her path helped and, from Lady Tedinton's petulant expression, Kate thought her new enemy was probably having an even less satisfactory evening than she was. She allowed herself a brief smile of triumph when they finally left the Tedintons' ballroom, quite certain there was a metaphorical dagger in her back this time.

Chapter Five

'There it all is then, shipshape and neat as you like,'
Ben Shaw, the other half of the firm of Stone & Shaw
Shipping that he and Kit Alstone, now the latest Earl
of Carnwood, had set up long before his lordship even
dreamt of inheriting the family wealth and titles,
informed Edmund the next day. As this came after an
exhaustive tour of the warehouses and the new enclosed
dock Stone & Shaw were building by the side of the one
they'd already outgrown, then a return to the elegant
offices they now kept in the City for a résumé of the
firm's finances and projections for future profit, Edmund
could only agree with him.

'Even I can see that for myself, thank you,' he told
his formidable friend and business associate and wondered why Ben Shaw thought he needed reassurance
that, while he was at the helm, Stone & Shaw would
turn a fine profit for any investors lucky enough to be
admitted into the select ranks of their stockholders.

'If you didn't come and see it all for yourself every now and again, I wouldn't have much respect for you as a man or an investor, and I dare say we'd never have done business together in the first place,' Ben told him.

'So long as I don't try to interfere in the way you run the enterprise from day to day, I presume?'

'Aye,' Ben admitted wryly, 'you've the measure of me on that front, my fine young lord, and that's plain to see.'

'Not as young as I was,' Edmund defended himself automatically, although such teasing bothered him much less than it had when he was first admitted into the august boardroom of Stone & Shaw, probably because he had been thought likely to become part of the family Ben Shaw protected and loved as fiercely as if they truly shared ties of blood, by marrying Kate Alstone.

Would his refusal to become part of that family, now he'd finally returned to the *ton* with the aim of taking a suitable wife who wasn't Miss Alstone, mean an end to such an unexpectedly comfortable and profitable friendship? If so, he'd regret it deeply, Edmund decided, and settled down for an excellent glass of burgundy and a companionable cigarillo, determined to enjoy them and this unlikely friend while he still had the chance.

'Speaking of your relative youth, or lack of it, when are you going to get down to the business of finally wedding and bedding that stubborn girl of ours?' Ben came straight out and asked the question Edmund had been dreading all morning.

'I'm not,' he admitted bravely, considering Ben was the largest and most formidably tough man Edmund had ever encountered and could probably mill him down without even having to break his stride.

Coming under the steady examination of a pair of grey eyes that suddenly looked as if they were determined to see into the very depths of a man's soul wasn't the most comfortable experience of Edmund's life, but he held his ground and managed not to sigh with relief when Ben sat back in his chair and watched him blandly instead of reaching for his neckcloth and attempting to strangle him with it. 'Because?' was all Ben said while considering this new state of affairs.

'I can't imagine a worse fate than being in love with a woman who merely tolerates me, especially if we were to be bound inextricably together for life, can you?' Edmund replied, thinking of the Tedintons and barely managing to hide a shudder at the idea of being trapped inside a marriage like that one.

'No,' Ben admitted, 'but it beats me why you've now decided she won't do when last time you were in town you were so madly in love with her you couldn't even consider wedding anyone else.'

'Beats me as well, but maybe I finally saw the truth of the matter, before she got so bored with turning me down that she decided to accept me just for a change of scenery.'

'I think you would have discovered you had underestimated her if she did so,' Ben said sagely and Edmund wondered if the unconventional giant did indeed know Kate Alstone far better than he did. He'd once lavished such minute attention on her every mood and gesture that it seemed a sad reflection on Edmund's judgement and so-called powers of observation if he'd failed to understand her after all that effort.

'No, for I won't ask her again, so the situation will not arise,' he insisted, denying himself the luxury to hope that he was wrong about her after all. 'I lost my taste for being a tame lapdog to her some time over these last three years.'

'Then if she weds another man, you'll be entirely indifferent?'

No! The certainty of it roared through him like a sudden bitter tempest on a summer day. He'd hate her, and the cur she married, until his dying day.

'Not entirely,' he admitted out loud.

'Not in the least, you young fool,' Ben informed him roughly. 'Had my Charlotte even threatened to promise herself to another man, I'd have torn him apart limb by limb and danced on his lousy body, then taken her to bed and loved her until she saw some sense. So either you don't love Kate and never have, or you still do and owe it to yourself and her not to end your life in Newgate dangling on the end of a hangman's rope. Although, I suppose in your case, my lord, it would be a jury of your peers and a silken noose at Tyburn instead of a hempen collar.'

Despite Ben's mockery of his rank and what he'd make of the stern resolution Edmund had made to find himself a suitable wife this year and forget Kate Alstone if he ever found out about it, Edmund didn't feel excluded from the select ranks of Ben Shaw's friends. Either the unconventional giant didn't believe Edmund could turn his back on his passion for the wretched female he'd once thought so firmly lodged in his heart he'd never shift her, or Ben was determined to stand his friend, irrespective of those other loyalties.

'I've no taste for martyrdom,' he admitted at last.

'As well Kit Alstone's occupied elsewhere, then, for he's a damned idiot when it comes to his precious family and those he truly loves. He might decide you've dishonoured Kate's good name and challenge you to a duel if you don't wed her after all, for if ever I met a hot-headed fool when he's in a temper, it's my lord Carnwood.'

'She's the one who turned me down time and again, not the other way around,' Edmund protested.

'Well, I did say he was a damned fool, didn't I?'

'And you think me one as well?'

'I never claimed to understand any of you great lords of creation and I can't say that a closer acquaintanceship with the two of you has improved what I already had very much.'

'And I don't see how you intend to get away with that hackneyed line any more, considering we all know who your father is now,' Edmund said with rash courage, for it was also common knowledge that Ben Shaw was no respecter of titles and ancient privilege.

'Let's hope the Marquis of Pemberley stays so busy with his new wife that he won't interfere with your plans then, whatever they are, for he's devilish fond of Kate as well,' Ben warned, discussing his natural father with an ease neither of them had ever thought to hear when he'd still been so convinced he hated his lordly sire.

'Aye, it's bad enough having his wife's attention fully fixed on me, without adding Lord Pemberley's eagle-eyed scrutiny to the mix—along with Lord and Lady Carnwoods' thrown in for good measure,' Edmund admitted ruefully.

'Don't delude yourself I'm too busy to interfere myself, will you?'

'I never delude myself that badly, but what beats me is why,' Edmund said.

'Because I don't believe you can really turn your back on the headstrong minx after you fell in love with the little devil at first sight, and don't forget I was there to see you behaving like a mooncalf when it happened, so don't try to deny it. I've met men who could cut themselves off from a woman they once cared for like that, as if she'd never existed or was cold in her grave, but you're not one of them. Kate cares for you more than either of you seem to know, and I don't think you're fool enough to turn aside from the magnificent female she'll become if she weds the right man, if only she'll just throw caution to the wind and accept you at long last.'

'Thank you for thinking I am that man, but I'd have to be fool enough to ask her first. So what holds her back from being that woman anyway then, Ben?'

'And you once claimed to be in love with her?' Ben said with a hint of scorn in his deep voice that made Edmund flinch, despite knowing it was Kate who had been so set against falling in love once upon a time rather than he. 'I can't but marvel at fine young gentlemen who call infatuation love, then flit from girl to girl, like strutting peacocks waving their tail feathers, with not a worthwhile thought in their silly heads.'

'I certainly thought myself in love with her three years ago, until she convinced me it was hopeless; if that makes me vain and idle, then so be it.'

Ben gave Edmund another of those searching glances, then nodded as if making up his mind about something. 'I never really thought you guilty of those vices, so Kate obviously made a fine fist of whistling your mutual happiness down the wind, but have you ever stopped being furious with her long enough to wonder why?'

'No, I just realised my one-sided love would make our lives a farce, even if I managed to persuade her to say yes instead of no in some moment of weakness.'

'If you really loved her, you wouldn't have given up at the first hurdle.'

'Hardly that.' Edmund was stung into justifying himself as he looked back over that wild springtide when they'd both been painfully young and he'd been alternately effervescent with hope and cast into the depths of despair by Kate's inability to see how finely suited they could be, in bed and out, if only she'd open her eyes and see the rich possibilities of it all.

'I grant you she's stubborn and can be damnably difficult to either drive or lead at times,' Ben conceded.

'Difficult? She's nigh impossible,' Edmund told him with a bitter exasperation he thought he'd conquered, but it seemed that his friend was right and he still had strong feelings toward Kate Alstone, even if foremost among them was currently vexation, closely followed by something darker and angrier and born of three wasted years apart that he refused to examine more closely right now.

'There are one or two good reasons why she's not exactly the easiest female to live with at times,' Ben said almost apologetically, which in itself was enough to render Edmund momentarily speechless.

He shook his head over what those reasons might be and must have looked as puzzled as he felt. 'I can't imagine what they might be,' he replied at last.

'Then apply the brains God gave you and use your imagination, Edmund. Have you ever stopped to wonder how you might feel if you were brought up as a much-loved and indulged child of a happy family instead of a noble and indulged orphan? Then imagine that, one by one, you lost every person in the world who was dear to you one way and another, all but your little sister, whom you then had to fight like a tiger to protect from the suddenly hostile world around you. Kate and Isabella Alstone lost their parents, their brother and, to all intents and purposes, their elder sister in quick succession when Kate was little more than ten years old. Their grandfather, who should have protected them both and loved them all the more, was so wrapped up in his own selfish grief and fury at the fates that he abandoned those two little girls to the so-called care of his daughter, Lady Ennersley, and *her* daughter, and I wouldn't trust either with my pet dog, let alone the comfort and education of two innocent and supposedly helpless young girls.

'Take my word for it, Edmund, those two unnatural females are the worst harpies I ever met, and I was brought up near the rookeries and certainly know a harpy when I see one. They constantly belittled and even beat Kate and threatened to do the same to her little sister, except Kate used to get in their way so they couldn't reach her, which of course meant that they chastised her instead. They also robbed them of all those two little girls held dear, refusing to let them even see Eiliane Rhys as she was then. I know my darling stepmama tried time and again to wrench them both out of their icy grasp, but old Carnwood ignored the plight of his own grandchildren and refused to do anything to stop his daughter or the devil's spawn she gave birth to making their lives a misery for far too long.

'Those two heartless witches told them he hated them for living when his son and then their brother died and maybe they were even right, for he never made any effort to look to their welfare until it became more comfortable to act on Eiliane's constant nagging to at least send them to school rather than to refuse to do so. Their aunt and cousin also managed to convince Kate that nobody but the servants cared what became of them, and that even they only gave a damn what happened to them because they were paid to. If not for my darling wife, Shuttleworth, those girls would have remained alienated and adrift even at the school their old fool of a grandfather eventually sent them to, solely to get them out of his way and to stop Eiliane's constant letters and enquiries about them, and calm the hornet's nest she stirred up among his wider family to shame him into action.

'Now *I* respect Charlotte's judgement and my own instincts well enough to be certain there are very deep and passionate feelings hidden behind Kate's cool façade, even if you can't see it. To the wider world she's a confident and desirable young beauty with riches and privileges at her fingertips most young women would envy her, but if that's all you see when you look at her, Edmund Worth, maybe you don't deserve her after all. You might be better off with a less complex and difficult woman if you're merely in search of an easy life with a conformable wife who'll exclaim over your cleverness hourly and give birth to a pack of spineless brats you can hand your wealth and titles on to before you finally die of boredom.'

Perhaps as a fortunate, if often lonely, orphan he *had* been guilty of envying Miss Katherine Alstone her loving family and so had failed to look beyond the cool indifference with which she met the eyes of the world. He knew better than to dismiss the counsel of a man he respected, Edmund decided, and neither could he ignore the opinion of Ben's wife, a woman of such extraordinary character, integrity and unusual looks that he couldn't help but admire her, from a safe distance.

'Maybe I'm *not* the man you take me for, and perhaps I don't deserve Kate Alstone as I should if I can't gain her love, but I never managed to knock down that wall of touch-me-not indifference you claim she's hiding behind, Ben, even when I was trying my damnedest to demolish it.'

'I suppose you know what they say about faint heart not winning fair lady?'

'All very well, but three years ago my doglike devotion did nothing to win her affection or convince her she can trust me. I hope you don't expect me to sit at her feet for another three, risking being kicked aside every time she wonders if another pet might not suit her better.'

'Maybe she doesn't want a pet in the first place, then.'

'What does she want then, man? I'm damned if I know any more.'

'Just that—she wants a man and not a lapdog. She's a sensible female and finds them pettish and yappy and who can blame her? I'm relieved my wife has never shown any sign of falling for the breed.'

'From what I can tell she just adopts strays, and the larger and uglier the better.'

Edmund recalled his visit to their eccentric household last week with a reminiscent grin. Mrs Shaw had lately taken in a hound of very mixed breeding and huge size, who bayed at all her visitors and buried his bones under her best furniture, whilst protecting her and hers from all and sundry, even though she didn't actually stand in need of any protection so far as he could see.

'My point exactly,' the lady's husband agreed smugly.

Edmund wondered what the *ton* would make of the son of a marquis, even one born the wrong side of the blanket, who smugly claimed kinship with a mongrel of the most mixed variety and dubious origins. Possibly Ben's very indifference to his own blue blood, and most of his father's peers along with it, explained why he wasn't just tolerated, but lionised by all but the most stiff-necked of them. It seemed to him that there was nothing quite so intriguing to most of the *ton* as someone so genuinely unimpressed by their elegant show and lofty traditions as Ben Shaw appeared to be.

'So next time I call on Miss Alstone, you think I should growl menacingly at all other visitors who dare to enter Lady Pemberley's drawing room?' Edmund asked with a rueful grin. 'Then perhaps I could pin any gentlemen I don't like the look of up against the wall with teeth bared, whilst I attempt to bay loudly at the same time and dribble down their shirt fronts or all over their precious Hessians while I'm doing it?'

'If you could leave out the drooling, that will probably go down better,' Ben said with a reminiscent shudder and Edmund almost pitied him that aspect of the over-enthusiastic Prometheus, as Charlotte had christened her latest waif.

'Maybe, but I am what I am, Ben, and have never been good at pretending to be otherwise, I'm afraid,' Edmund admitted ruefully, almost ashamed of himself for lacking the guile to storm and bluster sufficiently to gain Kate's attention at last.

'No need, you're rich, titled and personable, Shuttleworth, so why would you need to be other than what you are? Just show Kate how much you've grown up since you fell all of an adoring heap at her feet three years ago. Make her see that you've become your own man while she wasn't paying attention before you give up on her, that's all I'm suggesting.'

'All?' Edmund echoed faintly, but he grinned at his unexpected mentor just the same and left after an interesting as well as an enlightening morning in a thoughtful frame of mind.

It might have been possible to set his face against the very idea of loving Kate and abhor her inability to see what was in front of her pert nose when he was a hundred miles from her and spare her incendiary presence, Edmund admitted to himself as he walked away from Stone & Shaw's neat offices. He might even have found a sweet and biddable wife to put in her place if only she'd stayed away this Season. Kate was too near now; too real and right in front of him night after night, proving how much less life with that sweet little wife would be than one with her. Maybe it wouldn't be fair to offer another woman so little when she might find an untainted young spark to make little paragons with instead. And how could less ever be good enough, despite his three-year-old resolution never to let Kate Alstone trample roughshod over his dreams again?

Despite the vow he'd made to himself to forget her, he still yearned for her in his bed and at his board night after night in his dreams and in his deepest, darkest fantasies. If he couldn't beat his obsession with her, why not use it to trap her with her own scheming? He'd seen her summing up the young bloods and even the personable widowers in search of a wife to look after their restless and motherless broods and had wanted to strangle her for looking about her for a suitable, coldly selected, unloved husband. Still, he might be able to use her stubborn misreading of her own character and get her up the aisle before she realised they could never be so little to each other if they both lived to be ninety.

Hadn't apparent indifference got him a lot further already than devotion ever had? He recalled the feel of the sway and dip of her lush but streamlined body against his in the dance and gave a reminiscent grin. If she was to be lured out of her ivory tower, wasn't he already halfway to tumbling her into his arms instead? With such a promising start he'd be a fool if he failed to draw the real Kate even further out from behind those defensive barriers of hers.

The prospect of a future he'd resigned himself never to achieve was heady, but the last thing he wanted to do was risk more humiliation at Kate's hands. Next time he asked her to marry him he'd make quite certain the skittish redheaded torment was ready to say yes at last. So there had to be a very long way to go before he could be sure his last offer was met with eagerness, rather than the absent-minded kindness she might show a boot-boy who'd spilled lamp oil on the furniture and was being tiresomely emotional about the whole tedious business of clearing it up.

Edmund had walked through the City and into Mayfair, probably only escaping being robbed because he'd dressed plainly for his trip round Ben's empire. Potential thieves took one look at such a distracted gentleman and decided he was either mad and too much trouble to bother with, or a poet or an artist caught up by his muse and therefore too poor to be worthwhile. He'd experienced such a revolution of feelings since he'd set out from it this morning that he got back to Worth House in Grosvenor Square only to find he couldn't settle to anything, so he took his favourite hack out in an attempt to calm his seesawing feelings instead.

Did he really love Kate Alstone? That was the question that trumped all the others, he decided, as the black gelding finally won free of the mêlée and Edmund allowed him a little more freedom. Deciding it wasn't too late to ride into the countryside to avoid the curious and the sociable when the evenings were drawing out and there was a moon tonight anyway, he set the powerful animal on the road to Richmond and tried to keep at least half his mind on their going.

When he'd first met her, perhaps he'd still felt less than other men, because he was the last of his line and couldn't join one of Wellington's regiments to fight Bonaparte, or follow Ben Shaw and the Earl of Carnwood's example and forge his way by his own efforts. Even as a boy he'd known he couldn't leave his land and his people masterless and abandoned to the uncaring hands of the Crown as the Prince Regent, with his voracious appetites and gargantuan debts, would strip every asset the Worths had built up so diligently over centuries, then sell it piecemeal to whoever offered the most money.

Had his secret insecurity, when he'd been forced to turn his back on the army he'd once longed to join and dutifully go to Oxford instead, made him doubt himself, until he'd felt Kate's rejections were all he really deserved? If it had led him astray about himself and the woman he wanted to love for life, then he cursed it. Ben Shaw's shrewd summary of Kate's well-hidden fears and insecurities had made him see at last why she might hold back from love, or any other emotion that would leave her vulnerable to hurt. He raged against the very thought of how badly hurt she had been and fervently wished he'd been the one to punish those two she-devils instead of Kit Alstone. Everyone knew he'd banished the old earl's daughter to a remote estate and ordered her to stay there on pain of losing even that, and the lady's daughter had been told to live abroad with the secret husband she'd apparently been wed to ever since her seventeenth birthday, despite her subsequent and bigamous marriage to another man.

So why hadn't Edmund had the confidence to see through Kate's almost absent-minded tolerance of her eager court and him in particular when they'd first met? What excuse did that young sprig have for not looking into her dark blue Alstone eyes and finding the real Kate she still hadn't dared to fully become lurking under all that wary indifference? That Kate was lion-hearted and passionate and he wanted her fierce protection and all that pent-up love she was so wary of giving for his children, and a share of that last commodity for himself as well, or he'd end up envying them and that would never do.

Well, he could see her now and had her firmly in his sights at last. He was his own man now, too, and if not the dashing hero he'd once dreamt of being, he was strong enough to shoulder his responsibilities and even enjoy them most of the time. He'd got his estates running at a healthy profit and restored the depleted fortune managed, or mismanaged, by his various trustees until his majority, so if he could take on all that and succeed, why not have one last, reckless throw at winning the woman he's always wanted above all others as well?

He grinned at the memory of how he'd managed to confuse Kate recently without even trying; now he was in earnest, keeping her off balance and paying attention long enough to claim her heart and her hand suddenly didn't seem so unlikely after all.

Chapter Six

'*What* a brilliant catch Lord Shuttleworth will make
some lucky girl, now he's obviously looking out for a
more *suitable* wife,' Kate heard one of the chaperons
behind her whisper rather loudly to her crony a week
or so later and knew perfectly well that she was meant
to hear every word. After all, she had refused to marry
the lady's impecunious elder son in no uncertain terms
at the end of last Season and that did put a doting mama
off a girl rather badly.

It was true, of course, that she'd watched Edmund
dance with all the prettiest and most eligible débutantes
the Season rejoiced in night after night and could vouch
for the fact that, while all seemed to agree he was a very
fine gentleman and would make an even finer husband,
some were shamelessly eager to march him up the aisle
of St George's, Hanover Square, at the double.

'Indeed, my dear—he's so rich, so well born and *so*
handsome that he's without a doubt the finest catch to be

had this Season,' another lady, who persisted in thinking Kate had deliberately eclipsed her elder daughter's début, and blamed her for that poor girl having to marry a mere mister with only two large country estates and a town house to his name, asserted. 'The Tedinton woman seems quite set on cuckolding her poor husband with him, but that won't bar him from marrying well. My dear little Felicity is too young yet, but your girl hasn't made enough effort to captivate such an eligible young lord up to now, my dear; you should remind her of her duty to her family.'

'Darling Charity is quite determined on her Mr Holt and he on her, so Henry will agree to the match in the end, I dare say, and Lord Shuttleworth can marry where he pleases so far as I'm concerned,' the first lady replied placidly enough, since Mr Holt was commonly held to be a very wealthy man and she was obviously a realist.

'It's a well enough match, I suppose, but Shuttleworth would make a very fine feather in any mama's cap,' the second said wistfully.

'Especially Lady Tedinton's,' the first lady said with a shrewd and significant nod in the languorous and lovely Countess of Tedinton's direction.

'That, my dear, rather depends on whether she's intent on wearing him on her bonnet or her sleeve,' her friend replied with heavy significance.

'Surely not even she would do that, especially during her daughter's come-out Season when it would be more fitting if he caught the chit rather than the mother?'

'The girl's only her stepdaughter, don't forget, and

not ten years younger than the painted hussy her father married in some fit of madness. Tedinton should have known it would end in disaster once he'd made such a ridiculous second marriage.'

'That woman can't pull the wool over the ladies' eyes, even if the gentlemen hang on every word that falls from her painted lips. She's little more than a strumpet and not a very well-bred one at that.'

'I pride myself on always being able to read a person's true nature, despite any shoddy façades they may care to throw up to confuse people. Even Tedinton won't be able to fool himself her affairs and her low appetites don't exist for ever, for all that she's a beauty.'

'True, but she's nowhere near as clever as she thinks she is. The woman has risen too high and now thinks she can have whatever, or whomever, she wants. Such arrogance will prove her downfall one fine day and it won't be a moment too soon for me when she tried to condescend to me last time we crossed each other's paths.'

'Well, I doubt she'll try it twice, my dear, but there's no mistaking exactly what, or rather whom, she wants right now,' the other lady replied meaningfully. Lady Tedinton was watching her stepdaughter chatter animatedly with Lord Shuttleworth whilst reclining on a nearby sofa and eyeing him as if she'd like to pounce and never mind how many spectators saw her do it.

'Her thoughts are written all over her face, for all she thinks we're too stupid to read them, yet he looks more entranced by the girl. Tedinton would be a fool to turn down such a match on the say-so of a wife who wants Shuttleworth herself. So that match would put the cat among the pigeons, and set others with their eye on him in their place once and for all,' the first lady said sweetly.

Kate did her best to look serenely unconscious of their spite while she fervently hoped they were wrong. She wasn't well acquainted with the girl, but she was pretty enough and might be charming as well for all she knew. However, she was clearly no equal match for Edmund Worth. He deserved a woman who wouldn't bore him before the honeymoon was over and, if he met that lady, Kate supposed she'd have to shrug her shoulders and look about her for that perfect husband a little more diligently than she was doing at the moment.

'Certain ladies need to realise that it's never wise to be too finicky and risk coming back Season after Season, don't you agree, dear?' the second of her detractors continued relentlessly, with a significant nod in Kate's direction she pretended not to see.

'Luckily our darling girls are in no danger of finding out that pert opinions and overweening vanity will almost certainly land them on the shelf for good.'

'Quite—I never could abide such precocious chits myself,' her friend agreed while Kate planned their imminent demise in minute and purely theoretical detail, to keep from verbally grinding them under her chariot wheels as her restless temper demanded she must.

'Our dance,' pronounced Mr Cromer concisely at just the right moment to stop her leaping to her own defence in a reckless fashion.

'Indeed,' Kate replied gratefully, having come to

value his sparse conversation over the last weeks, as he began to court Miss Transome in earnest.

Who would have dreamt a few years ago that Amelia Transome and Kate Alstone would ever come to enjoy each other's company so much, when each had eyed the other during their début and decided they had little in common? Now Kate valued Amelia's kind heart and generous nature and wondered at herself for not seeing past her chatter and fluttery manner before. And at least Amelia regarded Mr Cromer dancing with Kate as the lesser of two evils, since she couldn't dance every dance with him herself. In her company at least he wasn't being giggled over or eyed speculatively by one of the eager newcomers or their husband-hunting mamas, and Kate felt at ease with at least one of her dancing partners, so all three were content. Yet Mr Cromer had a good friend in Lord Shuttleworth and every now and then Kate would glance up and find him standing by the other gentleman's side and watching her, as unreadable as he was unsmiling while he did so. His lordship hadn't asked her to dance again and she told herself that she was relieved.

'Shuttleworth ain't serious about that chit, y'know?' Mr Cromer informed her during one of the country dances.

'He gives a very good impression of it, then,' she replied, just as if she had every right to feel bitter, which she most certainly did not.

'Chivalrous to a fault, always was. Easing her path into society quiets his conscience, I suppose.'

Then it was true. Edmund *had* been Lady Tedinton's

lover and evidently he still felt guilty about that and, considering the wretched woman was another man's wife, so he should. How could he have fallen for that heartless female's overblown charms? No, there was no need to wonder about *that*; Kate only had to flick a look at the sultry beauty doing her best to look faintly amused by her stepdaughter and his lordship to know exactly why a gentleman would find such lazy sensuality irresistible.

Yet Kate thought from the downward curve of her pouting lips that the lady was secretly furious at his defection. Turning the situation over in her mind, Kate shivered as she contemplated the sort of marriage she'd fooled herself she wanted. The very idea of casually following in the footsteps of Lady Tedinton and taking lovers once she'd borne Edmund's heirs made her want to weep now. Then, imagining how she'd feel if they'd actually wed and she'd found out about the exotic Lady Tedinton afterwards, she felt a strong temptation to go into strong hysterics. So maybe it was as well this was neither the time nor place to consider what her revulsion at the very idea said about her own feelings toward Edmund Worth.

'Bestholme,' Mr Cromer remarked obscurely after they'd finished their dance and he was escorting her back to where Eiliane and Miss Transome were sitting.

'Yes?' Kate said encouragingly.

'Fortune hunter,' he warned with a shake of his head for emphasis.

'Ah, I thought so,' she said with a grateful smile.

It set the cap on a hateful evening that Mr Bestholme

seemed even more desperate to corner her attention when she refused to take to the dance floor with him. He besieged her with sly comments and overfamiliar touches whenever he could force himself closer to her by using the crush of guests as an excuse and if she didn't get away from his damp, cruel hands and hungry eyes soon she was going to be sick. Eventually she disgusted herself by taking to her heels and fleeing his far-too-persistent and public pursuit, even resorting to the ladies' withdrawing room where even he wouldn't have the gall to follow her.

Sure the man would think nothing of compromising her into marriage if that was the only way he could get his repellent hands on her fortune, she quit her temporary sanctuary and trespassed into the private part of the house to plan a rapid retreat to Derbyshire and the safety of Kit's fearsome protection, if her determined evasion of Mr Bestholme didn't persuade the human leech she wasn't going to be tricked, pressured or just plain forced into marriage.

It seemed a coward's way out even to her, but it sounded so tempting after the last few weeks of disappointed hopes and mistaken dreams. To be in Derbyshire with spring softening even the starkly beautiful peaks with its lovely bounty, to breathe in good clean air and be able to ride all day without having to be civil to a soul if she didn't choose to meet one, seemed like heaven just at the moment. And what a relief it would be to escape the nagging feeling that three years ago she'd turned away the one man who could have made leaving her beloved Wychwood for a new life as his wife and mother of his children a wonderful adventure, rather than an impossible sacrifice.

Yet even while she was searching through possible excuses for running away, mentally planning her journey and thinking up a story that would convince Kit and Miranda when she got home that she was perfectly well and happy, just jaded with London and the social Season, she knew she couldn't do it. There were her detractors to outface and, more important than any of them, there was Izzie, who would be here very soon—how could Kate not be here to witness her little sister's social triumphs and enjoy her lively company once more? It might hurt far too much that Edmund had decided to look elsewhere for a bride and a lover, but she was an Alstone and would not turn tail and run at the first setback put in her path by unkind fate.

There was Eiliane to consider as well, of course, and, come to think of it, she was oddly distracted tonight and unlike her usual sharp-eyed self for some reason. Her chaperon had hardly seemed to notice Bestholme's increasingly bizarre behaviour tonight and Kate frowned as she wondered belatedly if there was something seriously wrong with her dear friend and mentor. Then she had her two newest friends to see safely wed, of course, and Amelia Transome had gallantly deployed her most determined chatter on Kate's behalf tonight in a selfless way that commanded equal loyalty. Even Mr Cromer had put his stalwart silence between her and Mr Bestholme as often as he could without seeming too particular himself, but nothing had put the awful man off his single-minded pursuit of her fortune.

Kate could practically hear the ill-natured gossip breaking out all around her if she went back into the ballroom to make sure her chaperon wasn't sickening for something. Awarding herself five minutes of peace and quiet would do no harm, she assured herself cravenly, and stole on through the half darkness of the private rooms of their host and hostess's town house with a guilty sense of playing truant from reality and fortune hunters, as well as intruding on their privacy.

Edmund eyed the assembled company and almost wished he'd stayed in Herefordshire this Season after all. Yet the fine hairs on the nape of his neck were prickling as if trying to warn him of some danger the rest of him was slow to pick up. Lady Tedinton, with her silly pretence that he had already been her lover and would shortly be so again, was a damnably inconvenient complication he'd certainly not bargained for and he'd had to waste far too much time tonight avoiding her very obvious lures and any hint he might be susceptible to them. He did his best not to meet *her* gaze as he searched the room in vain for a glimpse of Kate's glorious red curls, but something told him he'd soon have to take the time and trouble to convince Selene Tedinton once and for all that she meant nothing to him and never would, in terms even she couldn't misinterpret as part of the game she so loved to play.

'Something's amiss,' Cromer informed him brusquely as he joined him with a worried frown on his face.

'There's always scheming afoot at affairs like this

one,' Edmund responded coolly, even if his friend's unease only added to his own.

'Miss Transome claims that Lady T. and Bestholme are up to something,' Cromer said with resigned acceptance that Amelia's sayings and doings were more important to him than he'd dreamed they could be until recently.

'Any idea what?' Edmund asked, suddenly very interested in them as well.

'Don't know. Unholy pair at the best of times. Welcome to each other, except the Tedinton woman keeps looking at Miss Alstone as if she'd like to kill her slowly, then stamp on her grave. Miss Transome's convinced the woman's hatching a scheme to put Miss Alstone out of the picture for good so far as you're concerned.'

'She's mistaken her adversary then,' Edmund said curtly.

'Or her quarry.'

'Yes, she couldn't be more wrong there,' Edmund replied softly.

'Going to stand here gossiping all night, then?' Cromer prompted.

'No, I'll deal with the harpy in my own good time, after I've tracked down Miss Alstone and seen her safely back to her chaperon's side once more.'

'Aye, she's been gone too long for her own good. You go and find out where she's up to and we'll cover your backs as best we can.'

'Thank you, the confounded woman is a damned nuisance at the best of times and this isn't one of them,' he said grimly. 'Sometimes I'd like to strangle her.'

'Better marry her as soon as possible instead—obviously made for each other,' his friend said with understated irony that was currently wasted on Edmund as he fumed at Kate's protracted absence.

'I'll think about it,' Edmund said tersely and with a casual look about him to locate the Marchioness of Pemberley and Bestholme, who was, luckily for him, still in the ballroom and not pursuing Kate around the half-lit gardens or goodness only knew where else she might be hiding herself.

Satisfied Kate's chaperon was engrossed with old friends now and blissfully unaware that anything was amiss, he left by way of the card room as if he hadn't a care in the world, even as he fought an irrational fury that Kate hadn't come to him for help instead of bolting for the shadows. After searching the quieter rooms of their host's residence, he was beginning to think trouble existed in Miss Transome's overheated imagination when he caught the faint, unmistakable scent of Kate Alstone lingering in an otherwise deserted corridor leading towards his host's library. He stilled his already near-silent footfall and listened for any further sign of the elusive, overly independent female.

Despite knowing very well she should return to the ballroom and prepare to endure a whole evening of dodging Bestholme as stoically as she had it in her to manage, Kate had wandered furtively on through private rooms she knew very well she shouldn't intrude into. The farther she got from the ball, the more she felt like a hind with the noise and threat of hounds and huntsmen fading behind her and the harder she found it to turn about and go back. She scoured a dark room for unexpected fortune hunters and allowed herself a huge sigh of relief once her eyes adjusted to the darkness and she still found no sign of the repulsive creature—nor any hidden galleries or dangerously secluded corners he might spring out from.

Sinking into a snug high-backed chair by the unlit fire, she wondered if the lady of the house sat there to embroider or read whilst her husband laboured over his speeches in the House of Lords, which were apparently earnest, detailed and well intentioned, but guaranteed to empty that august chamber almost as fast as a cry of fire. It made a rather appealing picture of two lives entwining over the years so that, even if she didn't share his interest in politics, her ladyship sat and kept her lord company whilst he pursued one. Shifting in her chair, Kate wondered if Eiliane had been right all along. Maybe marriage wasn't a military campaign from which all emotion must be sternly banished and all hope of anything better shorn ruthlessly away in case it proved false.

Too late for such a conclusion to make any difference to her situation, she decided sadly, but she still felt irrationally betrayed by Edmund's defection when she had absolutely no right to. Such a shame that she'd spurned him so emphatically during her first heady Season, when she'd been too young to realise just what wonderful possibilities were being offered her and grab them with both hands. Now he was so indifferent to her it felt as if some long-anticipated treat had been withdrawn and her life was suddenly limited and dry for the lack of it. Squirming in her comfortable seat, Kate braved an answer to so many of the questions troubling her and it only made matters worse. Edmund, who no longer wanted her, who despised her for turning him away, who seemed determined to court a sweet and suitable wife not in the least bit like Kate Alstone—somehow he mattered uniquely to her and it was obvious to anyone who had two eyes to see with that she no longer meant a thing to him.

Cursing her younger self for refusing to see that he'd make her an ideal husband and lover, Kate felt unable to just sit and contemplate her own idiocy and jumped to her feet to pace restlessly. She couldn't put her hand on her heart and admit it was irrevocably his and therefore broken beyond mending and, as he now watched her with hard disillusionment instead of adoration in his silver-green eyes, that was just as well. Yet Kate had an uncomfortable suspicion she'd been testing Edmund's devotion from the moment they first met, and considering it had proved such a chimera, maybe she'd been right not to trust it enough to agree to marry him.

Doing her best to be honest with herself now her future looked bleak, Kate stopped her perambulations and tried to face her own faults as unflinchingly as she was prepared to pick over Edmund Worth's. Impatient with herself for being unable to consider him, or her feelings for him, with dispassionate coolness, she was about to pace her host's fine Persian carpet when a sound in the corridor outside made her freeze in her tracks. Just making out the soft tread of a gentleman's evening shoes on the marble floor outside, Kate muted a huff of impatient fury and turned to face the wretch who'd been chasing her all evening with defiant determination and the fireside poker.

'Preparing to beat me off with more than just words this time, are you, my dear?' the intruder asked her blandly and relief and something far warmer than that ran through her at the very sound of Edmund's voice. It made her feel young and silly all of a sudden as she had to put her hand over her mouth to stifle a chuckle.

'Only if you really annoy me, Lord Shuttleworth,' she said, her heartbeat thundering in her ears for a very different reason now and her fear flying as wild curiosity about darkened rooms and their unknown possibilities took its place.

'Maybe you should carry it at all times to fend off importunate suitors then?' he said as he took it gently from her and returned it to its stand.

'I can think of at least one person I'd like to leave with a few good bruises,' Kate said darkly and saw him frown even in the semi-darkness.

'Just say the word and I'll do it for you.'

'And then be forced to meet the repellent man at dawn as if he deserved to be rated a gentleman after all, my lord? I rather think not,' she told him crossly and just the thought of him risking all he was to a pistol ball made her insides go as cold as if she'd swallowed an icicle.

'I can take care of myself,' he told her abruptly.

'I dare say you can, but I'll manage without your assistance on that front all the same. I do like to sleep at nights, you see?'

'So do I, although you've robbed me of a great deal of that commodity since we first met,' he informed her softly and Kate realised how close he suddenly was to her only at the instant when he slid a strong arm round her waist and pulled her against his muscular frame so easily it hardly even occurred to her that she might resist him.

'Have I? How very inconsiderate of me, Edmund,' was all the response she seemed able to offer, which was very odd of her, considering she'd come in here to avoid similar attentions from another man.

'Yes, it was. So don't you think it's high time you shared a little of my sleeplessness to make amends?' he murmured huskily.

'Maybe...' she began, but it was too late and he stopped her mouth by the simple strategy of kissing it until she forgot what she was going to say and almost everything else as well.

Chapter Seven

At the advanced age of one and twenty Kate had experienced only the most respectful of chaste salutes to compare this one with and they were no help at all, she decided hazily. She supposed having such a powerful guardian hovering like Nemesis in the background must have kept her ignorant of such dangerous delights until now. If Edmund had kissed her like this three years ago, she'd almost certainly have been married to him virtually ever since, but had either of them been ready for such heady enchantment then? It was a question she'd never be able to answer since he hadn't kissed her until her wits were shot and her body singing with some wild hope she didn't dare name until tonight. Abandoning any effort to reason with herself, she snuggled even closer to him, whilst raising too-willing lips to lure him back to her the moment he seemed about to recover his senses and back away.

'Edmund,' she murmured his name reproachfully,

protesting any distance between them and wantonly hoping he could be persuaded to do it again.

'Katherine?' he replied, lingering on the syllables of her name as if it was a sensuous luxury in his mouth.

'Kiss me again?' she begged shamelessly.

So he did and this time there was nothing reverent and respectful about his wickedly knowing mouth as it opened hungrily on hers and, as soon as she echoed him in instinctive response, he plundered it ruthlessly. For the first time Kate felt the true allure of being seduced as well as seducing, with a man's firm mouth and hot demands suddenly a wonderful promise, rather than a threat of terrible vulnerability or base subjection. She shivered in anticipation of something even more mighty, a force that could take her under and drown her in passion and sweetness, so she did her best to make sure she attained it by sneaking her hands up and about Edmund's strong neck, then shocking them both by moaning against his lips when his tongue invaded her mouth and her knees turned to water.

It was heat and light and sustenance and she couldn't currently imagine ever needing any other. He ran lingering, approving hands down the supple line of her slender back and she all but purred with satisfaction when he reached the firm swell of her buttocks and settled there for a hot, breathless moment before he swept that incendiary touch back up to mould her even closer into his kiss. Gasping with delight as his wicked tongue darted in and out of her wanton mouth in a rhythm even she recognised as primal, for all her ridiculous innocence, she clung as if he was her rock in a very stormy sea indeed.

Then he allowed them the sumptuous treat of lowering his hand to cup her breast and Kate wondered how she managed to stay standing for the rush of heat and temptation that rocked through her like a force of nature. She heard his breath catch at the willingness of her tightened nipples, obvious under the richness of silk and his exploring fingers and she stuttered out a sigh of delight when he explored one of them further until she moaned once again. All thought of where they were and what risks they were taking of being discovered fled as even the distant sound of music faded from her consciousness and all that mattered to her was him. Edmund, her almost-promised lover, hers. At last there were no questions in her head except for how soon the searing ache at the heart of her could be appeased with something he and no other could grant her. Caught up in her first taste of headlong, driven passion, she keened softly at the bolt of demand for more that ran through her like hot fire.

Head reeling from her innocently erotic responses to his runaway loss of control, as soon as he felt her mouth respond to his with untutored enthusiasm, Edmund tried hard to draw back, to let his longing hands fall from her magnificent body and put distance between them that his own harder, even more eager body certainly didn't want.

'No, stay,' she urged, her voice husky and shaky and utterly in tune with every one of his feral instincts to possess her and carry her off to his lair and keep her there for ever. 'Kiss me again,' she demanded, so lost in what they'd set alight between them that he doubted she remembered her own name, let alone his.

'If I do there will be no going back for either of us,' he managed to grate out between lips stiff with wanting and needing to do exactly what she demanded.

'Edmund,' she whispered and it was an agreement, not a denial.

Triumph roared through him as his body tightened even more painfully. He struggled to leash his own out-of-control instincts and the need he'd kept under such a mighty curb ever since he'd met her in the face of her suddenly so wild, so natural, so truly Kate-like urgency. The lure of lowering her on their host's fine carpet and thrusting into the warmth and welcome she was innocently laying out for him tempted him until it felt like too much of an effort, too much of a betrayal not to give in and take her to their mutual ecstasy.

He tensed to do as they both wanted and seize her by that ridiculously slender waist of hers and soothe and stoke her passion until neither of them had any choice but to let themselves sink onto the floor of this room in a stranger's house and rut like a pair of spring-tortured animals. He'd always known she would be matchless and sweet and impulsive and unashamed in her wants and needs, if she ever let herself be the passionate and extraordinary woman she had it in her to become. Now that Kate was free from the restraints the miseries of the past had forced her to curb her true, passionate self with, she was utterly breathtaking as she took fire in

his arms and demanded an intense seduction neither of
them would ever want to forget.

And here they were, exactly where they should not
be, with risk and scandal dogging every step along the
way, and all it would take to set it off was someone else
feeling the urge to wander as she had wandered and find
them out. They were trespassing in the shadows of their
host's private rooms, with an open door at their back and
hundreds of curious guests far too eager for any slight
scandal that presented itself to their eager ears and eyes
a matter of mere yards away. Reluctantly he restrained
the ravenous wolf within him bond by painful bond,
until he could gasp in a huge breath of cooling air and
set his forehead to hers, drawing on an unexpected stock
of true tenderness that surely only she could unleash in
him at such a time.

'Not here, lover,' he murmured, 'and certainly not
now.'

'Where then, and when?' she demanded, the tremble
in her low-voiced demand threatening to undo all the
good he'd managed to do them.

'In our marriage bed, after all is made right between
us in our own eyes.'

'It *was* right,' she protested bitterly, drawing away
from him as if his touch repelled her now and he cursed
her contrary, headstrong nature, even as he knew very
well it was one of the things that made him want her so
unbearably that he'd take her on virtually any terms.

He wondered if he'd made a mistake after all by not
seducing her as if she meant no more than a quick and
lusty roll in the hay to him. Yet every instinct that wasn't

primitively crying out for her and a release from this nigh-overwhelming frustration shouted just as loudly that he'd have lost a crucial part of her if he'd sunk into her and brought them both to a quick and savage climax on the floor in a virtual stranger's house with so much risk all around them.

'Not until you know exactly what you want from me and why,' he told her implacably.

'I want *you*, and I want you *now*,' she challenged him furiously.

'But *why*, Katherine, *why* do you suddenly want me so much?'

'Because...' She almost let something betraying slip out, but stopped herself just in time, as she always had when it came to her feelings for him, whatever they might be, and now he doubted she knew any better than he did.

'Because I'm irresistible, because I make your world shift and then brighten whenever I come into the room? Or is it just because I'm the first man to get past your ice-queen defences and make you feel the possibilities of being a real woman?' he made himself ask in a voice husky with wanting to do just as she urged, to forget anything else and let the devil take care of afterwards.

Luckily she was far too innocent, far too confused to read his true state from that gruff enquiry, for if she truly ignored the scruples that had backed them away from the precipice and rubbed her roused body against his, butted her mouth against his and demanded more, he knew he'd be beyond controlling his response to her, beyond fighting this reckless need that tore at his self-control and snapped at the fetters he was trying to put on both their demons.

'I really can't imagine,' she told him with such a superb attempt at frosty dignity he almost applauded, except that would drive her further back behind her defensive ramparts and he couldn't allow that now they were so close to getting where he'd wanted them to be for so long.

'Oh, I think you can, Kate,' he murmured.

'So you can prove to me I'm just a foolish woman like any other you might care to kiss in the dark? I think you just did that,' she said quietly and all hope might have drained out of him, if he hadn't reminded himself that everything about their recent encounter argued the exact opposite, if only she wasn't so innocent. She didn't know the difference between mere lust and the nigh-overwhelming passions and heady emotions they'd just lit in each other.

'If that was all I wanted, I could have done it perfectly well three years ago and got it out of the way,' he said flatly.

'Arrogant, boasting braggart that you are?' she gritted furiously.

'Adult, realistic man that I am now,' he corrected and did his best not to grin at her as she sucked in a mighty breath in order to denounce him comprehensively enough to slake her wounded pride. 'Quiet!' he ordered abruptly.

All Edmund's senses were alert again as he remembered the world outside this silent, darkened room and cursed himself. He shouldn't have taken such a reckless risk with Kate, shouldn't have got so close to seducing her and himself in this risky, hole-and-corner fashion. His ridiculous susceptibility to her hadn't withstood the purely tempting fact of her, alone and unguarded and almost sad in the darkness. She'd gone straight to his head like fine wine, just as she had the first time he'd ever set eyes on her, and it tore so painfully at his heart to see her pensive and lonely that he finally accepted Ben was right. He could never turn his back on her and all she meant to him, despite the nearly three years of effort he'd wasted trying to evict her from his heart. He cursed himself for making that discovery in such a place as he heard another whisper of sound from outside his host's study.

'Don't you—' She never quite managed to counter his abrupt order since he clamped an impatient hand over her mouth and forced himself to at least try to ignore the feel of it, soft and moist under his palm, since he wanted his senses alert for whoever was creeping about outside.

He saw a wicked glint come into Kate's eyes even through the gloom, as if she knew very well that the connection between them had not been severed and probably never really would be now. She narrowed her gaze and let her sharp and sweet tongue lick his palm, even as she breathed in quite happily through her nose and watched him like a houri. No, he couldn't succumb to her mischievous allure, the gnawing temptation to kiss and take and to hell with the consequences. Evidently he was as fast under her spell as ever, but he wasn't going to be discovered here with her, because the decision to marry him or not would then be sidestepped and void as it became inevitable, and that would let her off the hook of having to admit how she felt about him. Marriage of convenience indeed! he scoffed silently. How could she be so wilfully blind to her own passionate nature?

'Someone's coming.' He risked getting even closer to murmur in her ear and felt her senses jar and her mouth tense enough for him to risk taking his hand away.

Casting about him for any avenue of escape, he noted the locks on the long windows into the garden with something like despair. For a moment there seemed nothing for it but to face whoever was coming and announce his immediate engagement to the woman he'd wanted for so long, but he wasn't inclined to let whoever was coming dictate their fate. Seeing a door into some lesser office ajar, he towed Kate inside before she could protest, or dig her stubborn heels in and brazenly await discovery, so he'd have to marry her without the admission of love he was determined to wring from her.

Kate peered through the crack in the door that was all Edmund had left them by rushing her in here and could just make out the faint glow of a single candle. She blinked against even that much brightness after the virtual darkness of the shadowed room and flinched away from the idea of being discovered cowering in here like a guilty felon. It would make so much less of what they had been doing, until Edmund had recalled what a gentleman he was, and even now frustration and awe tugged at her newly awakened senses. She swallowed an unladylike curse that they'd been interrupted, just when she'd been hoping he might seduce her after all. Instead they'd only gone a heady, headlong stride forwards, then sharply back to dull respectability again. She was undoubtedly fast and wanton, and maybe in the morning she'd feel suitably ashamed of herself, but just now she'd trade the last three years of dull respectability for three hours of sensational discovery in Edmund's far-too-noble bed.

Her rebellious reverie was interrupted by the noise of a candlestick being carelessly plunked down, then the unmistakable sound of a man pacing. She should have been relieved that Bestholme had stopped searching for her, but wished whoever was marching up and down the book room at Jericho instead. Releasing a pent-up shush of breath in an exasperated sigh earned her a sharp nudge from the annoying man at her side. Even as she stung at his silent rebuke, she caught the sound of two voices murmuring and realised someone else had entered the room while she was working herself into a fine rage against fate and Edmund's overactive conscience.

Then she heard Bestholme's rather nasal tone after all and shuddered, but could hear little more until the furtive pair came closer to their side of the room and she hoped it wasn't because of some give-away sound she or Edmund inadvertently let slip. Wondering why, if this was an assignation, they didn't just shut the door and be done with it, or go and bother some other clandestine lovers with their unwanted presence, Kate shifted from one foot to the other to ease her cramped limbs and longed for them to leave.

'I'm sure there's nobody out there and I vow it's like

making an assignation with a little old lady who's afraid of her own shadow, meeting you in secret and pretending all night that we mean nothing to each other, even if it does relieve the boredom of a very dull evening, but why won't you do just this one little thing for me, George?' Kate heard a distinctive husky voice murmur.

Whatever was Lady Tedinton doing here, risking whatever scraps of her tattered reputation she had left to her? And what on earth could she be asking an apology of a man like Bestholme to do for her? Deciding she was fated to overhear other people's conversations tonight, Kate listened shamelessly, but when Edmund's strong hand felt for hers in the darkness she clasped it gratefully and clung to the warmth and comfort he was silently offering.

Suddenly she didn't need him to tell her the rumours of him and the unscrupulous woman standing only yards away from them being lovers were merely lies; a tale the peculiar female had no doubt thought up to puff up her own consequence. Not that Kate suddenly thought him a perfect Sir Galahad. No doubt he'd taken at least one or two willing beauties into his keeping in the past, since he wasn't a monk or a saint, even if the mere thought of him doing so hurt far too much for comfort. There was a core of integrity about him that would not let him couple with a woman who held her husband and his family in such contempt that she didn't care if most of society knew she'd cuckolded him repeatedly.

'It's a hell of a risk, Selene,' Bestholme replied at last after considering whatever that 'little thing' might be for a very long moment to two listeners, forced to breathe so

shallowly that Kate for one felt almost suffocated by her
desire not to be heard and discovered by so unattractive
a pair.

'But I'm so very weary of warming an old man's bed,
Georgie. Please, say you'll do this for me, lover? I so
long to be free,' her ladyship wheedled in a little-girl
voice that somehow made their discussion all the more
sinister.

'No, I'm not risking putting my head in a noose to
set you free in order for you to try to wed a man who
has no more interest in you than a stone statue might
have. Tedinton's fortune would go to his heir anyway
and I dare say your jointure would be tied up so tight
not even the Lord Chancellor could get his hands on
it. You'd end up worse off and alone, and I can't afford
to keep you, you're far too extravagant and altogether
costly a creature for me, my dear.'

'That repellent brat is a minor and makes no effort
to ingratiate himself with anyone and I'm certain you're
quite wrong about my jointure. Algy thinks the world
of me and will leave me a rich woman.'

'He might be a ridiculous old fool, but he's far more
possessive than you choose to realise. He won't leave
you a target for men like me after he's gone, and the boy
has a pack of embittered relations all longing to avenge
the slights you've heaped on them these last ten years.
The truth of it is that you've grown lazy, Selene. The
world doesn't revolve around you and what you covet
for now, despite your belief you only have to scheme for
whatever you want to get it.'

'Just do this one little thing for me and I'll make sure

that high-nosed Alstone bitch has no alternative but to marry you,' the woman cajoled and even as Edmund's hand tightened on hers to offer comfort and denial of what the scoundrels were discussing so coldly, Kate had to put her other hand over her mouth to stop herself shouting out a protest at such a repulsive strategy and add the furious caveat that she wouldn't marry Bestholme if her very survival depended on it.

'And precisely how do you propose to do that?' Bestholme asked.

'I'll whip up such a scandal she'll beg you to wed her by the time I've finished.'

'You don't have the power, Selene my dear. Haven't you realised by now that nobody as heedless as you are will ever hold sway among the *ton*? I doubt they mind your blatant peccadilloes with other men, or even the fact you married a fool for money for most of them did the same when it comes down to it, but you're about as subtle as a town crier about your contempt for your husband and his cronies and he's widely liked, for all he's a senile old fool, and you, my dear, are not.'

'Never mind preaching me a sermon and to hell with what a pack of pompous fools think, will you do it?' Lady Tedinton replied in her lazy, malicious drawl as if they were discussing some minor favour instead of cold-blooded murder.

'I'm still listening,' Bestholme replied as if bored, but indulging her.

And so am I, Kate was tempted to shout and step out of hiding to confound the unlovely pair, but she shuddered at the very idea of confronting such a sordid pair of rogues and wasn't it as well to know exactly what they were planning?

'Quiet,' Edmund mouthed a warning against her ear, but how had he known?

Kate was so busy struggling against the incendiary effect of just his breath on her ear lobe, his mouth so close against her neck she could almost feel the words form on his lips, that she missed Lady Tedinton's first few words and frowned fiercely at him in the pitch darkness. How could she be so wrapped up in her response to his closeness that even the small matter of the murder of Lord Tedinton faded against the fierceness of the fire Edmund had lit between them with those few passionate kisses?

'All you'll need to do is be found with the silly chit in a scandalously dishevelled condition, then you can inform everyone you were just celebrating your engagement a little prematurely,' she was saying in a scornful tone. 'Even Carnwood won't gainsay you when the silly wench is obviously in need of a husband.'

'And you think I'm incapable of thinking up such a simple scheme myself, Selene? I'm almost insulted,' Bestholme responded in that cold, indifferent voice Kate now knew was not an affectation, but reflected his true self.

'You're still being dunned and always begging so-called loans off me to pay off your endless debts, so you evidently don't have the nerve to carry it out.'

'Whereas you have the nerve and not the brains?'

'Think so if you dare,' Lady Tedinton hissed and Kate shuddered at the casual evil of it all.

'I do dare, but that's why you keep coming back to me, isn't it?' Bestholme demanded and there was the sound of a brief scuffle and then a horribly needy moan as Lady Tedinton demonstrated the truth of what he said.

'Take me now,' she growled.

'No, it's too risky,' her lover argued and gave a low chuckle that made Kate shiver at the cold lustiness of their loathsome need for each other, 'and I like you desperate, Selene. By the time Tedinton has pawed you all the way home and tried to mount you like a man, you'll be glad to meet me in that very convenient summerhouse he's had built in the garden for us, if he only knew it, and feel a real man between your legs again at last.'

'I hate you,' she informed him throatily and there was another of those horrible interludes as Kate heard them kiss noisily and even caught the sound of fine cloth tearing as they went at each other like beasts.

'I like the way you hate. Now tidy yourself up, then get back to the ballroom and persuade that old fool to take you home early. I'll go the other way and come back through the garden, so nobody will know you were with me. It's only the fact I'm supposed to be courting a fortune that keeps my creditors off my back as it is, so who knows what they might do if they found out about you, my lovely doxy?'

'Foreclose?' Lady Tedinton asked as if discussing the weather and Kate felt sickened at the sound of her lover's flat-handed slap, presumably to somewhere that didn't show. 'I could come to you in the Fleet,' she offered

throatily, as if violence made her more eager and Kate
wondered if she might disgrace herself and Edmund by
actually being sick, then considered the consequences
and managed to control her revulsion after all.

'No, try informing on me to get me sent there and
you'll rapidly discover what a mistake you've made. Just
behave yourself and go on keeping that senile old idiot
sweet, then be where I told you to be by dawn, Selene,
or I'll take my pleasure elsewhere. There are plenty of
younger and more obliging mistresses than you who
can be had for a lot less trouble than you cause me,'
Bestholme warned carelessly.

'I'll be there,' Selene Tedinton replied urgently.

'I know,' her repulsive lover drawled huskily and Kate
heard his footsteps recede while the light faded as he
ungallantly took his candle away, leaving his mistress
still in the dark.

A few moments later there was the swirl of silk and
satin and an exasperated curse, then softer footsteps
receded towards the ballroom until all seemed silent
and empty in the room beyond this airless office they'd
been trapped in.

Chapter Eight

'Have they really gone?' Kate whispered as quietly as anyone could whilst making a sound at all.

'I hope so, since you're restless as a cat and nowhere near as silent,' Edmund grumbled back.

'I was quiet as a mouse and resent your aspersions, my lord,' she informed him with as much dignity as a lady could assemble whilst shut in this cupboard of a room with the unbelievably infuriating Viscount Shuttleworth and forced to listen to murder and her own forced marriage being planned outside it.

'Then for heaven's sake do it softly for a change.'

Kate stamped a soft-soled foot on the runner and hoped Bestholme really had left and so wouldn't hear the faint thump it made against the oak floor underneath. If being angry with Edmund for very little reason helped keep her from falling into hysterics over what she'd just overheard, then Kate was all for it.

'Virago,' he chided impatiently.

'Tyrant,' she flashed back at him.

'Come on, I've had enough of lurking in the dark like a thief,' he growled in an exasperated masculine rumble and towed her as abruptly out of their hiding place as he'd hauled her into it in the first place.

'Just as well they really have gone,' Kate carped even as she clung to his hand like a lifeline. 'We'd have been in a fine pickle if he'd stayed here in order to give her a head start for the ballroom.'

'He's not that much of a gentleman and we're in a fine pickle anyway,' he told her seriously.

Thinking back over the last however long they'd now been away from the ballroom and propriety, Kate could only agree with him. 'How are we going to stop them?' she asked shakily.

'We aren't.'

'Then you're prepared to let that harpy and her disgusting paramour murder her husband without even lifting a finger to stop her?'

'No.'

'Then what are we going to do?'

'*We* are going to do nothing. When you cease your incessant nagging and let me think, I dare say *I* will eventually find a way to stop them without a scandal.'

'And I just sit about simpering while you stamp about brooding and proving what a clever gentleman you are?'

'You're a single female with a reputation to consider.'

'Bah! If I were a married woman without any shreds of one left to me, you'd still find a way of excluding me,' she fired back at him, struggling to free her hand from his at last, although it felt very comfortable in the misogynistic, contrary man's hold and part of her really didn't want to stand alone after such an evening.

'Yes, I would,' he told her implacably.

'Why? I'm not a fool or a hysterical female given to fainting and die-away airs.'

'No, just because you're you,' he told her rather obscurely, 'and you'll be busy,' he added by way of a diversion.

'Busy?'

'Planning our wedding,' he said and Kate felt the odd sense of detachment she'd been suffering ever since he'd stopped kissing her finally threaten to overwhelm her.

'I thought you just said "our wedding",' she said faintly.

'I did.'

'But how can I do that when we aren't going to be married, Edmund?'

'Because we are, Kate.'

'Solely because you just kissed me in a private room where nobody could see us? That's complete nonsense and nobody will know what we've been doing if we don't tell them.'

'They will when we return to the ballroom together in a state of disarray and hint very strongly that we'll shortly be announcing our engagement. I may despise Bestholme and his whore, but I'm not above borrowing that scheme now the devil's in the driving seat.'

'Nonsense, if you go ahead and I follow you into the ballroom a little later, nobody will dream we were

together all this time, or that either of us heard anything we shouldn't have tonight. Nobody need be any
the wiser.'

'You have a simple-minded faith in the gossips suddenly turning incurious about all you say and do that
I could find almost admirable, Miss Alstone. If only it
wasn't so misplaced and silly,' he told her, suddenly back
to the aloof and superior Lord Shuttleworth he'd been
towards her since returning to town and Kate refused to
ask herself why his icy tone hurt and the hard look she
could imagine in his eyes cut through her so coldly. 'You
have now been absent for far too long to just shrug it
aside and pretend you've been innocently drifting about,
and I don't want those two black-hearted villains realising you overheard their assignation,' he went on relentlessly and Kate felt her palm itch to slap some sense
back into him.

'Then what do you suggest that I do instead, you
infuriating man?' she gritted through clenched teeth.

'Be thoroughly compromised by me, or prepare to
embrace life as a social outcast,' he informed her so
laconically she felt that odd sense of not being quite
connected with the real world threaten her again.

'You can't do this, Edmund, you'll be dragooned into
marrying me if we appear together in such a state as
you suggest and we both know that you don't want to
wed me any more,' she protested in a fierce whisper.

'Better that than risk that unsavoury pair realising
you were wafting about listening to out-of-the-way conversations, Kate,' he declared not very encouragingly.

'How flattering,' she told him crossly, wishing she

could turn her back on the infuriating monster and walk away.

'Find a bit of steel to stiffen your backbone, for goodness' sake, Miss Alstone,' he chided like some large and handsome gadfly sent to plague her by a malign fate.

'Why should I resign myself to such a fate when you obviously don't have the least desire to marry me?' Kate managed to say in defiance of her inner idiot, who was demanding stridently that she accept eagerly and be glad he felt honour-bound to marry her after being so sternly set against it.

'Needs must when the devil drives,' he said coolly and must have decided he was done with useless words and it was time for action before things got worse.

He hustled her out of a side door and into the garden proper before she could find breath or words to protest with and urged her inexorably closer to the long windows of his lordship's fine ballroom, but not close enough for propriety, of course. The further they got from that darkened room the better, even if it was leading them closer to marriage, Kate decided numbly, and cursed herself for not fighting this more strongly. It was hard to fight temptation when it beckoned so wickedly.

'You could leave me here alone,' she whispered softly in defiance of her own eagerness for any sort of marriage with him, even this forced one.

'So you could be quizzed from now until next Christmas on the identity of your cowardly lover?' he murmured back, and anyone watching them would probably mistake them for fellow moon-led idiots lured out here by such promising darkness, she decided crossly. 'Go back in that room alone after spending such a long time away from it and your chaperon, and you'll be ruined without anyone having to plot against you,' he continued relentlessly, 'and in acute danger once that harpy realises you could have overheard her plot to murder her husband, whilst you wandered about in the shadows so carelessly that anything might have happened to you.'

'And being a perfect gentle knight you're sacrificing yourself instead?'

'No, being a pattern-card of perfection was so dull that I gave it up,' he declared flippantly.

'Along with me?' she murmured, then could have kicked herself for letting him know how much his recent rebuffs had hurt her.

'I thought I'd save myself the pain of enduring another crushingly polite refusal,' he told her and Kate hurt at the careless apology in his deep voice. 'I dare say marrying you won't be so bad once I get used to the idea again,' he added.

'And if you think I'll stand by idly while you have affairs with other women you will be sorely disappointed, Edmund Worth,' she informed him in a fierce undertone.

'That's entirely up to you, dear Kate. If you keep me otherwise occupied, I probably won't have the time or the opportunity to stray,' he observed and silenced her with another mind-stealing kiss.

Furious, she did her best to bite him, so he deepened his kiss and dared her give whatever she might have had the wits to withhold until now. Defeated by her own need of him, her body seemed to meld itself to

Edmund's powerfully lean one of its own accord and wild heat burst into instant life again. She angled her wanton mouth to his in a way she should think appallingly fast but didn't. *Never mind fast,* her deepest buried instincts warred with her training, *he'll still marry you now, even if he doesn't really want to.*

She couldn't make herself break away, even with that chilly thought in the back of her mind, but she clenched her hands at her sides and refused them the luxury of his lithely muscled body. It didn't abate the searing wildfire flaming through her like a force of nature, but it made her feel a little better about herself and the self-control she'd once prided herself upon.

Unimpressed, his hands ran over her in an unashamed exploration and she loved it. She'd always denied being capable of deep feeling, in her ignorance of how elemental and out of control she would be with the right man. Now he let his wicked hands find a way between them, despite her body's ridiculous efforts to plaster itself against him like a poultice, and Edmund ran an approving thumb over a raised nipple that immediately hardened and begged for more without permission from her. She had to fight not to moan and cry out a frantic demand for more, for everything. If not for the half-painful gnaw of need, the half-wondrous goad of heat at the heart of her, of course she would put distance between them and escape the purely physical spell he'd cast over her, yes, that was just what she would do, in a minute.

This was the wild and passionate Kate he'd always known existed beneath that façade of serenely composed beauty. Edmund managed to find enough willpower from somewhere to put a distance between them and convince himself painfully that he'd discovered enough about her most secret passions for now, in public or almost public as they were. He forced his hands away from her delicious body before his fascination with it broke his self-control. She was flushed and breathless, her soft gasps for air drawing his attention to her lush, but firm, young breasts, rising and falling rapidly against the low neckline even a single lady could wear by her fourth Season without being considered intolerably fast.

Her eyes were wild and more beautiful than he could ever recall seeing them even in his dreams as they blazed with feelings he would give half his fortune to read fully. Her lips parted as she fought to get her breath back and his eyes lingered on them with hungry fascination as she slicked them with her sharp little tongue. If he wasn't to throw himself on her and ravish her on the lower terrace of his hostess's garden, he must get their engagement rolling relentlessly on before she lost that starry-eyed, just-kissed look and remembered all the doubts and fears that inhabited her contrary thoughts whenever he wasn't in a position to haze them with merciless passion. An image he'd best not dwell on if he wanted to get the next few minutes over with without causing an even bigger scandal than the one he had in mind.

'Come,' he ordered brusquely as he towed her back to the shark-infested waters of the *ton*, before she balked.

'I still can't see why…' Miss Alstone seemed about

to take over from his wild Kate, so Edmund summarily tugged her into the ballroom and put an end to her nonsense.

'Good heavens!' Cromer exclaimed at the sight of a stormy-eyed, very thoroughly kissed Kate on Edmund's arm and just managed to suppress a grin. 'They're quite right about that dangerous moonlight,' he mumbled as he stepped back to let the company see what it had done to so cool and collected a couple.

'Good heavens, indeed, and yes, very right,' Edmund replied calmly.

'I don't think they had much to do with it,' his Kate mumbled tartly and Edmund wondered if he was suffering from shock and hallucinating when she didn't just tear herself away from him and flounce off. It wasn't every day a man heard murder plotted, and with Kate pressed so close he'd struggled to listen to a word of it. He'd wanted her so mercilessly and now he nearly had what he'd longed for so deeply within his grasp at long last, what had happened so far tonight almost seemed unreal to him for a few moments.

'I hope you'll congratulate us, Cromer, for I refuse to wait any longer after three years of waiting for a yea instead of a nay, even if her former guardian and brother-in-law hasn't agreed to it yet,' he said with a possessive look at Kate.

'Carnwood cutting up rough, is he?' Cromer asked obligingly, managing to look astonished while his eyes told them he didn't believe a word.

'You see? Everyone thinks I'm your ideal husband,' he whispered in Kate's ear and felt her tense, as if she might jump away and deny every last truthful hint of how they'd been amusing themselves since they left the ballroom that he was building up so carefully. 'Try it and I'll kiss you right here,' he threatened softly.

'I hate you,' she told him between clenched teeth and he met the heat and fury of her furious glare with a satisfied smile.

'Hate away, my fierce Kate,' he murmured and heard a sentimental sigh from somewhere close by.

'Mountebank!' she condemned in a spitting under-tone, but still made no effort to pull away or give his apparent devotion the lie.

Looking as if he was trying very hard to come down to earth, Edmund considered his friend's previous question. 'No,' he replied to the clever lead, 'but I can't tear myself away long enough to go up to Derbyshire and ask him.'

'Should think you've obtained his permission often enough in the past,' Cromer said.

'So I keep telling Miss Alstone, but it took me until tonight to convince her I can't endure to wait and be wed with the full fanfare and fuss of a grand wedding. I'll have to go and beard Carnwood in his lair now she'd agreed at last that our wedding must be soon, then maybe we can get on with being my lord and my lady at long last.'

'Short notice, gossips bound to twitter like starlings in an apple orchard,' his taciturn friend warned sagely and Edmund gave an expressive shrug before looking significantly about him at the eagerly whispering throng.

'I've waited long enough,' he said loudly enough for

most to hear him and enjoy a fresh wave of delighted speculation.

He smiled wolfishly at Kate, hoping his eyes conveyed a warning to back him up now this was all but irrevocable. She really had the most extraordinary eyes, they were truly ultramarine, he decided distractedly, savouring the word on his tongue as he almost murmured it aloud. Very blue, he translated, and was in grave danger of falling into the wondrous depths of them and not caring where it took either of them. Most blue, he corrected in his head, and freed himself of their spell just in time to stop himself kissing her passionately in public.

'Well, here's a fine to do,' Lady Pemberley observed, apparently torn between laughter, delight and a chaperon's duty as she hurried towards them. 'Impatient children,' she chided as if mildly exasperated.

'You could hardly expect me to be patient when Miss Alstone finally agreed to wed me at last, my lady,' he responded, fervently hoping Kate would play up to his act and not revert to that contained sceptical aloofness she used so often to set the world at a distance just at the wrong moment.

'Yes,' she managed rather lamely instead, 'his lordship is *most* impatient.'

'So I see,' Eiliane Pemberley responded drily, with a comprehensive scrutiny of Kate's wildly curling hair and scandalously creased gown before her sharp eyes met Edmund's with a challenge.

'Perhaps we should send that notice to the *Morning*

Post and so on soon, Lady Pemberley?' he asked with
apparent satisfaction before she could speak it.

'I believe that might be for the best,' her ladyship
agreed blandly, despite the dagger look his Kate shot
her. 'Imperative even,' Eiliane added implacably, giving
Kate just as sharp a warning look in return. 'It's high
time we ordered Kate's bride clothes to be made up and
St George's, Hanover Square, isn't at all easy to book at
this time of year, even for you and this haughty young
woman, if that's where you decide you both want to
marry in the end.'

'I'm not haughty,' Kate protested hotly.

'No,' he drawled, caressing her hand as it rested in his
with a rightness he hoped she wouldn't deny any more,
even when they were alone. Playing with her gloved
fingers absently, he smiled with sleepy-eyed approval.
'You're very far from it if I remember rightly, and I have
an excellent memory,' he murmured intimately.

'Forgive us, ladies and gentlemen, but all will become
clear to you when a certain announcement is published shortly. I cannot say more now, I fear,' Edmund
announced to nobody in particular with as elegant and
ironical a bow as a gentleman might with his tawny
locks still awry from his lady's fingers and his neckcloth
askew.

'Since you wicked children decided to pre-empt
proper formalities, perhaps you should have your
betrothal dance now?' Eiliane suggested just loudly
enough for the cool clear sound of her voice to rise
over the hubbub.

Lady Wyndover looked as if she might be considering

the unlikelihood of it all, then nodded, before indicating the orchestra should play a waltz for her scandalous guests. Kate let her steps shadow Edmund's as closely as usual. She was so confused by the suddenness of it all she couldn't say what her feelings were at gunpoint, but most of their fellow guests evidently thought it a love match.

'Keep dancing,' Edmund scolded softly as her steps began to falter as weariness threatened to make her wilt like an overheated lily. 'Don't you dare flag and let Bestholme and that witch suspect everything is not exactly as it should be between us,' he berated in a stern whisper.

Sympathy might have made her collapse in his arms and require to be taken home, but he could be a little gentler, Kate decided. He was looking at her now as if it was only a matter of time before she swooned or did something equally feminine and therefore foolish, so she glared at him instead.

'You're the most irritating male I ever came across, Edmund Worth,' she informed him even as she smiled up at him as if the sun rose and set in his eyes.

'At least I'm pre-eminent at something, then,' he drawled back, as if he found her stubbornness and bad temper mildly irritating and amusing all at the same time.

'I really and truly hope that you're one of a kind then, my lord, for I'd hate to think the human race was afflicted with two such.'

'Didn't your long-suffering relatives teach you it's

rude to abuse your acquaintances in such a forthright fashion, Kate?'

'You're not an acquaintance, you're my betrothed.'

'I can see why you put off gaining one until now if this is how you intend to treat me from now on,' he countered, giving her a supposedly warm smile even while his cool willow-green eyes warned her he wasn't joking.

'I could jilt you at the altar if you'd like me to,' she offered half-seriously.

'Banish the idea from your mind right now that you can escape this marriage, Kate, or I'll walk off and leave you standing here with your mouth open. You made an idiot of me once too often three years ago for me to let you do it again.'

'I never meant to make you feel an idiot then, my lord,' she said and a heavy feeling of regret chilled the pit of her stomach as he looked unconvinced.

He looked at her austerely, as if seriously wondering what she was currently using for brains. 'That's moot, but there's no going back for either of us after tonight, so all we can do is get on with it,' he said brusquely.

'I'll do my best to make you a good wife,' she said stiffly.

'And that's all a convenient husband can ask of his lady, is it not?' he seemed unable to resist saying as the dance finally came to an end and he bowed over her gloved hand as gallantly low as if he was utterly besotted with her and thought her a queen amongst women.

'Quite,' she replied repressively and just about managed not to kick him soundly on the shin, or tread very deliberately on his toe.

The noble effort it cost her must have shown on her face if only because he was close enough to see more than anyone else. He grinned at her, that old, infectious grin she'd once taken so carelessly for granted, and it gave her a bittersweet heartache for the ease there could have been between them, if only she'd been less of a fool when they'd first met.

'I wish we could be friends again,' she said wistfully, only to see laughter fade from his unusual silvery green eyes and the chill return, as if she'd no right to ask.

'I want you, Kate. I'll be faithful for as long as you return the compliment, but I'll never be your lapdog again.'

'I can't imagine you as anyone's willing slave nowadays, my lord, but I would have us be comfortable together at least.'

'Do you think your elder sister and her husband find mere "comfort" in their marriage?' he asked her as if the very word offended his mouth.

'No, I think they each consider that the sun rises and sets in the other,' she informed him steadily, 'but I doubt they'd thank me for saying they were anything so mundane as merely comfortable together.'

'Then why should we settle for less?'

'Because we're not in love,' she was goaded into declaring exasperatedly.

'My point exactly,' he murmured in her ear as they returned to Eiliane's side and she couldn't glare into his challenging eyes, for fear of letting the world see this wasn't the fairytale romance they'd just been at such pains to pretend it was.

'You don't fight fair, my lord,' she murmured instead as she met his eyes with every appearance of dewy-eyed wonder.

'No,' he breathed for her ears alone as he raised his hand to let it whisper down her cheek in a regretful, lover's salute as if he couldn't bear to completely let her go whatever the conventions, 'that would be because I fight to win, Miss Alstone.'

'Win what?' she asked with genuine puzzlement as he let his hand drop and she shivered as her every nerve seemed on the alert and desire almost made her shake with the effort of resisting a foolish driving compulsion to be in his arms again.

'You, Miss Katherine Alstone, body, heart and soul,' he murmured as he once more leaned towards her as if he might kiss her and Kate was sure she heard several of the ladies huddled nearby to get the best view of them sigh sentimentally.

'First you'd have to want me,' she whispered.

'Oh, I most certainly do, sweet Kate, make no mistake about that,' he drawled and she could see the truth of it in the flash and burn of such raging hot desire in his eyes that it made them look intensely green all of a sudden.

Involuntarily her mouth opened and her lips were so dry she just had to lick them, watching him gaze at her tongue as if he wanted to catch it with his own and then... Best not to think of that then, not with such a very interested audience hoping to see the self-possessed Miss Alstone melt into boneless idiocy in front of their eyes.

'I suppose we'll see you tomorrow then, my lord?' she said foolishly, so muddled by the mix of fiery passion with that edge of angry desire that kept flaring between them that falling back on platitudes was the only option open to her.

'You can be very sure of that,' he replied, 'but the night isn't over yet.'

'It is for me. Do you think we could leave now, Eiliane? I'm so very tired,' she turned and asked her friend, eager for some peace and quiet in which to gather her scattered thoughts.

'And at least I can accompany you home without arousing speculation, now we're engaged all bar the shouting,' Edmund said with an ironic smile.

'Oh, I suspect there might still be shouting,' Lady Pemberley said, evidently considering Kit Alstone's reaction to the news that his sister-in-law and former ward had behaved so scandalously. 'But, yes, we can go home now and your escort is always welcome, Lord Shuttleworth, especially in these strange and uncertain times.'

'What it is to be wanted,' he said with a smug look of *faux* self-importance that made Kate smile and Lady Pemberley inform him she'd always known he wasn't the straightforward young man he too often pretended to be.

'If I were that simple, I'd have stayed on my estates nursing my broken heart and missed the prospect of a lifetime of marital strife with your lovely charge, Lady Pemberley,' he parried lightly.

'Just as well you didn't, then,' Eiliane replied as he handed her into the luxurious carriage her husband had brought on the occasion of their marriage.

'Yes, isn't it?' he said with such cordiality Kate eyed him with suspicion.

'My love?' he prompted with such bland patience she once more felt her foot itch to kick him as she looked at him with a sharp question in her eyes. 'Could you get into Lady Pemberley's splendid equipage before the horses collapse from boredom or one of us catches an inflammation of the lungs, do you think?'

'Oh, yes, of course,' she replied, doing so with such haste she nearly fell over her own feet. 'I'm so clumsy that I seem to constitute a danger to myself and others tonight. It really is most irritating.'

'I don't know,' he murmured as he managed to climb into the carriage with all the grace she'd failed to find. 'I quite like it, and perhaps it's a sign that I've finally knocked that exquisite balance of yours out of kilter at long last.'

'And that's something about tonight's events I certainly need to hear about in more detail, my lord,' Eiliane informed him in her sternest chaperon's voice.

'Later, if you please, my lady. We have a great deal to explain and only a short carriage ride to do it in, if you won't consider letting me come inside to enlighten you properly when we get there,' he cautioned and Kate could feel the tension in his powerful body as he sat opposite her, but evidently couldn't bring himself to relax into the generous squabs of Eiliane's carriage.

Chapter Nine

'If I were a proper chaperon I'd probably occupy the whole drive back with a stern lecture about your disgraceful behaviour,' Eiliane said ruefully and then fell silent.

Kate thought of all that had happened since she'd left her temporary home tonight and all hope of relaxation left her in a heavy sigh she hoped was inaudible above the noise of the horses' hooves and the rattle of iron-rimmed wheels on cobbled streets. Obviously not, because Edmund's strong fingers reached for hers and his hand engulfed hers to offer simple comfort before the sound of it had hardly left her lips. She felt at least some of the horror of hearing two conscienceless rogues scheme murder, then almost couple with each other, subside under the warm reassurance of his touch as he massaged the chill stiffness from her fingers.

'Thank you,' she murmured as they drew up outside the Marquis of Pemberley's town mansion.

'No need for thanks when I intend enjoying a very thorough exploration of everything about you before we're very much older, my Kate,' he breathed into her ear before he jumped down to hand them down with such elaborate ceremony she wondered crossly if he was trying to infuriate her, or if it just came naturally to him.

Considering the smug look he gave her after she stiffened her shoulders and marched up the shallow steps in front of him, she concluded he knew exactly what he was doing. Nobody watching them would suspect she'd suffered anything more shocking than an impetuous engagement tonight, and she swept into the cosy and private sitting room Eiliane had annexed for her own use, unsure whether to be grateful or furious that he'd manipulated her so easily once again.

'You're clearly a master of strategy, my lord,' she informed him when the door was finally shut and that fact alone made her realise that Eiliane already thought of him as family.

'Edmund,' he corrected as if it really mattered. 'But I'd never lay claim to so much guile,' he denied with an unreadable look she found oddly disturbing.

'Never mind that, I demand an account of your adventures,' Eiliane said with a sharp look at Kate's dishevelled gown and Edmund's disordered locks, 'or should I say *mis*adventures?'

'The latter,' he affirmed. 'Tonight Kate decided to wander off and explore Lord and Lady Wyndover's personal rooms, with far too little consideration for their privacy I feel I must point out, as that fact seems to have escaped her.'

'I *was* being harried unmercifully by Mr Bestholme,' she argued.

'You could have looked to me to remedy that, but you risked far worse instead of lowering your pride. I found her sitting in his lordship's book room in the pitch dark, Lady Pemberley, where we had a slight altercation before I heard someone padding furtively about in the proscribed fashion for the evening,' he explained, then raised an eyebrow at Kate as if waiting for her to argue. He nodded when she didn't, as if that confirmed an idiocy she plainly couldn't defend and proceeded to explain whose tryst they had overheard to her shocked chaperon.

'Oh, heavens above,' Eiliane gasped, 'what did the two unprincipled rogues say while Kate was listening to every word?'

'For goodness' sake, Eiliane, I'm not a child,' Kate protested.

'You are an unwed female,' Edmund answered as if that explained everything.

'But not an unfledged one,' she argued.

'So you might think, Miss Alstone, but I beg to differ.'

'Really, my lord? Pray what would you ask of a *fully* fledged lady then?' she asked with as much irony as she could fit into a few short words.

'I'll tell you after we're married.'

He was undoubtedly the most infuriating, self-satisfied, would-be superior male she'd ever come across and with a brother-in-law and guardian like Kit and his best friend, Ben Shaw, lurking like a man-mountain in the background, she'd met a fair few of them.

'Never mind quarrelling, what did they actually say?' Eiliane asked and Edmund explained distractedly, as if his mind was suddenly busy elsewhere. 'What a truly awful person that woman must be at heart,' Eiliane said hollowly.

'My reaction exactly,' Kate said, getting to her feet with a resentful glare at her newly affianced husband, who ignored her and solicitously poured Eiliane a restorative glass of brandy.

Considering the stark contrast between his gentle way with Eiliane and his abrasive manner towards her when she'd actually heard the whole horrid conspiracy for herself, Kate blinked back inexplicable tears and eyed his broad back resentfully.

'I should have chosen my words more carefully,' he reproached himself as he handed Eiliane the glass.

'I don't see how it could be wrapped up comfortingly, but could you see them, Kate?' Eiliane asked shakily.

'No, because, if you remember, I was immured in pitch darkness in little more than a cupboard with Lord Shuttleworth,' Kate explained patiently. 'If I had known how densely populated his lordship's book room might become tonight, I would have stayed in the ballroom and endured the evening more gladly.'

'A lot of nonsense is talked about premonitions and portents,' Edmund said rather grumpily, as if hurt by the idea that she would rather have come home tonight a free woman than his affianced bride in all but a few formalities.

'Forgive me for finding my situation less than enjoyable, my lord,' Kate replied sarcastically, for suddenly she felt very tired and didn't know how much longer she could endure his impatience when all she wanted to do was nuzzle her head against his shoulder and seek any comfort he cared to give her.

'I might if I wasn't part of it,' he explained with a rueful look that understood too much about her ragged emotions.

'I didn't ask you to declare yourself in front of several hundred people,' she defended herself wearily.

'I suppose you expected me to just abandon you to the condemnation of all those who thought you'd gone sneaking off to meet some lover? I was the one who compromised you, after all.'

'It wasn't your fault,' she said, trying her best to get him to see that it was his loss of freedom she found so intolerable, not her own.

'That's odd, because it felt as if it was to me,' he said with a flash of sardonic humour that warmed her, despite her resolution to resist his charm, at least for the rest of the evening.

'Aha!' Eiliane said with what sounded to Kate like rather a contented sigh for a supposedly outraged chaperon to utter. 'So you forgot to tell me the most pertinent details of the whole affair, did you? Somehow I thought you might have done.'

'Maybe,' Kate admitted warily, seeing the I-told-you-so glint in her friend's eye.

'Almost certainly, considering the state you were both in when you appeared out of the garden looking as if you'd taken up where Adam and Eve left off, Katherine Margaret Alstone,' Eiliane scolded.

'We are engaged,' Kate defended herself recklessly, 'so surely Edmund and I can kiss each other without you and half the *ton* getting all of a-flutter about it.'

'You were certainly *not* engaged, nor anywhere near it until tonight and well you know it, my girl.'

'That's a private matter between the two of us, don't you think, Lady Pemberley?' Edmund said gravely and Kate wondered how her friend felt about being on the chilly side of his exquisite manners for once.

'It might be if you hadn't made such a fine show of it in public, young man,' Eiliane parried bravely, but Kate could have told her from the resolute set of his jaw that she'd get no more from Edmund about their more intimate affairs.

'Do you actually want us to wed, your ladyship?' he asked coolly.

'It's been my dearest wish since I first set eyes on you together, my lord, for some odd reason that escapes me just at the moment,' Eiliane admitted.

'Then why not leave best alone, ma'am?'

'Because Kate and her sisters are the daughters of my heart, despite their headstrong ways and knack of getting into any trouble that's brewing.'

'And we all love you so very much, Eiliane,' Kate assured the woman who'd done her best to mother her since her own mama died.

'Something in my eye,' Eiliane explained gruffly to

Edmund as she returned Kate's fierce hug. 'I hope you intend to make her very happy, my lord.'

'It will be my duty as well as my pleasure,' he promised quite solemnly.

'Then I'm content,' she said, as if he'd just made a vow she intended to hold him to for the rest of her life, and that she might even come back and haunt him if he broke it after she'd gone.

Edmund nodded and tried not to wish Kate was resting her fiery head so trustingly against his shoulder instead of Lady Pemberley's. Maybe one day she would be that unguarded with him, but for now he had her promise to wed him, and her passionate response to every sensual demand he'd made so far.

'You should go to bed and rest,' he told her abruptly and wasn't surprised when she raised her head to glare at him as if he'd suggested she take poison.

'Why?' Kate asked, standing up in order not to be towered over. 'I've only endured the revolting attentions of a fortune hunter, overheard his repellent clandestine assignation with a so-called lady of my acquaintance and then been forced to listen to their murderous schemes, before narrowly escaping ruin by a man who would rather marry virtually any other woman in England than me. So the last thing I want is to sleep while you and Eiliane plan my life without so much as a by-your-leave.'

'I wouldn't like to wed any of the royal princesses,' he said with unpardonable levity and Kate seriously considered throwing the contents of Eiliane's glass at him, since her friend had left it untouched, but she decided he didn't deserve even that much acknowledgement of his ill-timed humour and drank it off in one swallow instead. 'Can't take her drink very well, can she?' he observed as Kate choked and spluttered on that reckless gulp of fine cognac and incandescent fury.

'I should be thankful for small mercies if I were you,' Eiliane advised sagely, 'and if you intend to go on like this, my lord, I'd learn to duck very swiftly indeed if I were you,' she warned, with a cautionary look at Kate's flushed cheeks.

'I shall not lower myself to throw anything at *him*,' Kate snapped even as she felt the warmth of the strong spirit seep into her cold belly. 'He thinks he's going to get his way by making me so furious I'll forget to be horrified by what I overheard tonight and storm off to bed so you can arrange my wedding without any inter-ference from me, and it's *my* future, too,' she ended. Yet even she had trouble following the logic of her own argument.

'Did it work?' Edmund asked with what looked like academic interest.

'Nearly,' she gritted between white teeth and forced them apart as she willed her hot temper to die down and her fists to unclench.

She *wouldn't* be ruled by her passions. No, that hope didn't work after tonight. She'd lived by them all evening and there was little prospect of getting them back in a neat box and throwing away the key.

'I'm perfectly recovered now, so shouldn't we be dis-cussing this rationally?' she managed to ask as if she thought it was true.

'I suggest we send appropriate notices to the newspapers and hope Carnwood won't take offence when I explain what took place tonight,' Edmund said far too calmly, considering she was still in turmoil.

'That's not what I meant and you know it,' she snapped.

'Planning to jilt me even before I manage to get our names on a special licence, my dear?' he asked and met her eyes with a bland look before shaking his head. 'Not possible, I fear. We could have a pair of potential murderers on our tails as well as an assured scandal if we don't go through with it.'

'This isn't what I meant by rational discussion of our future and you know it.'

'I long ago gave up on being rational with you, my dear, so let's return to our plans, shall we?'

'We could if only I knew what they were.'

'I suggest getting ourselves up the aisle before the tabbies have time to work themselves into a frenzy and Bestholme realises we might not have been seducing each other the entire time we were absent from the ballroom tonight should be our priority.'

'And if he does realise it, then it will all be for nothing.'

'Oh, surely you exaggerate? I can say without undue vanity that you'll be marrying to advantage before the end of this Season. Which is exactly what you planned to do at the outset of it, rather than endure ending another Season unwed, is it not, Miss Alstone?' he observed coolly and Kate blushed under his ironic gaze.

Was she so transparent, so lacking all subtlety? She

felt bitterly ashamed of her scheme to secure a convenient husband even as she was asking herself why. After all, arranged marriages were often made between eligible *partis*—except they were usually made by the families and not the victims. Now why had that damning word suddenly sprung into her mind?

'I would have been just as advantageously wed three years gone by if you'd had your way at the time,' she pointed out.

'Oh, the follies of extreme youth, Lady Pemberley,' he said, unfairly dragging Eiliane into their argument and Kate had no doubt which side of the line that turncoat would jump. 'Moonstruck young cubs such as I was then should be ordered out into the world to discover the realities of life, instead of being left to make idiots of themselves at the feet of capricious young ladies, don't you think?'

'Maybe if the Continent had been less chaotic, we could have sent you on a grand tour until Kate came to her senses,' Eiliane replied.

'Traitor! We could send him on one now instead,' Kate muttered darkly.

'In the hope you'd escape your fate when I came back?' he said sardonically.

'No, in the hope you wouldn't come back at all.'

'This is no time for petty quarrels,' Eiliane chided and Kate fumed all the more.

'No, we have the rest of our lives to indulge in them after all,' Edmund replied.

'How I look forward to it,' she replied with an artistic sigh.

'Then at least we'll never be bored,' he said with a rueful grin.

'At the moment a nice, comfortable attack of *ennui* would suit me very well, but will it work?' she said rather obscurely.

'Will what work?' he asked warily.

'Throwing dust in their faces.'

'Oh, that—it depends on what they decide to do next, I suppose.'

'How reassuring.'

'You're not the sort of female who wants a pat on the head and a parcel of pretty lies, my dear.'

'I'm not *your dear*.'

'I think we'd better hope you are, Kate. We'll endure an unhappy marriage if it turns out that you're not.'

'Then why marry me at all?'

He watched her as if fascinated. 'I never took you for a fool, however I railed at your obduracy when I begged you to marry me and got a polite "no, thank you" for my trouble, but maybe I'd have been better off respecting your intelligence less from the outset,' he said as if in the grip of a startling revelation.

'Are you telling me I'm *stupid*?'

'I'd never be so ungallant. Lady Pemberley, I appeal to you—did I even hint that your protégée is a lack-wit just now?'

'No, and I should have to reproach you for such a slur, my lord.'

'It won't work, so you might as well stop provoking me,' Kate said.

'Have you got anything interesting to say about

our betrothal, then?' Edmund asked as Kate reminded herself she wasn't going to indulge in a redheaded temper.

'I believe it takes a proposal from the gentleman, then acceptance on the part of the lady to constitute a betrothal. At no time tonight can I recall receiving a formal offer of marriage from you, my lord, or accepting it.'

'Knowing that I laid myself at your queenly feet more times than either of us care to remember in the past will just have to suffice. I promised myself that last time that I'd never beg you to marry me again and it's one vow I fully intend to keep.'

'Which doesn't bode well for our future,' she said quietly.

'I dare say we'll rub along well enough,' he said with a careless cheerfulness she hated. 'You're a fine woman and I'm in dire need of an heir or two, so you'll hear no complaints from me. Just see to it that you abide by your vows and I think we'll suit like ham and eggs at the breakfast table.'

'How very reassuring,' she answered faintly, wondering if she was meant to be flattered.

'You wanted a marriage of convenience,' Eiliane reminded her sneakily.

'I did, didn't I?' she replied numbly and tried to comfort herself with the memory of Edmund's fiery kisses.

How silly to find she wanted an impassioned lover after all and not the detached and sardonic husband he promised to be. Regret threatened once more, along with bitter nostalgia for the ardent, love-struck young aristocrat he'd once been. That Edmund had bombarded her with flowers, thoughtfully chosen trinkets and sent with them fervent assurances of his enduring love. Fool that she was, she'd brushed him aside as if he was an importunate boy, instead of a young man who'd one day become this mature Adonis and break too many susceptible feminine hearts, including her own if she let him. Some Adonis, she reminded herself as she straightened her shoulders and met his unreadable grey-green gaze. And some enduring love when, three years on from swearing she'd break his heart for ever if she refused to marry him, he was watching her as if she were a specimen he was studying for a paper at the Royal Society.

'Have we got a bargain, Miss Alstone?' he asked mercilessly.

'It would seem so, Lord Shuttleworth,' she agreed, refusing to let her eyes fall while she admitted he was to be her fate, for good or ill.

'Then I'll take a kiss to seal it with, saving your presence, Lady Pemberley?'

'Oh, I'll turn my back, never fear,' Eiliane said blithely and Kate glared at her friend as she did just that. 'I swear I can feel that furious glare of yours, Kate,' her ladyship murmured irrepressibly.

'I'm quite sure you can,' Kate muttered vengefully.

Then she forgot her annoyance with her inefficient chaperon as Edmund's lips once more took hers in a potent, passionate kiss that rendered her breathless and defenceless before Eiliane had hardly finished turning away. Shock, she assured herself. That was why she melted into his masculine arms as if formed to fit them. Yielding to the pressure of his firm mouth on hers, she opened her lips and let him invade the softness within. Her breath caught and her hands clenched in a vain attempt to stop them creeping up to caress his strong neck and ruffle his vital golden-brown hair, where it curled irrepressibly into his nape and tempted exploration.

He knew all the same; she felt it in the smile he let form against her willing mouth, the way he shifted to bring her body so close even she couldn't mistake his arousal. It was blatant, startlingly explicit as she felt melting heat threaten to rob her of the use of her legs until she clung to him and yielded everything. His passionate enjoyment of her femininity made her feel unique and special, and she needed to know there was something more in their future than duty and the mutual respect she'd once thought so important.

'That's enough kissing to seal half a dozen bargains,' Eiliane observed, even though she was staring appreciatively at a portrait of her husband as a young man that hung in pride of place over the mantelpiece and obviously not at all bored with the sight. Kate could have sworn she heard a satisfied sigh as Eiliane added another triumph to her matchmaker's tally.

'I've had enough of everything for one day, so you may do as you please about announcements, my lord. I'm tired and confused and I can't do this any more,' Kate confessed with a catch in her voice she hated anyone to hear.

'Aye,' Edmund agreed. 'Go to bed now and ring for

a posset to help you sleep. You need rest after such a day, and the one we'll face tomorrow.'

She must be exhausted for his concern to threaten tears, Kate decided. 'I'm not a child,' she managed to remind him shrewishly when she turned at the door to take one last, incredulous look at her new fiancé, not quite sure if she'd dreamt up such a handsome one after the last weeks of uncertainty and self-doubt.

'That much is blatantly obvious,' he drawled, letting his eyes wander over her flushed cheeks and heavy eyes, now the darkest of blue with the richness and potential of what could be between them left over from that last kiss. He went on with his scrutiny of her supple young body in a way that left her in no doubt he relished every single slender curve and elegant line of her and couldn't wait to take his bride to his bed and begin his marital duties.

'I fear there's a great deal to be done in the morning,' Edmund added when he finally managed to tear his gaze from her tingling form.

'A very great deal,' Eiliane agreed gravely.

'So you will call on us, then?' Kate asked and could have kicked herself for sounding so betrayingly eager.

'I don't know, I thought I might go and order a new pair of boots, or perhaps a visit to my tailor and then a stroll to my club to see if I could meet up with a few old friends to pass an idle hour or two reasonably pleasantly instead,' he was stung into replying. 'Of course I'll be calling on you as soon as I decently can and, if you're still asleep after such a wearisome night as this one has been, I'll wait until you're awake and plague Pemberley instead,' he added roughly as soon as he saw she was half-inclined to believe him.

'Oh, very well then,' she said and found herself wishing stupidly that he was coming upstairs with her, to kiss her gently into sleep as a lover might after they'd worn out the night with loving, even if he only slept chastely beside her for the brief sliver of night still left to them now.

'Until tomorrow, ladies,' was all he could say or do until she really was his to take to bed whenever and wherever they chose, his jade, silver and wildfire gaze told her, as it lingered on her once more and it boldly caressed and promised her all that and more until she shivered with anticipation.

'Goodnight then, Eiliane, Edmund,' she muttered and made her legs carry her away, before her wicked desires led her to say something foolish.

'Goodnight, lover,' he murmured intimately as she went past.

Almost as if, she reminded herself indignantly as she heard the echoes of the door closing behind her, *almost* as if he already had the right to strip her of her ball gown and explore every inch of woman underneath it bit by sensuous bit, while he worked her into an incoherent mess of passion and eagerness for his ardent attention. Trying not to agree with him, she ordered her weary feet upwards and went to bed dreaming of him instead of the evil she'd overheard or the scandal their betrothal would probably be entangled in by morning.

Chapter Ten

'Was teasing and tormenting poor Kate after such an extraordinary evening as she just weathered altogether fair of you, Lord Shuttleworth?' Eiliane mused as she was left facing a rather self-satisfied viscount.

'Not at all, but it made her forget those two villains and their foul schemes. I could hardly take her to bed and divert her with a night of untrammelled passion under your respectable roof instead, now could I, Lady Pemberley?'

'Not from want of trying, so far as I could tell just now.'

'You mean you didn't position yourself cunningly enough so that you could see everything that went on between us in yonder mirror without Kate knowing it, my lady? How very noble of you.'

'You're so sharp you run the worst risk of cutting yourself I ever came across in a man,' she condemned with a strong hint of admiration.

'If I were that clever, I'd have taken myself off on that tour of the Continent the instant Boney set out for Elba in the year fourteen and it was open to travellers again for the first time in years, my lady.'

'Since you're about to become an adoptive godson to me, you really must call me Eiliane from now on instead of all this my-ladying, but do you mean it?'

'Do I mean what, Eiliane?'

'You have a very annoying habit of answering a question with a question that could make me regret taking your side in all this after all, I hope you know?' she said with gentle malice and he grinned back at her as if they understood each other perfectly. 'I meant, of course, do you truly regret not leaving the country before Kate made her come-out? If you really don't wish to marry her, you'd best confess it straight away so we can get you both out of this betrothal without ruining Kate's good name, or putting you beyond the pale.'

'Is that even possible after tonight's almost-announcement? It sounds beyond the wisdom of Solomon to me.'

'Most things are possible if one goes about them in the right manner, but one has to know first if they are also desirable, my lord.'

'Back to that, are we?'

'If necessary,' Eiliane replied implacably, letting her absolute loyalty to Kate show, even if she would think her protégée illogical as a London mob if she thought about letting this fascinating young lord slip through her fingers once more.

'No, I'm very satisfied with the outcome,' he replied

seriously enough, 'if not exactly delighted by the way it had to be achieved.'

'Good—it's my belief Kate doesn't know her own mind.'

'I doubt I'll ever know what goes on in her contrary head, but I intend to guard her happiness with my life. How else would I behave towards my wife after all?'

'Being a man of honour?'

He shrugged and looked as if honour was the last thing on his mind, but she could believe it if she chose, and Eiliane hid a smile of catlike satisfaction. None of this had happened quite as she'd expected, but Kate was engaged to a man of wit and character who wouldn't let her lead him about by the nose at last and, for now, that would do her very well.

'You'll have a fight on your hands, on more than one front,' she warned.

'I dare say I'll weather it.'

'Remember that Kate's really a very different creature under all that stubborn reserve and contrary coolness, Edmund Worth, one who could be badly hurt by a husband who didn't understand her.'

'I'll never willingly hurt her, I can promise you that at least.'

'Then I'm content.'

'Would that I were, too,' he replied obscurely, before bowing and wishing her a good night. Lady Pemberley retired to her splendid bedchamber just before her lord ran lithely up the stairs at a speed many men half his age would envy to join her and diverted her attention from anyone's marriage but their own.

* * *

Edmund chose to walk home, despite the offer of his carriage from the Marquis of Pemberley when that gentleman returned home very late and found him about to depart. Apparently his lordship had been dining with some obscure official who probably had more real influence than the Prince Regent and his entire circle of raffish friends put together. The marquis obviously moved in the most exalted of political circles and, if he didn't watch his step, Edmund might be at risk of joining them. He reported his engagement and received his lordship's hearty good wishes, as well as a half-serious threat to horsewhip him if he ever made Kate unhappy, which he took in good part as he silently agreed that he'd deserve it if he didn't, before he finally set out for home.

He wasn't as weary as he should be after such a night and took a convoluted route home through Mayfair, where dawn was already stealing into shadowy corners and town-bred blackbirds and song thrushes were chirruping in readiness for performing a dawn chorus in the parks and gardens along his way like an orchestra tuning up. He needed to walk himself into at least a few hours' sleep against the day ahead of him, so he strolled on through the dawn and the already stirring city, considering how different his life was now from when he set out for an evening spoilt by the familiar frustration of watching Kate dance and flirt with other men.

Kate had responded to him with such headlong enthusiasm tonight, or last night or whatever it was now, just as she had in his wildest dreams so many times in the past. Not being able to take that passionate response to its logical conclusion had left him with an inevitable burn of frustration and a spike of exhilaration that would keep him from sleeping properly until his wedding night if he let it. After all, self-restraint and denial were feelings he should be all too familiar with, but now Kate had tacitly agreed that their becoming lovers would be the most wondrous thing this side of paradise and it was newly minted.

Fighting both of them until he'd got his ring on her finger at last would be a gargantuan struggle, but in the meantime, he intended to make her think harder than she wanted to about that blazing attraction. Yes, if he was to suffer weeks of longing for her until he could finally slake it in their marriage bed, she could spend them considering why she belonged in no other bed but his. The very idea of her marrying another man made him so angry that his staff tiptoed about him when he finally got home and whispered knowledgeably that his lordship must be disappointed in love again to return home looking so grim.

'Good gracious, Welland, where on earth is everyone?' a familiar voice in the corridor outside Kate's bedchamber demanded next morning.

She did her best to bury her head under the pillow and pretend last night had been a disturbing dream, but her memory told her she was undoubtedly engaged to Edmund Worth and nobody could have imagined those deeply sensual kisses they'd shared so enthusiastically that her body throbbed eagerly at the very memory, before she told it sternly to behave itself.

'Surely they're not *still* abed on such a lovely morning, especially when I managed to rise from my sickbed with the dawn to post here hotfoot,' the annoyingly happy and altogether too-awake voice outside asked again.

So her sister Isabella really was yelling wrongheaded observations as unsubtly as ever and it wasn't a nightmare as she'd hoped, Kate decided grumpily. She reluctantly removed her head from its down-and-fine-linen sanctuary and rang the bell. If she was going to have to cope with Izzie in what sounded like tearing spirits, then getting dressed seemed not only called for, but just plain essential.

Evidently Eiliane agreed with her, for half an hour later all three ladies were installed in the morning room, drinking tea and eating breakfast while they came to terms with the day.

'Don't tell me you travelled all night just to get here at such an unearthly hour and badger us out of our nice, comfortable beds?' Kate queried as Isabella continued to look rudely healthy and annoyingly serene whilst tucking into an enormous plate of ham and eggs.

'Then I won't, sister dear. Being a proper and sensible young lady now that I must make my come-out at last, and knowing what a life of dissipation you two lead, we stopped in Windsor last night and came on this morning in an attempt to cosset my failing strength, rather than arrive scandalously late to an empty house last night.'

'You don't look very weak to me,' Kate said with a sceptical sniff, wishing she had half as much energy as her little sister, who was glowing with her accustomed health and vitality once more after her recent illness.

'I either had to promise to behave like a Bath breakdown and coddle myself all the way here, or submit to setting out on my journey with the entire Mausley family in attendance, with most of Richard's university friends threatening to act as outriders. Agreeing to spend a couple of nights on the road was a small price to pay for escaping such a ridiculous fuss. We would have taken for ever to get here, what's more, and I'd already had enough of Bath and all those silly young boys.'

'Proving importunate, were they?' Kate asked cynically, knowing the effect her sister's deceptively angelic countenance had on susceptible young gentlemen.

'Maddening,' her sister agreed without any sign of vanity or gratification.

'Never mind all that,' Eiliane put in impatiently and Kate braced herself for the announcement she was sure to make. 'I hope Lady Mausley didn't send you all this way alone, however much fuss you kicked up about being properly accompanied,' she said anxiously, confounding Kate's fears she was about to describe last night's misadventures and unknowingly putting her in her place at the same time.

Isabella rolled her eyes at the very idea and sighed. 'Would that she had,' she said disgustedly. 'If you care to look upstairs, you will find that Emily's maiden aunt is currently lying down in your best guest chamber, doing her best to recover from the extreme fatigue of driving here from Windsor this morning at a pace quite suitable for the average funeral. Her companion, who also happens to be Miss Mausley's former governess and as ancient and formidable a lady as you'll ever encounter, is attending her along with Miss Mausley's maid, who could sour milk with a single glance at the best of times and apparently this isn't the best of times. The Mausleys' coachman, two footmen and a postillion are being stowed wherever they can be found room even in your grand residence, my lady, and they are all awaiting what I hope will be a very speedy recovery and a swift return to Bath of the whole caravanserai.'

'Well then, Fanny Mausley certainly sent you off in style, so I'll grant she's a proper and caring hostess, even if she did carelessly allow you to get the mumps in the first place, love.'

'She certainly didn't have anything to do with that, as I picked them up all on my own and, so long as she did actually send me off at last, that was all I really cared about,' Isabella said ungratefully and went over to investigate the covered dishes on the sideboard for further sustenance.

'She was probably worried you'd eat her out of house and home after so many weeks of ransacking Bath and the surrounding area for supplies,' Kate observed with a shudder as she watched her sister pile her plate with yet more ham and eggs.

'I'm hungry and I'd dearly like to know just what's put your hair so out of curl this morning, sister dear,' Izzie demanded. 'I hope you haven't been overindulging?'

'Of course I haven't and, if I had, it would be my business and none of yours.'

'Now there you're quite wrong, for it won't help my

début if I have to go about London apologising because my older sister's become a toper and could disgrace us at any moment.'

'I don't think many are rash enough to think any of us all that respectable in the first place and I certainly haven't taken to the bottle in your absence, little sister, and therefore I'm not feeling in the least bit liverish,' Kate replied, the temptation to enjoy a refreshing family argument threatening to topple her dignity at any moment.

'Then you must have got out of the bed the wrong side, sister dear, for you look about as happy about my return as a lion with a thorn in its paw.'

'Of course I'm pleased to see you, I was really worried about you,' Kate admitted gruffly and almost let herself weep lachrymosely over her little sister when Izzie jumped up to hug her fiercely.

'There really was no need to be,' Izzie assured her cheerfully as she plumped down on her chair once more and looked genuinely delighted to be back with her family. 'In fact, it was downright embarrassing to catch such a childish illness and have to go about looking like a gargoyle for a week or more.'

'I wager you managed to look lovely despite it, considering you have an annoying habit of coming out of any potential disaster smelling of roses,' Kate assured her and traded an indulgent smile with Eiliane as Isabella returned to her abandoned breakfast with vigour.

'And so do you,' Izzie assured her absently between mouthfuls.

'Not this time, I didn't,' Kate muttered darkly, but her sister's hearing was famously acute and Isabella shot Eiliane an interrogating look when Kate became so absorbed in buttering a slice of toast she somehow couldn't spare time to meet her sister's eyes.

'It's not my tale to tell,' Eiliane observed with a shrug, so Kate glared at her instead.

'I accepted Shuttleworth's hand in marriage last night,' she announced baldly in order to get it over with and proceed with weathering her sister's much-too-acute scrutiny of her averted face.

'Then why are you being so cross-grained about it? In your shoes, I'd be jumping up and down with joy to secure a fine husband I could love and respect, instead of growling and grumbling into my breakfast as if I'd just lost a guinea and found a farthing.'

'Then *you* marry him,' Kate snapped, then wished she could climb into a hole in the floor and pull the carpet over her when she realised Welland, Eiliane's usually imperturbable and meticulously correct butler, had opened the door after only a brief knock in order to admit her new fiancé to this supposedly joyous family occasion and just in time for Edmund to hear her disastrous comment.

He paused at the sound of her defensive remark and watched her blush with cynical eyes, before he raised his eyebrows to let her know he'd heard. He turned to smile at Isabella, as if seeing her again had put the sunlight into his morning. Maybe it had, Kate thought in complete horror at the very idea of Edmund falling under her enchanting little sister's spell. Something even more uncomfortable than horror jagged under her confusion as well, but she wasn't prepared to think about what it could be, not while her ridiculous remark still echoed between the two of them and the possibility she'd just hurt him again, or even that he might now think twice about wedding her after all, dragged painfully at her thumping heart. Even Eiliane looked unusually daunted.

'Well, I'm delighted to welcome you as a brother, even if my sister is feeling as grumpy as a bear with a sore paw this morning, Lord Shuttleworth. You're going to make an excellent addition to the family in my opinion,' Isabella declared brightly and bounced out of her seat again to give him another of her impulsive hugs, as if she had no idea her sister had just dug herself a tiger trap and fallen headlong into it.

Kate scowled at her cooling piece of toast and hoped he wouldn't take that embrace as anything more than an exuberant expression of joy and sisterly solidarity on Isabella's part.

'At least gaining a sister, and such a lovely one, by marrying into your family will go some way to soothing my wounded soul after your sister's begrudging acceptance of my suit, Miss Isabella,' he told her with one of those old, unaffected smiles as he returned her sister's embrace and Kate tried to pretend neither of them were there while she fought off a ridiculous, primitive stab of jealousy even she couldn't pretend was indigestion after such an interrupted meal.

He might have kissed her with sensuality and passion last night, but somehow the sight of him looking so genuinely pleased to see Isabella again made her long for the days when he'd greeted her with such warmth as well. Reminding herself she'd always returned his delight with either suspicion or indifference, she felt ashamed of her eighteen-year-old self and did her best not to regret the passing of the eager youth Edmund had been then. She had nobody to blame but herself if her attempts to set him at arm's length had worked so well he probably believed her ridiculous invitation to Isabella to marry him herself just now had been sincerely meant.

'It's not begrudging, precisely,' she qualified, waving her toast in the air in what she knew was a most ill-mannered fashion to emphasise her point. 'It's more a matter of being annoyed that you considered me so compromised that you must marry me whether you want to or not,' she explained earnestly and made Isabella more interested in her sudden engagement rather than less so.

'I should have got the coachman to whip up his team and get here last night after all, despite Miss Mausley's delicate nerves, for it sounds to me as if you two had an evening I'm sorry to have missed. Are you going to tell me what you got up to, or leave me to speculate wildly?' Isabella asked, wide-eyed and eager for any detail she could coax or trap them into providing.

'It's got nothing to do with you,' Kate intervened hastily, before Edmund could yield to the melting appeal Isabella suddenly managed to add to her wide-eyed and supposedly innocent stare.

'We left the ballroom for half an hour, quite separately, then re-entered it looking scandalously dishevelled by

one another after a very improper interval, so I broadly
hinted to the company that an announcement of our
engagement would follow very shortly,' Edmund told her
flatly and, shorn of all its twists and turns and the dizzying, unexpected seduction of his kisses, Kate hoped it
sounded a workaday enough explanation to halt Izzie's
rampant curiosity in its tracks for once.

'You did all that?' she asked Kate incredulously as
it became plain her curiosity was bolting headlong for
the wide-open spaces after all. 'No, Kate, please don't
tell me that you got carried away by *passion*? I really
never, ever did come across anything quite so shocking
in all my life, sister dear, and you, Lord Shuttleworth,
are obviously a very superior kisser indeed.'

Kate shot her sister a furious look, then spared one
for her new fiancé when she saw him appear ridiculously
pleased by that accolade, then try to look modest and fail
abysmally. It was true enough, so perhaps he had some
reason to preen himself on his skill in that dubious art,
but he could at least try to pretend to be ashamed of the
bad example they'd set her sister.

'Charlatan,' she muttered as Eiliane made room for
him to sit at the breakfast table, then rang for more
coffee as if he was already part of the family.

'Shrew,' he countered and, plumping down in the
seat next to her as if there was nowhere he'd rather be,
he gave her a casual hug and pressed a quick, hard kiss
on her open mouth that unfairly shot straight to her legs
and rendered her incapable of getting up and walking
away with dignified hauteur after all.

'*Very* superior,' Izzie observed approvingly and Kate

came back to her senses to find all three of them staring at her as if expecting something spectacular.

'Can I eat my toast now?' she asked sarcastically and hoped they were safely put in their places by her feigned indifference.

'No,' he denied her ungallantly and, seizing it, made a show of biting along the surface she'd absently nibbled at, as if eager to put his mouth everywhere hers might be even in the mundane act of eating her breakfast instead of his own.

She might have found his posturing of the devoted lover seductive and warm, promising so much for their marriage she'd instantly forget his enforced captivity. Unfortunately she knew he was putting on a show for Izzie and his ability to parody a lover's devotion made Kate feel edgy and, contrarily, a touch betrayed.

Watching Edmund and Isabella determinedly plough their way through a mountain of food as if they'd both just walked here from Windsor, Kate tried to consider if her sister would make Edmund a better wife, but found the idea horrifying. Then she wondered numbly when she'd become so jaded she refused to indulge in even the simplest pleasures without examining them for flaws? Food could be one of those pleasures, when not indulged to excess. So it must be sheer perversity that was making the coddled egg she absently helped herself to taste like dust and ashes in her mouth. Swallowing coffee hastily to help it down, she joined Eiliane in watching the experts at work instead.

'I'd rather keep either of them for a week than a

fortnight,' Lady Pemberley observed with a smile that understood too much of Kate's seesawing emotions.

'It's just as well that the kitchens are restocked from your marquis's vast estates at such regular intervals,' she said with a wry look back that agreed, yes, she did stand in need of a little sympathy and support. Yet if this was an ordeal, how could greeting the legions of callers they must expect this afternoon with a serene countenance and an unrevealing smile be described?

'I'll tell them to send an extra cartload every week if we're to entertain a pair of hungry wolves for breakfast each morning,' Eiliane joked.

'Nonsense, I was only sharp set after so many weeks of being offered nothing but invalidish pap,' Isabella emerged from her coffee cup to inform them. 'If I ever even see a bowl of gruel again I swear I'll throw it out of the nearest window.'

'You poor thing,' Kate said blandly, 'did they lock you in a garret as well?'

'They might have wanted to, because I made a sight sure to frighten small children, but Emily's mother really did offer me a bowl of gruel one day, I swear it.'

'Only the once, I suspect,' Kate observed wryly and Izzie grinned back with a nod that somehow re-established their usual easy accord, one they'd surely need in the face of the changes about to take place.

'She's usually quite a sensible woman, so, yes, only that one time.'

'Mrs Mausley was probably terrified what my lord Carnwood would say if his ward went into a decline in her care. I expect you were looking pale and interesting at the time as well,' Kate teased her sister.

'Probably—most inconsiderate of me not to have had the mumps when everyone else did at school, was it not?'

'Yes, especially as I remember you being unbearably smug while *I* went about looking like a gargoyle instead, so maybe I should have caught the first stage to Bath to soothe your fevered brow and gloat just a little after all, little sister.'

'Not if you ever wanted it to become un-fevered you shouldn't.'

'True.'

'And if you'd come to stay with the Mausleys as well, you wouldn't have had the opportunity to scandalise the *ton* outrageously as well as finally becoming engaged to Edmund at long last, so I for one am very glad you stayed away.'

'As am I, dear sister-in-law-to-be,' Edmund said with such politeness Kate couldn't say whether he actually meant it or not.

'Well, of course you are,' Eiliane said as if there was no question about it, and for once Kate wanted to live in dreamland as well and smiled her thanks at her. 'That being established beyond doubt, I think we should retire somewhere a little more private and discuss strategy, don't you?' Eiliane added with raised eyebrows and Kate wondered which of them she was intending to exclude.

'Oh, very well,' Isabella said with a sigh, 'it's perfectly plain you wish me to go away so you can discuss all the interesting things you won't tell me, so I'll just go and annoy my maid by getting in the way of her unpacking instead, shall I?'

'If you would, just for half an hour or so, my love. Then all three of us really must visit Celestine as a matter of urgency and never mind preparing for morning calls. The *ton* will just have to wait.'

'We must?' Kate asked with a sinking heart, for ordering a bridal gown and her trousseau seemed so inappropriate just now, when she'd said such a foolish thing about her marriage, just as if it wasn't exactly what she'd wanted all along and perhaps now even needed.

'Of course we must,' Eiliane said implacably and Kate avoided Edmund's eyes, unsure if she would see mockery or fury at her apparent reluctance in them.

'And I dare say I'll need a new waistcoat or so as well,' he said blandly and she was no closer to knowing his true feelings towards their upcoming marriage.

'Half an hour, then?' Isabella said with a sympathetic look for Kate that told her what her sister thought of his lack of enthusiasm.

'At the most,' Kate replied, thinking she could very likely stand no longer.

'It's like pulling teeth; anticipation is almost always worse than the act itself,' Edmund assured her with a perfectly straight face.

'Except for the small fact that it's also painful almost beyond words.'

'Not necessarily and, even if it is, the agony is brief, then comes the euphoria of finally being rid of it.'

Now why did Kate suddenly think they weren't

talking about dentists at all and why should his eyes take on such an intensely silvery light until she wasn't quite sure if they were green at all any more? Which was all very confusing of him and his eyes; she was almost sure she wanted him to go back to being polite and reliable, instead of the mocking devil he'd become some time in the last three years.

'I really hope you two know what you're talking about, because I certainly do not,' Eiliane interjected.

Chapter Eleven

As they were about to be sucked into the whirlwind of relentless activity the Marchioness of Pemberley generated whenever a new project presented itself to be organised, Kate wondered if this was the time to mention any doubts, but Eiliane sat down at her husband's impressive desk and drew a blank notebook out of the top drawer as if everything was set in stone.

'Not a new one, we'll have to get married now,' she joked feebly to Edmund.

'We had to get married the instant we appeared in Lady Wyndover's ballroom in a state of disarray. Don't even think about backing out and leaving me to explain you preferred social ruin to becoming my wife,' he said in an unamused undertone.

'It was a feeble joke, not a declaration of intent.'

'Never joke about our marriage,' he said dourly, as if near the end of his tether as well as his patience with her.

'I've endured enough taunts about your repeated refusals these last three years to last me several lifetimes.'

Kate flushed and mumbled something vaguely apologetic.

'If we might get on with the business in hand, then?' Eiliane asked, her expression almost as impatient as Edmund's. 'Isabella will not give us long, so if you two intend to marry with indecent haste we'd better get on with arranging it.'

'I'll have to go into Derbyshire and ask Carnwood's permission before there's an official announcement,' Edmund said with a frown.

'Shouldn't I accompany you to tell him I've changed my mind?' Kate asked.

She felt distinctly unlike herself in far too many ways and had done ever since Edmund had kissed her last night. So what did it say about her that stumbling on a pair of very guilty lovers and a plot to murder a man had left her feeling distressed but reasonably composed, yet one sensuous kiss from Edmund Worth had sent her floating in such a cloud of unreality she still didn't recognise herself next morning?

'Certainly not,' he countered sharply.

'Why?'

'Because we've scandalised enough people already without adding to it by infuriating your brother-in-law and former guardian and upsetting your sister,' Edmund said with exaggerated patience, as if addressing a slow child who probably wouldn't understand him.

'But we need not go alone.'

'And what about your other sister?' he asked, as if she

was confirming all his worst suspicions by suggesting they uproot Isabella now she was safely returned at last and obviously in robust health as she prepared to make a spectacular début.

'Isabella will stay here, of course, even Lady Pemberley can hardly present her if she's not here to be presented,' she replied patiently, as if he was the idiot.

'Then who will chaperon *you*?' he asked, still with such insufferable reasonableness she felt her temper rise and forced herself to count to twenty.

'There's sure to be someone,' she said with a shrug, 'some proper and respectable female who'd be willing to lend us countenance if she thought it would avert even more scandal. Emily Mausley's aunt might even be prevailed upon to do so in such a worthy case for an instance, or what about Miss Carton, she's certainly respectable enough for all three of us,' she said brightly, glad she'd recalled the stern and efficient lady who came in three days a week to help Eiliane with her many good causes and her correspondence.

'I need Miss Carton here,' Eiliane protested. 'I couldn't think of managing without her for the fortnight it would take you to post to Derbyshire and back with any degree of comfort. It's folly to even think of going, Kate. Shuttleworth can ride there and back in a few days if he's unburdened by coaches and luggage and your maid and his valet, as you'd have to take them with you if you were to travel in that sort of state. No, it's a ridiculous idea. You must stay here and face the intrusive questions until your betrothal is officially announced. It will be unpleasant, but you're not one to shirk a task because you don't like to make an effort to deal with it, I hope.'

'That's really not fair, Eiliane, you know I take my responsibilities seriously,' Kate defended herself.

Being heiress to a large estate in Ireland, as well as owning several smaller holdings in England and the small fortune invested in funds left her in her parents' will, weighed heavy on her shoulders now she was one and twenty and felt obliged to make decisions she'd been very happy to leave to Kit in the past.

'I agree that you're as good and concerned a landlord to your tenants as anyone can be when a few hundred miles and the Irish Sea keeps you from meeting most of them, my love, but it's high time you stopped being such a coward where your own life is concerned, Kate. You must learn to deal with more personal problems like a mature adult instead of a frightened child.'

'I have, I am,' she defended herself stubbornly and glared at both of them.

'Then let's get on with that list of things that must be done which you're so eager to begin, your ladyship, before I must set out for Wychwood,' Edmund intervened with a sigh that told Kate he disagreed with her about the emotional maturity she'd just claimed for herself, but wasn't inclined to dally and argue just at the moment. 'I should probably have left already if I'm to get as far as I'd like to with my journey before it's dark,' he added impatiently.

'Surely you don't intend leaving without a letter from me to explain everything to Kit and Miranda and assure them of my agreement to your offer?' Kate objected.

'Absolutely not,' he barked as if she'd suggested sending a primed bomb in his saddlebags. 'First you want some unfortunate lady who has just travelled here from Somerset, probably against her own inclinations and purely out of duty to a guest in her family's care, to pack up again and hare off to Derbyshire at your say-so and at a few moments' notice. Now you think it's a perfectly sound idea to blithely inform your pregnant sister that I've compromised you to the point where a marriage between us is a more or less foregone conclusion among the *ton* and presumably you then intend to rely on her to prevent Carnwood killing me in a duel when he finds out how upset she is about just how close to the wind you sailed with me last night on the Wyndovers' terrace?'

Feeling that horrible sinking in her stomach again that had plagued her on and off since Edmund appeared in town this spring, suddenly as indifferent to her as if he'd never begged her to marry him in the first place, Kate decided she'd weathered enough for one morning.

'No, I'm not,' she snapped, 'for if Kit kills you, at least it'll save *me* the trouble.'

'Vixen,' he informed her with a wry smile, but at least that frozen look had left his eyes, so did he still care for her after all? This was hardly the right time or place to find out.

'So what does that make you?' she asked snootily instead.

'A fool, I suspect, considering I'll be setting out to ride my poor horse into the ground in order to beg your brother-in-law and former guardian for your hand, Kate Alstone. Despite the fact I'd probably do better to buy a passage for the Americas and a new life in exile, instead of staying here and marrying a stubborn, ill-tempered termagant who'll do her best to lead me a fine old dance for the rest of our days.'

'Much better, so why don't you?'

'Because annoying you for the rest of our lives promises to be so much more amusing, and my estates and tenants need me, even if yours apparently don't. Now, I believe we've used up half our time with arguing already, so shall we occupy the rest by doing something useful?'

'You two may do so, but I'm going to find my younger sister. Remember her? The other sister I don't consider whenever I'm putting my own selfish needs before anyone else's? So I'll bid you goodbye, my lord, and leave you to plan the rest however you please and tell me about it afterwards. I suppose I'll see you after your epic ride to Derbyshire and back, whether I want to or not?'

'That you will, my love, that you will,' he informed her suavely and escorted her to the door and bowed over her hand, as if they'd been discussing their wedding in delighted harmony for the last quarter of an hour.

'One thing I do know after the last few weeks, my lord, is that I'm certainly not your love,' she muttered as Eiliane became ostentatiously absorbed in her list-making.

'All the last few weeks have proved conclusively is that you, my lovely Kate, don't know your own mind, let alone whatever happens to be skulking about in mine.'

'And that you think you're very clever,' she informed him crossly.

'You wrong me; only a complete idiot would marry you after what you put me through three years ago and expect any peace out of it.'

'Then I suggest you decide now whether you're capable of such a noble self-sacrifice after all and a long ride with all the bother of a visit to my brother-in-law to no useful purpose.'

'I never said I wanted anything as humdrum from life as peace and quiet though, did I? So it will serve a very useful purpose to me,' he replied in a low voice that sent an unwanted shiver of desire down her back, despite her threatening temper and secret reluctance to part from him. 'Stop teasing me with such un-Kate-like shilly-shallying when we both know the die is cast,' he added.

'But I wasn't teasing, Edmund,' she said silkily and he laughed.

'I know and that's what makes it so irresistible. Most men prefer to fight for what they want most from life, sweetheart, and you really ought to remember that very pertinent fact in your dealings with my sex and adjust your behaviour.'

'As I'm fated to marry you in a matter of weeks, I won't be dealing with any other gentlemen now, so their peccadilloes can be of no importance.'

'But *I* am a man, Kate, and expect my peccadilloes to be vital to you for the rest of our lives. So important that they completely exclude any other gentleman's,' he said smoothly, but there was an implacable purpose in his silvery green eyes that made her shiver.

'As *I* am a true lady, I will certainly never be aught but faithful to my husband, your lordship,' she told him stiffly, but something flashed between them as his gaze heated and promised her such untold intimacies when they truly became man and wife that her head spun and her breath came short and shallow.

'And I'll be as devoted to my wife as you allow me to be, Kate,' he promised ambiguously and she shivered as he bent over her hand and kissed it as formally again, as if society were watching, and not an unconventional marchioness pretending to be fascinated by the view out of the window and her notes for a spring wedding.

'Goodbye then, Shuttleworth,' Kate managed to say as if it was three years ago and she was as indifferent to his staying or going as she'd managed to pretend even to herself that she was then.

'Goodbye, my dear,' he corrected her gently enough, before surprising her by pressing another of those hard, hotly uncompromising kisses on her softly opened lips after all.

Whilst his mouth on hers was all she wanted to explore, enjoy and seek more and yet more intimacy with, as he drowned her senses in infinite possibilities until she was oblivious to everything else, Edmund calmly opened the door behind her back. Then he relinquished her mouth with a lopsided grin that admitted yes, kissing her was a very pleasant, if time-consuming, occupation before he gently pushed her out into the corridor. With jolted incredulity bordering on fury, she numbly watched him turn and face Eiliane's bland smile of enquiry as if he'd just put the cat out, even as he gently shut the door in Kate's face to exclude her.

Never before had one of the Marquis of Pemberley's finely crafted and highly polished mahogany doors been subjected to a glare of such burning hatred. Never had Kate wanted to kick one of them so badly that her foot hurt in sympathy and anticipation until today. Simmering with fury and righteous indignation, she stood on the other side of that satin-smooth door and clenched her fists to stop herself beating them against it in a tattoo of wild frustration. Instead she turned smartly on her heel and tried to contain her rage and wounded pride as she marched up the stairs and sought her own spacious bedchamber to pace in agitation, until she was fit to seek out her sister without snapping Isabella's nose off when she didn't deserve it.

Isabella greeted her with a determined expression on her lovely face that told Kate she hadn't escaped an inquisition. 'If you think I'm going to tamely accept the tall story that you and Shuttleworth just fell into each other's arms last night like a belated Romeo and Juliet, Katherine Margaret Alstone, you've never been more mistaken in your life,' her sister informed her sternly.

'We might easily have done,' Kate defended herself, deciding she'd have to do better than that if she was going to escape having to tell Isabella the whole story.

'After he asked you to marry him so many times that first year even I stopped counting, and you refused every single offer he made when he was more romantic and ready to love you than he appears to be now? I wasn't born yesterday or even the day before that, sister dear.'

'I've had a change of heart.'

'Unconvincing,' Isabella declared and tapped her foot impatiently.

Kate sincerely hoped she was wrong and wasn't it almost true? 'He's grown into more of a man than the rest of my suitors put together,' she heard herself say and it was true and yet a little less than the whole truth. She'd spent several weeks metaphorically measuring eligible bachelors against her requirements of a perfect husband and failed to be impressed by any but Edmund, but there had been others these last few years who would impress the most finicky and discontented of ladies, and none of them had made her heartbeat flutter and her knees go weak with need, which right now seemed most unfair of them.

'Well, that can hardly be considered difficult, since you've turned away every overtly masculine and potentially demanding man you met since you made your come-out,' Isabella echoed her thoughts mercilessly. 'Little wonder they gave up on you and decided to marry someone less challenging and a lot more amenable after a few weeks of your ice-queen act, Kate. I suspect Lord Shuttleworth only ever seemed an acceptable escort to you in the first place because he wasn't yet the mature and rather impressive man he is now when you made your come-out. He's certainly nothing like the love-struck youth you met three years ago any more, is he?'

'I said all along it was a mistake for Miranda and

Kit not to find you a new governess when Charlotte married Ben, for you've obviously been spending far too much time minding my business for me and too little on your lessons these last three years. I'm sure that I never got left to my own devices in London far too much when *I* wasn't even out. You must have been given far too much liberty to know so much about eligible bachelors now and you're only just making your début and should therefore be innocent and sweetly naïve, not a budding fishwife who thinks she knows everything there is to know about other people's private business,' Kate snapped.

'Heaven forbid I should ever be as innocent as Miranda evidently was when that worm lied and wheedled and seduced her into eloping with him in that scrambling fashion,' Isabella said with an expression in her eyes that made Kate's heart sink.

She'd fought so hard to shelter her little sister from the full impact of their elder sister innocently believing Nevin Braxton's self-serving, cynical lies. Even now she shuddered to think of the terrible consequences of what should have been just a silly youthful infatuation, when Miranda eloped with a villain before being abandoned by him, after being stripped of her innocence, her pride and even her health while he gaily spent the quarter-day rents for the whole Wychwood estate he'd somehow managed to steal away with her on wine, women and more unspeakable pleasures that Miranda would never dream of discussing with her little sisters.

'Both of us have her example in front of us to make us wary, Izzie, but you only need to watch Miranda with

Kit, or Charlotte with her Ben, to know that not all men are lying villains.' With incredulity Kate heard herself defend that overwrought emotion some called love, the very one she'd spent so long avoiding and refusing to truly believe in.

Only yesterday she would have probably applauded Isabella's hard-headed refusal to be taken in by passions that threatened to fog the intellect and blind a person to all the faults the object of that passion might possess.

'Suddenly you're singing a very different tune,' Isabella confirmed with some satisfaction and Kate wondered if her devious sister had manufactured this whole scene to get her to do just that. 'About time, too,' she added and smiled smugly.

'I'm just making observations,' she excused herself lamely.

'Liar.'

'At least I'm not a precocious brat who thinks she knows far more about other people's business than they do themselves,' Kate retorted, infuriated that her sister was right. The moral high ground she'd thought so settled and immutable under her feet shifted every time Edmund gave her one of those hotly assessing looks, or a provoking smile that promptly sent her wits to the four winds.

'Neither am I,' Isabella replied with annoying, very conscious calm in the face of the childish provocation Kate had just resorted to in order to change the subject.

'Neither are you what?' Kate asked shortly, already

having had her temper severely tested by her betrothed this morning and deciding she'd had enough.

'A precocious brat,' Izzie replied coolly and proved it.

Arrested by the truth of that declaration, Kate finally took in the absolute certainty that her whole life was about to change for ever. Isabella was a beautiful and composed young woman, almost guaranteed to become the toast of London society as soon as she stuck her nose inside the first ballroom and Kate was going to marry a man who'd thought himself in love with her what seemed like for ever ago, just when he seemed to have decided he didn't want to wed, or perhaps even like, the woman who'd cost him so much wasted time and frustration. Edmund had certainly cooled towards her during those three years of absence and, before last night, had seemed more intent on watching her with cynical amusement and a lazy smile than begging for her closest attention and her hand in marriage.

He'd obviously found little enough to like about her when he was subjecting her to that mocking scrutiny these last few weeks and it was obvious even to her that he'd been hunting for a wife whose greatest virtue would very likely have been *not* resembling Miss Katherine Alstone. Apparently he'd learnt to distrust her since they'd parted on his last passionate offer to love her and her refusal of that offer. She recalled a few more heated memories from last night and decided he'd managed to overcome it long enough to kiss her senseless and want her almost ravenously all the time he was doing it. The whole topsy-turvy situation was enough to give any female the urge to fall into hysterics, she decided, and met her little sister's gaze with some of her confusion probably all too evident in her own.

'Edmund's clearly no longer a besotted youth, eager for any kind word I care to offer or a duty dance or two when I'm not otherwise engaged, and you obviously don't need me, either,' Kate admitted hollowly. 'Nothing about my life or that of most of the people I care about is as I thought when I came to town this year.'

'Shuttleworth's certainly not a youth, and whether or not he's besotted with you largely depends how you treat him, I suspect, but I'll always need you, Kate. Perhaps in a different way now I'm not the vulnerable little girl you fought so hard to protect, although just a child yourself. We're both women now and all three of us Alstone sisters could be closer than ever, if you'll let yourself need us as deeply as we'll always love and need you.'

'Whatever do you mean, Izzie? I've always loved you both so much.'

'Only that you did what you had to do when Miranda ran off with that awful Nevin Braxton and Grandfather refused to even hear her name mentioned again, let alone allowing her any contact with us at all, despite you being so very young yourself. When our dear brother, Jack, died, it left us at Wychwood, grief-stricken and lost as we were, and you stood up to Aunt Ennersley and Cousin Cecelia's bullying and carping and even somehow persuaded Grandfather to send us to school to get us away from them. Both Miranda and I needed you to be far more grown up than anyone had the right to ask you to be at such an age then, but I'm a woman now, Kate, and Miranda is so blissfully married neither of us need worry about her happiness ever again, with Kit there to see to it so ably.

'You can stop worrying about me, and it's plain as the nose on your face that Miranda is almost insufferably delighted with her earl. Maybe one day she'll even stop feeling guilty that such a youthful folly took her away when we needed her most. What I'm trying to say, and probably making a ham-fist of it, is we love you deeply and heaven knows you've proved you love us, but you don't need to fight the rest of the world any more. Miranda and I want you to be *happy*, Kate, so please let Edmund Worth love you as ardently as he's wanted to from the first moment he laid eyes on you, and make sure you are just that for the rest of your days.'

'It's too late,' Kate said bleakly.

'Don't be ridiculous, you're about to marry the man.'

'Only because he thinks he compromised me beyond repairing while rescuing me from my folly. He's been doing a very good job of ignoring me all Season whilst he flirted and danced with the prettiest of the current batch of débutantes. He was obviously trying to make up his mind which one to marry and it certainly wasn't me he expected to walk up the aisle towards him at the end of the festivities, Izzie.'

'Yet he gained *your* attention by proving himself not to be an eager young puppy to be kicked away or taken for granted any longer, if he was ever as tame as you thought him to be in the first place, of course, which I doubt.'

'I really don't think that was what he was trying to do, Izzie. Indeed, Edmund made it very plain to me from the instant he set eyes on me again this year that he no longer cared one way or the other *what* I thought of him. He was seeking a pretty and conformable wife, and he certainly wasn't looking in my direction to find her since I am patently neither pretty nor conformable.'

'No, you're beautiful and spirited, which makes you far more interesting and exciting to be around, but did you really care what he thought of you, Kate? You didn't seem to during that first Season when he followed you about like an overenthusiastic dog guarding a bone.'

'I've missed him,' she admitted rather grudgingly.

'And if you'd been caught behaving improperly with any other man than Edmund, you'd have meekly married him instead?' Isabella demanded ruthlessly.

'Perhaps,' Kate mumbled as if she were the younger of the sisters by several years and didn't want to own up to some iniquitous deed she was ashamed of, even while her mind screamed an unequivocal 'No!' So apparently she'd rather face disgrace and social exclusion for the rest of her days than wed anyone but Edmund, Viscount Shuttleworth, which seemed close to disastrous when he could put her out of the room with such breathtaking arrogance, then go back to discussing details of their wedding with Eiliane as if they didn't concern her in the least.

'Then you're an idiot.'

'Well and so I am. Eiliane thinks me one, you obviously agree and Edmund hasn't stopped glowering at me since I was stupid enough to agree we have no choice but to marry each other after all.'

'And you're just meekly accepting the majority decision on your sanity, are you, sister mine? That really doesn't sound at all like you.'

'It's not, but I don't *feel* at all like me at the moment, Izzie,' Kate admitted her confusion at last and surprised herself by feeling considerably better for doing so.

'Good, then there's clearly hope for you yet.'

'I fail to see why my feeling confused about it could mean my marriage to Edmund is any more likely to succeed.'

'I know, that's what makes the whole situation so irresistibly amusing,' Isabella said annoyingly and refused to expand on her cryptic statement any further.

Chapter Twelve

'The Earl of Carnwood and Viscount Shuttleworth, your ladyship,' the Pemberleys' butler announced solemnly six days later, then he reluctantly shut the door after that noble pair before he could observe the full effect of his announcement on the ladies.

'Good heavens, whatever are *you* doing here?' Kate demanded of her brother-in-law as soon as he stepped into the room. She noted that, even though he was as tall and powerful and full of life as ever, the Earl of Carnwood quite failed to overshadow Edmund as he should have done just with his impressive physical presence.

It wasn't much for her to ask of a brother-in-law and ex-guardian, she chided him silently. All he'd needed to do to make her feel a lot better about her seesawing emotions and uncertain temper was to put a pampered young aristocrat in the shade for her with his effortless poise and that air of barely contained energy Miranda obviously found so irresistible. Not that she had the least desire to lust after her sister's husband, of course, especially now he was no longer her guardian and she'd come to regard him as an elder brother, but Kit could at least have done her the favour of putting her betrothed back into the Edmund-shaped slot she'd once managed to make him fit into so neatly.

'Where else did you expect me to be at a time like this?' Kit replied harshly, as if only just restraining himself from shaking her, which might well be the case since he'd probably hated travelling every last mile that now separated him from Miranda and their children, both born and still just about unborn.

'We were managing perfectly well without you,' she defended herself, unable to conceal the fact that her gaze was locked on Edmund as if she was waiting for whatever danger he posed to reveal itself so she could jump the other way.

Except he was her affianced husband now and shortly she'd no longer have the luxury of avoiding anything about him. The delicious shiver that accompanied that inescapable truth distracted her so shockingly that she heard Kit's impatient reply as if from a vast distance.

'So well that you got trapped in such a deep hole by drifting about someone else's house as if you owned it, that Edmund was forced to dig you out of it at the cost of his own freedom,' Kit accused her crossly.

'I take it you both had an unpleasant journey then,' Eiliane finally managed to say with the manic cheerfulness of a hostess doing her best to cope with an impossible social situation and two travel-stained noblemen.

Both evidently thought their business too important to go to their respective homes so they could bathe and change before they strolled into a lady's private sitting room. Which made Kate's heart leap with apprehension for what they thought so urgent it couldn't wait just an hour to be dealt with in a more leisurely fashion.

'Indeed we did, Lady Pemberley. It was infernally damp and ridiculously hasty and I'd very much prefer to be at home with my wife, not caught up in some ridiculous bumble-broth of my sister-in-law's making,' Kit told Eiliane with only a slight softening of the formidable frown knitting his dark brows.

He continued to watch Kate as if she was about to add something equally silly and dangerous to the misadventure that had forced Edmund to pay him a hasty visit in the first place. She squirmed under his condemning gaze, despite feeling Kit was being ungracious and unfair, and that she'd done nothing particularly awful. It wasn't as if she'd gone into that room for any other reason than to avoid an importunate suitor and a nasty public scene when she would have been forced to repulse his obnoxious advances in no uncertain terms. Kit wouldn't have liked it if he'd been forced to gallop south to extricate her from Bestholme's predatory clutches and bear her home in disgrace, instead of agreeing for her to wed Edmund as he'd always wanted her to.

'Pray come and sit by the fire,' Eiliane invited soothingly and Kate knew she owed her friend fervent thanks for trying to deflect Kit's rarely aroused temper, before he gave her the full benefit of his pent-up frustrations.

'I allowed myself the luxury of ordering one lit today,
despite it being springtide according to the calendar, so
you can both enjoy my extravagance and I won't have
any standing on ceremony from you, dear Edmund, now
that you're almost a member of the family.'

Now one storm at least had been averted, Kate almost
caused another by nervously giggling at the contrary
effect Eiliane's invitation had on her two visitors. Kit
relaxed enough to mutter something about all his dirt
and had the very idea of him going across the square
to change before he could sit down and recover from
his hasty journey summarily dismissed. He shrugged
wearily and subsided into the comfortable chair by the
fire before gratefully stretching his long legs towards the
warmth with a long sigh of relief. Would that Edmund
followed his example, Kate decided wistfully, as he
stood aloof instead. He was watching her like a cat at
a mouse hole, which seemed rather harsh of him when
she was still trying to conceal the rush of pleasure her
first sight of him after several days apart had provoked
in her fast-beating heart and very confused mind.

How very unfair of the fates to allow her immunity to
his looks and charm three years ago and now make her
so ridiculously sensitive to his every look and gesture,
when he was far less charming, if even more formidably
handsome, than he'd been then. The fates had a great
deal to answer for, she decided bitterly, and pretended
to be absorbed in the list in front of her. Unfortunately
it was one of Eiliane's interminable ones concerning
their hasty wedding and she blushed foolishly at the
very thought of the future looming inexorably nearer

with every day that passed. It really wasn't ladylike to feel so wickedly curious about becoming a wife in every sense of the word.

A little maidenly shrinking at the unthinkable intimacies ahead of her would be far more proper, then she could forgive herself for being such a fool as to turn him down so often and so emphatically in the past. She shivered at the very thought of such incredible closeness between a man and his new wife entering the marriage bed together and wondered if it was possible to conceal her innermost thoughts and secret hopes from an intelligent and observant husband. She'd have her answer to that question all too soon and tried to look inscrutable when she glanced at him.

Edmund seemed more concerned with trying to read her deepest secrets in her face than with his own comfort, even after the hard ride he and Kit must have endured to get here so quickly. Kate squirmed under his examining gaze, just managing to meet it with more of an effort than she liked and she tightened her betraying fingers on her notebook lest he see how they were trembling.

'Was the journey so very bad?' she finally managed to ask.

'It was cold and wet as well as unpleasantly muddy,' he admitted at last and Kate couldn't dismiss the idea he might have enjoyed it far more if he'd been bound for Wychwood on any other errand.

'I'm sorry,' she offered stiffly.

'I really have no idea why,' he said with a ghost of

a smile, 'even you can hardly be responsible for the vagaries of the weather.'

Oh dear, none of this was going according to plan and how would they ever get on as man and wife if even a conversation about the state of the roads and the weather could turn from innocuous to personal in such a stilted, unpromising way?

'I was being polite,' she informed him crossly and had to control her temper when the contrary man evidently found the notion amusing and actually managed to look as if he might like to know her after all.

'Forgive me for not recognising the effort it cost you,' he teased with such a warm smile she couldn't resist a ridiculous need to grin back at him, just as if she'd been sitting here twiddling her thumbs since he'd gone and waiting for him to get back so she could simper at him like a besotted milkmaid.

'I'm not really so ill mannered, am I?' she asked.

'No, I recall being crushed by your exquisite manners on more than one occasion.'

'Then I shall endeavour to treat you with excessive rudeness from now on.'

'I'd certainly prefer that to the impenetrable politeness you once used to depress my pretences,' he said wryly.

'Then for goodness' sake sit down, you're giving me a crick in the neck as well as keeping the warmth of the fire from the rest of us.'

'Much better,' he murmured as he sat down cautiously on the sofa beside her with an apparent docility that no longer deceived her in the least.

Quite aware that very little about their supposedly private interaction had escaped either Kit or Eiliane, Kate decided a front of apparent serenity would serve her best against their rampant curiosity about her relationship with Edmund.

'So how is my sister?' she asked Kit as she handed him a cup of tea while Welland rounded up his acolytes and left the room once more, surprised not to have it thrust back at her while he demanded something more potent after such a journey. The Earl of Carnwood was in danger of becoming civilised, she decided wryly, and met his self-conscious glare with an innocently enquiring look.

'Well enough,' he admitted gruffly and sipped the fragrant Chinese blend Eiliane always insisted on having served with carefully concealed appreciation. 'It's quite refreshing after a long ride,' he defended himself and Kate saw Edmund grin at Kit's discomfiture with an openness that told her they'd reached a new equality on the road somewhere between here and Wychwood.

'Never having been overburdened with female relatives nagging me to forsake my wicked ways, I've always had the liberty of choosing which ways to pursue for myself, until now of course,' Edmund said with a polite bow and a bland look Kate didn't altogether trust.

Despite not believing she'd ever be allowed much say with regard to his behaviour, it occurred to her that she'd never seen him drunk, nor heard it whispered that he indulged in private debauchery even the gossips dared not be specific about, for fear of polluting their own tongues and reputations. Well, apart from that annoyingly persistent murmur about him and Lady Tedinton that she didn't believe for a moment, of course. Unfortunately she didn't have much faith in Edmund's implication that she alone would have permission to plague him about his foibles in future, let alone believing she'd be listened to once he'd made his mind up on any course of action he considered important.

'Lucky you,' Kit responded and Kate wondered how much difference even Miranda's opinions made to him once he had determined on something.

Since Kit's two sisters must have been responsible for any feminine nagging done before he and Miranda married, and her elder sister was a very decided female under all that serene beauty of hers, Kate supposed it was therefore just about possible for a strong woman to influence a masculine force of nature like Kit. The question being, of course, whether she had any chance of altering a course of action the equally stubborn male she was to marry might choose to embark on.

'One thing I'm not going to be moved so much as an inch upon, though, is the subject of your marriage,' Kit declared with the rock-hard set to his chin indicating a state of mind Miranda had learnt to circumvent rather than try to change.

'Then you disapprove?' Kate heard herself ask squeakily, even desperately, as if marrying Edmund had become the be all and end all of her entire existence.

'Of course I don't,' he replied and Kate wondered if she was the only one who heard the unsaid aside that she was an idiot to even suggest he might.

'What about our marriage, then?' she asked, and had

to physically stop herself reaching for Edmund's hand as if she needed his strength and support to face her brother-in-law's weary irritation with cool self-command.

'It won't take place in London,' Kit informed her bluntly.

Kate annoyed herself intensely once more by looking to Edmund for his opinion of that ultimatum before expressing her own. 'But what about Isabella?' she managed to say, unable to read his silver-green gaze and having to do all the work on her own after all.

'What about her?' Kit asked.

'It's her début Season and she's been late enough beginning it already, without her being dragged north to see me married and make it even shorter for her.'

'I propose that we ask her opinion of the idea before we start galloping off on wild-goose chases in either direction,' Eiliane suggested with the exquisitely breakable serenity of a lady who'd just spent the last few days hastily planning a fashionable wedding at St George's in Hanover Square that now looked very unlikely to take place.

'Well, where is she then?' Kit asked impatiently, as if Isabella had been deliberately obstructive in not refusing to stir an inch outside the front door until he reached town, especially when she hadn't known he was coming in the first place.

'Shopping—the Mausley family arrived in town the day before yesterday and you know very well that Fanny Mausley has always been Izzie's bosom-bow, Kit,' Kate said as pacifically as she could manage when she was beginning to feel rather impatient with her brother-in-law's weary irritability herself.

'And if only she wasn't such a breathy, overeager female, I'd be a lot more ready to forgive her for carrying my ward off on a hunt for fripperies when all I want is to get all this nonsense settled and go back home as fast as a pack of hired nags can carry me now I've worn out my own, and that won't be nigh fast enough for my taste,' Kit grumbled.

'It's not nonsense, it's my *wedding* and you sound just like the crabby guardian out of some Drury Lane comedy, overeager to get back to your acres and forsake the hurly-burly of the town for ever.' She managed to swallow her own annoyance to tease him and won a reluctant smile and a self-deprecating shrug.

'That's what the love of a good woman can do to a man, Shuttleworth, so be warned by my example and start *your* married life as you mean to go on,' Kit warned.

'Oh, I'll do that, never fret,' Edmund replied with a mocking glance at her that jolted Kate out of her mood of half-contented acceptance of her new lot in life and left her struggling to control her temper again.

'And *I* shall be forewarned,' she pronounced haughtily and had to conceal her ridiculously oscillating feelings for a very different reason when Edmund's smile turned openly sceptical. He seemed more intent on challenging her on every front than wooing her into accepting this marriage with good grace and it was just stupid to feel the least bit tearful about it.

'I do enjoy a refreshing tussle to whet my appetite,

especially when I know exactly how and where the engagement will end,' he murmured for her ears alone.

Kate marvelled at the conspiratorial glance she intercepted between Kit and Eiliane when she managed to tear her gaze from Edmund's and pretend to disregard his double-edged teasing. Surely they weren't deluded enough to think she and Edmund were in the midst of some besotted lovers' tiff just for the pleasure of making up their quarrel at the end of it? She could see nothing but some implacable purpose that involved his supremacy and her submission in his eyes, even if he was doing his best to use the sensual heat that had flared up between them as soon as their gazes clashed to get his own way. Struggling with a morass of contrary emotions, she wondered idly where cool and composed Katherine Alstone had gone, just when she needed her most.

This older, infinitely wiser and far more dangerous Edmund Worth called irresistibly to her senses and threatened to override her promise to herself never to fall in love, never risk her very soul for the traitor emotion that had lured her big sister into an elopement that had broken up their family and cast Miranda into a terrible limbo where she was excluded from everything she'd held most dear for five long years. Kate didn't love him, had promised herself *not* to love him from almost the first instant she'd laid eyes on him, she now realised. Yet just because she suddenly longed to learn the intimacies between a man and a woman that had previously been too secret and dangerous to risk exploring with him, that didn't mean she had to change her mind about everything else and become a meek little cipher to an unexpectedly powerful husband.

'Don't flatter yourself, my lord,' she managed to hiss back almost soundlessly.

'Oh, I don't, and I certainly never promise what I can't deliver, Kate. Surely you know me well enough to have realised that by now, my dear.'

'Well enough to know I'm not *your dear* any more,' she muttered.

'The longer our acquaintance goes on, Kate, the more I become convinced you've little idea what really goes on in your own head, let alone mine.'

'I certainly don't have a clue what goes on in yours,' she told him as fiercely as anyone could when trying not to be overheard by two very interested listeners.

'No, I really don't think you have,' he replied with such a delighted smile he almost charmed her into abandoning her cross-grained mood and smiling right back at him, before the implication of his words hit her and she frowned instead.

'Nor do I want to,' she told him ungraciously.

'Ah, but you will, Kate. You undoubtedly will, once we're finally husband and wife and I have you all to myself at long last.'

'That sounds more like a threat than a promise,' she faltered in a most un-Kate-like fashion.

'It probably is; you've made it into one by your own stubbornness over the years since we first met.'

'Nonsense,' she managed to scoff unconvincingly, all those spurned offers and ignored courtesies he'd once wooed her with so vainly piling up to mock her. Now she was to marry the wretched man anyway, she would welcome just a tithe of that worshipful dedication to her lightest whim he'd shown all those years ago.

'Luckily for you I can hear the sound of a small tempest arriving home, even through Lord Pemberley's substantial walls and fine doors, so no doubt your sister has arrived home from her excursion at last and we can find out if she chooses to stay here or remove to Derbyshire to witness our wedding.'

'At least she's got a choice,' Kate mumbled grumpily, but he didn't bother to reply.

'I told Fanny and her mama we would meet them at the theatre tonight, Eiliane,' Isabella announced even before Welland had the door open properly. 'I hope we're not engaged for some silly waltzing party full of giggling girls and spotty youths, for Kean is playing Hamlet and Fanny's brother has hired a box.'

'No need to ask if you're fully recovered, minx,' Kit told her, getting to his feet with a warm smile of welcome. 'And being as contrary as ever from what I can see. I can't help wondering why we bothered to go to all that trouble to arrange your début so carefully, since you're finding it all so tedious.'

'Kit! Oh, how lovely,' Isabella exclaimed, throwing the bonnet she was carrying by its strings into a corner and herself at her not-very-stern guardian, who caught her, then swung her round in an exuberant bear hug.

Kate couldn't help but contrast Kit's bad-tempered greeting for her with his delight at seeing Isabella. She didn't feel jealous of the open affection between them because she loved her sister too much to begrudge her the security of loving her guardian and brother by marriage, but it hurt a little that she didn't share such a warm relationship with him. Yet Kate realised fairly that she alone was responsible for keeping Kit at a distance, even if he had taken her aloofness at face value and stopped there.

'Contrary female,' Edmund muttered and she marvelled that he could read her so easily, while her shrewd brother-in-law and usually perceptive little sister were apparently quite unable to, which was probably just as well at the moment.

He smiled and shrugged as if he didn't know quite how he did it, either. Kate suspected that, as an orphan, even a very privileged and wealthy one, he'd learnt to watch and weigh up the feelings and motives of those around him from a very early age. He'd grown up with as little reason to trust others as she had learnt much later in childhood, yet he'd won his battle for his own unique place in the world and she felt as if she was still fighting for hers. Edmund George Francis St Erith Standon-Worth, Viscount Shuttleworth, really was an extraordinary man, she decided, and she wasn't quite certain she deserved him.

'Annoying man,' she replied placidly enough.

'And I couldn't possibly comment on your state of mind or temper,' he teased. Perhaps it was just as well Kit recalled he was weary and interrupted them before Kate could stare besottedly at her own fiancé, as if he meant more to her than he rightly should if they weren't marrying for love.

'Now we've got all that over with, and before I cross to my splendid mansion and change into equally splendid evening dress in order to escort you to Drury Lane tonight, brat, let's settle what's to be done next between us all, at long last, shall we?' Kit said as soon as they were all back in their seats and he and Edmund and Isabella were working their way through plates of scones and several cups of tea.

'Apart from Kean?' Izzie asked between mouthfuls.

'Of course, no waltzing party could ever compare,' he reassured her approvingly, probably as pleased as the rest of them that Isabella was so deeply unimpressed with her many social triumphs and showing no signs of letting all the admiration and fulsome compliments she was receiving go to her head. 'It comes down to you deciding what you wish to do most, Isabella,' Kit went on.

Kate was surprised that Edmund had let him take charge, until she concluded they'd already decided what the absolutes were between them and she did her best not to be irritated by such masculine arrogance when there were more pressing matters to be irritated about, like planning a wedding around the projected arrival of Kit and Miranda's very imminent baby. She and Miranda should never have become entangled with two such strong males if they wanted an easy life or to get their own way all the time, she supposed ruefully.

'Your sister and Shuttleworth are determined to be wed inside a month,' Kit went on, explaining the situation in his own inimitable manner, 'although some of us could call that indecent haste when they've been shilly-shallying about it for the last three years. Maybe he thinks if he doesn't get the contrary wench up the aisle very soon, she'll change her mind and jilt him.'

'Don't be ridiculous, Kit,' Eiliane intervened with a visible shudder that made Kate very glad she wasn't in the least inclined to follow such a course. 'None of us could show our faces in society for a very long time after such a lapse of courage and good manners on Kate's part.'

'You almost tempt me to do my best to persuade her to do just that then, my lady Pemberley,' Kit remarked ruefully.

They all knew that he had never done much more than tolerate the social whirl, probably mainly for his family's sake, and much preferred the company of the clever men and women he'd moved amongst before the *ton* ever dreamed of admitting the son of a bankrupt drunkard to their select ranks.

'Which would almost sway me to try to call you out one fine May morning, Carnwood,' Edmund almost joked in return.

'An interesting way to begin a closer relationship with your prospective bride's family, don't you think, Shuttleworth?' Kit replied and Kate was tempted to throw something at both of them for being so provoking.

'And, as I have no intention of reneging on my word now it's given, also totally hypothetical,' she chided both of them.

'True, and you're also right to glare at me in truly

Kate-like fashion. We're wasting time and there's precious little of that with the great lover here determined to march you up the aisle in double-quick time. The dilemma is, Izzie love,' Kit went on a little more seriously, 'that Miranda would dearly love to see our Kate married, which means the wedding will have to go to her since she is far too big with child to come here. Wychwood is Kate's home as well, of course, and therefore the right and proper place for her to be married anyway.'

'And Kate has no say in the matter, I suppose?' she asked, largely because she felt it was expected of her rather than out of any real disagreement with that assertion.

'Kate always has something to say about whatever matter is being discussed,' Kit replied drily, 'but is she going to argue that black's white, before agreeing to do exactly what she and everyone else wanted her to in the first place this time, or can we take that part of the proceedings as read and get on with planning this wedding of yours instead?'

'Why does everyone seem to consider me contrary to the point of mania all of a sudden?' she asked with what she hoped was a creditable attempt at lightness.

'I can assure you it's not sudden,' Isabella muttered darkly.

'Nor is it true,' Edmund defended her. Kate took in the lovely solidarity of being half of a couple for the first time in her life as his hand in hers, his warmth next to her, reassured her that even when her strong will clashed with his immovable conviction that he was right, they would still be more than my lord and my lady to each other.

It might not be love, it might not equal the almost headlong passion and devotion Kit and Miranda had for each other, or the deep, almost surprised joy Ben Shaw and his wife, Charlotte, her former governess, took in each other, yet her once-convenient marriage was going to become a far better thing than the shadow she'd aspired to at the beginning of the Season, Kate realised. She was so glad to have avoided such a dull travesty almost by accident, but not altogether sure she deserved what she had instead, which was Edmund Worth, probably the most eligible bachelor formerly on the marriage mart. The question was, did he deserve Kate Alstone, also very eligible on paper, but perhaps a little too distrustful and shrewish in fact?

Chapter Thirteen

'I should love to be wed at Wychwood, but as I want both my sisters to be there as well, perhaps we should wait until the Season is over?' Kate suggested.

'You are not putting off marrying Lord Shuttleworth for a minute longer on my account, Kate,' Isabella told her sternly. 'Besides which, I'll be completely weary of this whole silly business by the end of a month, and I certainly can't endure the prospect of waiting another to breathe some clean air and hear some reasonably sensible conversation again at last. Whenever you set the date, I will find a way to be there, Kate, even if I have to walk to Derbyshire dragging Eiliane and the marquis away from her balls and soirées along behind me.'

'You won't have to drag me. I'm feeling strangely jaded with them all myself this year for some odd reason,' Eiliane admitted and shrugged when they all stared at their famously sociable hostess. 'I suppose I'm just not as young as I used to be and lack the energy I once had,' she told them, which made Kate meet Izzie's concerned gaze with a shrug and a frown of her own.

Eiliane usually had almost boundless vitality and could outstay most of the younger set at the balls, concerts and soirées the London Season abounded in.

'Anyway,' Eiliane insisted, 'Pemberley and I will be there whatever date you decide on, Kate, my dear. Lord Liverpool will just have to manage without my husband for a few days while he attends to more important matters than the tedious affairs of state that wretched man keeps bothering him with.'

'Perhaps we'd best consult his lordship about when would be the best time for him all the same,' Kate suggested, reeling slightly at the idea that her wedding was more important than the fate of nations and Lord Pemberley's work for the government. 'And we must consult Mr Draycott about dates as well, because there's no point in us settling on one if Wychwood Church is not available when we want it.'

'Draycott sent a list of possible dates for us to argue about,' Kit recalled. 'Shuttleworth has it, I believe.'

'I do. Kate and I will meet with Lord Pemberley and discuss them, after we've decided which ones would suit us best for ourselves,' Edmund said, his eyes cool and challenging as they met the Earl of Carnwood's.

'Then everything is well on the way to being settled,' Eiliane interrupted brightly as if she really thought they might argue or worse in her sitting room, when Kate knew both were too gentlemanly to risk upsetting a woman they both held in such strong affection.

'So it would seem,' Kit said wearily and ran an

impatient hand through his unruly dark locks. 'Now I'm for Alstone House and a much-needed bath and shave, then a quick nap,' he said gruffly.

'And let's hope you come back in a better mood,' Isabella dared to tease.

'We can only hope so, as I still have to draft a suitable notice announcing Kate and Edmund's betrothal to send to the papers before I can bring about that wonderful transformation, don't forget, so I'll have to rack my brains and consult Lord Pemberley's secretary about the correct form first. You have no idea how much easier my life was when I was a carefree black sheep of the family, nor how much I look forward to shuffling off at least one of my responsibilities on to you, Shuttleworth,' he replied with a rather wicked grin before he took himself off to bring about those wonders.

Edmund bowed and left with a more conventional farewell to transform himself into the perfectly turned-out nobleman they were more familiar with than the travel-stained pirate he resembled just now.

'Well, really,' Isabella said indignantly once the three ladies were alone again, 'you'd think Kit would be a little more civil on the subject of Kate's nuptials and her future happiness, wouldn't you?'

'He's concerned about her,' Eiliane explained and surprised Kate herself with such a reason for his gruffness with her.

'Why on earth would he be?' she betrayed herself into asking as if she couldn't imagine why Kit cared one way or the other, so long as he was rid of all responsibility for her. Which was untrue, as she knew he cared deep down that she should be well and happy with whatever husband she chose to wed.

'Because he's not sure you and Edmund are marrying for the right reasons.'

'But that's ridiculous; Shuttleworth has been wildly in love with Kate ever since he first set eyes on her,' Isabella argued.

'But was Kate equally wild for him?' Eiliane asked with a steady look.

'I should have been,' she replied with a self-deprecating grimace. 'I could have been, if only I'd let myself see how different he was from all the others.'

'And from Nevin,' Izzie said and this time it wasn't a question. 'You were always afraid of doing as Miranda did and falling for a man who turned out to be nothing like he appeared, Kate. It's a problem we both have to face after watching that monster cajole and flatter and creep until he had Miranda believing black was white, after all. I was only a little girl at the time and far too wrapped up in myself to take a lot of notice of him, but Kate was always too acute for her own good, Eiliane, and much too easily hurt by everything that happened to us after he came.'

'I know, I should have been there, I should have come as soon as your parents died and certainly when I heard that your poor brother had been sent home from school after that wretched fever,' Eiliane condemned herself, as if everything that had happened to the Alstone sisters since before Nevin Braxton eloped with Miranda had been her doing.

'No, I've already told you that you're not to do this to

yourself!' Kate ordered furiously. 'Your first husband was ill at the time. In fact, the poor man was dying, so how could you just up and leave him while you came to Derbyshire on a fool's errand? You loved him, Eiliane, and he needed you. You must never again blame yourself for something my damnable cousin Celia and infernal aunt were responsible for.'

'You're ordering me about like some warrior queen, love, and do mind your language in case something like that slips out in public, even if it's a perfectly good description of the repellent creatures,' Eiliane said.

'It just makes me so angry to hear you blame yourself for not anticipating the evil those two thought up and carried out, as if you should have known about it all along,' Kate replied brusquely.

'And it's so very hard to make her angry, don't you agree, Eiliane?' Izzie put in with an angelic expression of sisterly patience on her lovely face and laughter lurking in her eyes.

'It was, at one time, far too difficult, Isabella,' Eiliane said as if it had been something that worried her far more than Kate thought it should have done, considering how wayward her emotions could be when she gave them full rein. 'But at last it seems much easier to goad her into all sorts of passions again, which is a blessing I'm profoundly thankful for.'

'And one I shall suspend judgement about until after she's wed and Shuttleworth can cope with her tempers and her wild ideas instead of us.'

'Why, thank you, sister dear,' Kate said ironically. 'I *am* still here, you know?'

'I do; you're hard to ignore.'

'Then kindly remember I'm still your big sister and that I know exactly where and when all your darkest misdeeds occurred.'

'Sometimes a person's memory can be too good,' Isabella replied with a very steady look that told Kate she wasn't referring to her own childish mischief.

'Yes, I'm finally beginning to realise that,' she admitted at last and felt as if a huge weight was lifting off her shoulders, along with the dark memories that had perhaps been allowed to shape her view of the world for far too long. 'I almost let them win, didn't I?'

'So long as you don't now, that's all that matters,' Isabella replied and Kate wondered how her little sister ever got to be so wise.

'I forgot one small detail before I left for Wychwood, Kate,' Edmund said when she came into the small drawing room of Pemberley House that evening. Kate finally realised why Eiliane had lost a glove, asked Izzie to go and fetch it for her and then suddenly recalled something else she'd forgotten, and had simply had to go and fetch it herself, leaving the newly affianced couple alone.

'Apart from my missing proposal?' she dared to joke, because treading on eggshells with each other for the rest of their natural lives was a prospect she couldn't endure, when one of the things she'd always liked the most about him was his wry and often self-deprecating sense of the ridiculous.

'No need for you to garner another of those when you already have a full set,' he told her resolutely. 'I've told you already that you can't have that, Kate, but maybe this will go some way for making up for the lack of it?'

He handed her a ring box and within it was the most lovely sapphire-and-diamond ring she had ever laid eyes on and she'd seen Miranda's, which until tonight had seemed unsurpassable.

'It's completely beautiful, Edmund,' she said, staring down at the amazing depth of colour the sapphires held and the pure clarity of the fine diamonds that sinuously curled around them in a lover's knot.

'I saw it years ago and knew then that it could have been made for you,' he told her uncomfortably, as if he was ashamed of the headlong youth he'd been then. She could have stamped on her own toe in fury at herself for doing that to him, except it would have made her fall over in a heap at his feet and, she reminded herself, she'd already promised herself that she wasn't going to do that.

'Thank you, but can I wear it?'

'I'd be highly insulted if you didn't,' he said with a wry grin.

She fumbled as she tried to take the lovely thing out of its bed of finest velvet with shaking hands and he did what she'd secretly hoped he might and took it from her to extract it neatly from its box and place it on her finger, presumably so she didn't drop it and condemn them both to an undignified search on their hands and knees.

'There you are, you see, I told you it could have been made for you,' he said as he played with her fingers and suddenly very little of Kate's attention was on the masterpiece of the jeweller's art on her ring finger.

'Edmund,' she said huskily and even she heard the note of yearning in her voice, but somehow no longer cared if it gave away how much she'd missed him.

'Did you really long for me so much that you're actually prepared to admit it, sweet Kate?' he murmured and drew her even closer.

'Yes,' she admitted, because as she was almost in his arms, her eyes heavy with longing and her lips parted and doing their best to invite his kisses, there seemed very little point denying it. She had missed him ever since he arrived in town this Season and she saw how changed he was from the lovelorn youth she remembered, then realised what she'd lost three years ago by refusing him so persistently that he'd finally listened to her and gone away.

'Good,' he said with exasperating masculine superiority and stepped away from her as Eiliane called something back to Isabella and they both stood on the stairs, very obviously pretending not to listen, but doing their best to hear every word.

'Good?' she muttered with a bitter glance in his direction. 'About as good as finding cherry-stones in a pie.'

'I *like* cherries, Kate,' he said in a ruthless undertone, his eyes on her lips as he licked his own, as if anticipating the ripeness of her mouth moist and eager under his. 'I long for them when they're so red and ripe and luscious, picked just fresh off the tree. Then I just want to bite into them and feel their sharp sweetness on my tongue again so very badly.'

'Very nice,' she said aloud, her tone flat and her eyes on his, flaring defiance at him for attempting to seduce her with words, under her supposed chaperon and her younger sister's very noses.

'Not just nice, Kate, but also delicious, pleasurable and compulsive,' he told her, placing a wicked emphasis on each description that made a shiver of anticipation run through her. 'We really must order sweet cherries at our wedding breakfast; I would so hate to do without their unique and piquant flavour at our celebration when we'll be setting out on our lives together at long last,' he concluded.

'I will order a tart especially for you.'

'What an obliging wife you're promising to become,' he parried and, even as he picked up her evening cloak, he took elaborate care to enjoy every chance to touch her as he caressed it into place over her nearly naked shoulders and exposed neck. Somehow he managed to drive her half furious with him and half inclined to swoon with frustrated passion at his feet all at the same time.

'And what a disobliging husband I seem to be chaining myself to,' she managed to say lightly for the benefit of their audience.

'You flatter me.'

'That was not my intention.'

'At least I'll soon be in a position to give you a few lessons in how to tell truth from fiction, Kate,' he said, looking inexcusably pleased with himself.

'First, my lord,' she informed him snippily, 'you'll need to find out what the differences between them are for yourself.'

'I thought we could do that together,' he said so smoothly that she glared at him in frustration, not quite sure if she wanted to slap him or kiss him.

'Come *on*, you two,' Isabella interrupted them impatiently, 'the farce will be over and the first act as well before we even get to the theatre if you don't hurry yourselves, instead of casting sheep's eyes at each other in that nauseating fashion.'

'Really, Isabella,' Eiliane rebuked her, 'that's such a vulgar turn of phrase.'

'But apt, they're nigh as annoying as Kit and Miranda and I never thought I'd be able to accuse Kate of thinking the world well lost for love.'

'I doubt you can now, either,' Edmund said with a wry smile as he finally took his hands away from Kate's shoulders and left her feeling horribly cold and bereft all of a sudden.

'Whether I can or not, please would you two kindly hurry? Even if you don't mind me glowering at you both for the rest of the evening for causing us to be late, I doubt very much if you'd endure Kit doing it with half as much detachment.'

Eiliane shuddered theatrically at the very thought and chivvied them all down the broad steps to her luxurious carriage before Kate could even think of a sufficiently crushing reply to annihilate her little sister with. Then, once they were ensconced in the carriage, she had the fiery consciousness of Edmund sitting next to her to struggle with, so they managed to arrive in Drury Lane with Isabella still uncrushed and almost unbearably smug as a consequence.

'I'll pay you back for that,' Kate managed to mutter to her when she thought the others too busy with polite manoeuvring as they descended from the carriage to hear either of them.

'You can try,' Izzie said before accepting Edmund's gloved hand to help her descend with more grace than she deserved to have at her command, at least in her older sister's opinion.

'Oh, you *really* should have known better than to say that,' Kate said menacingly, then promptly forgot the inventive punishments she'd been planning as she placed her hand in Edmund's in her turn.

She marvelled that her sister could do that as coolly as if it was just an everyday courtesy, which she supposed dazedly that it was between Edmund and her sister. Fire seemed to shoot through their joined fingers and along her oversensitive nerves to render her so open to the promise of it all that she was almost beyond using her legs in their accustomed fashion, let alone her sharp tongue.

'Now then, children,' Eiliane said reprovingly, as if she had no idea Kate was moonstruck, or bewitched, or whatever it was Edmund had done to her with that first kiss in Lord Wyndover's darkened book room. 'There is a time and place for nursery squabbles and such tit for tat and this is neither. There will be no lemonade spilt with apparent clumsiness over each other, nor will either of you step contritely on the other's hem as you climb the stairs to our box. Nor will Carnwood be further tried with your childish bickering after his wearisome ride to get here just when we all need him so badly, do I make myself clear?'

'Abundantly, I should think,' Edmund said, looking unforgivably amused that both sisters were trying not to look as chagrined as a pair of naughty schoolboys up before their headmaster.

'As a mountain stream,' Kate muttered.

'*I* wouldn't dream of behaving so badly,' Isabella asserted with such angelic innocence not one of them believed her.

'Then don't,' Kit greeted them as he strode forwards. 'Whatever it is Eiliane is threatening you so magnificently over, just don't.'

Isabella sighed. 'Oh, very well, I suppose we are a little too old for such things now,' she said regretfully.

'I very much doubt it, but I've had a long and rather trying day and am over a hundred miles away from my wife to make it all much worse, so I think I can safely admit my temper is currently on a fine trigger. So do you actually want to see this interminable rigmarole of a play or not, brat?'

'I do,' Isabella agreed with a look of such charming docility Kate wondered if her little sister should not be on the stage playing Ophelia to Kean's Hamlet, instead of just watching some less talented actress do it instead.

'You have no idea how lucky you are,' Edmund informed Kate as they were finally welcomed into the box the Mausleys had hired. She turned and looked enquiringly at him. 'You belong to such a close family that you can fight with your sister, be at outs with your brother-in-law and earn a mighty scold from your much-tried chaperon and mentor all in one evening.'

'And that's a privilege?'

'It is from where I'm standing,' he said with a smile of acknowledgement that, yes, it was an odd thing to envy her. 'I want my children to have it, too.'

'Have what?'

'That closeness, the chance to be knit into a family that will bicker and snipe at each other one moment and unite against the world the next to protect and love all the members of it as fiercely as tigers.'

'I don't think…' she began and then the implications of what he was saying finally sank in.

His children would be hers as well now and, through her, part of the wider family she was fortunate indeed to have grown up in. A family she'd failed to appreciate fully these last five years, since Miranda had come home and found Kit, then put the deep bond all three sisters had with each other at the heart of her own new family.

'I really don't think often enough, do I?' she continued with a rueful smile.

'Never mind, I dare say I've had more than enough time to do it for both of us these last three years,' he replied with an answering one that was much gentler than any he'd given her all Season.

'Oh, come *on*, you two,' Isabella summoned them impatiently, rolling her eyes in a pantomime of resigned exasperation at Fanny Mausley which she doubtless thought Kate couldn't see. 'Have you both become deaf as well as daft for each other?'

'Isabella Alstone, you will keep a still tongue in your head on the subject of your sister's private business, or risk being taken home before the curtain even comes up on the first act,' Eiliane snapped irritably and Kate spared a moment to wonder what ailed their usually even-tempered friend.

'Aye, be quiet, brat,' Kit drawled warningly and Isabella subsided onto the seat next to her best friend and managed to be silent for all of two minutes.

Once the main performance of the night began there was none of the usual murmurs and interruptions from the audience, who were as caught by the menace and turmoil stalking the state of Denmark on the stage as Isabella, who sat still and spellbound by the whole performance. It was a *tour de force*; even Kit had to admit that when the curtains closed for the interval. Kean had held his audience completely in thrall from the moment he stepped onto the stage and Isabella was voluntarily silent for all of a minute before she came out of her drama-induced daydream.

'Better than any ball,' she said as she finally left Elsinore for London.

'Don't look to me for an argument,' Kit said and even Fanny Mausley agreed it had been a very fine start to their evening, if a little gloomy, and now she could see why her brother had dragged them here when they could have danced all night instead, which was high praise, considering she adored the social whirl and all the glitter and gossip that went with it.

Young Mr Mausley had ordered refreshments delivered and looked very pleased with the success of his plan to please Isabella, even if her equally besotted suitors and friends of both families flitted in and out of their box to compare notes on actors and audience alike. Kate's ring was eyed enviously by ladies she knew would eagerly tell everyone who'd listen that the elder Miss Alstone had indeed captured the most eligible and desirable bachelor on the marriage mart as soon as they set foot outside the door. She did her best to be amused by her current notoriety and wondered for at least ten seconds if Isabella might one day discover her match in the obviously besotted but still painfully young Frederick Mausley, just as she had in Edmund, then dismissed the idea out of hand. Frederick had neither the strength of character nor the promise of grace and mature power Edmund had possessed at a similar age, if only she had let herself see it.

Chapter Fourteen

'So here you are, Miss Alstone,' Lady Tedinton drawled as she insinuated herself into the box and sat herself down in the chair next to Kate while she was still busy wondering how the woman's presence tonight hadn't registered with her until now. 'What a costly bauble you're wearing tonight, and how fortunate for you that you managed to catch such a fine fish in your net before your sister arrived in town to eclipse you.'

It must have been self-protective instincts that kept her ignorant, Kate decided, as she froze a visible shudder of revulsion in its tracks and faced her enemy as if having trouble recalling who she was. She managed a curt nod of acknowledgement and fought a hollow feeling in the pit of her stomach when she realised Edmund had left the box for some reason while she was having her ring inspected once more.

'Most young ladies who transgress the limits of acceptable behaviour pay for it with their reputations.

You are fortunate to belong to such a rich and powerful family, Miss Alstone,' the woman said silkily and how could Kate fight back, when she was supposed to be ignorant of the repulsive and possibly criminal behaviour her enemy indulged in when she thought nobody was listening?

'Indeed,' she said distantly instead.

'I was not so lucky,' her ladyship went on melodramatically.

Kate raised her eyebrows and allowed herself a pointed stare at the glitter of diamonds decorating her ladyship's throat, ears and wrists and the finest silk gown that clothed her and she hoped she managed to convey her incredulity, as well as her indifference to anything else the spiteful creature had to say.

'Tedinton rescued me from my encounter with a certain gentleman when I was much younger and probably more foolish than even you are now,' she went on, as if warming to the picture of herself as the *ingénue* she'd probably never been. 'As the sixteen-year-old daughter of a mere country squire with no fortune or aristocratic connections, I was easy prey for a cold-hearted seducer, although he was barely two years older than me when he got me with child and laughed in my face when I begged him to marry me.'

'How affecting,' Kate said expressionlessly.

'You won't look so smug when I tell you his name,' Lady Tedinton leaned forwards to whisper venomously.

'Will I not?' Kate asked carelessly, finding the whole

performance distasteful and a lot less convincing than any she'd seen on the stage tonight.

'It was Edward Worthington—such a neat alias for a nobleman to go carousing under away from his own nest, don't you think?'

'It might be, if I believed a single word you have to say.'

'Do you think I care what you think?' her ladyship asked with barely veiled hatred.

'Then why are you here?'

'To let you know exactly who and what you are about to wed.'

'How altruistic of you, Lady Tedinton, but I don't believe you care a snap of your fingers if I marry a paragon of all the virtues or Bluebeard himself.'

'Very well then, you tell me why he should be allowed to get away with what he did to me. He fully intends to marry you and pretend that his honour forced him to do so. How can he act as if he's so noble and upright and correct when he left me outcast and pregnant so young as if he had nothing to do with it? Well, I won't have it. I refuse to sit by and let him behave as if he never seduced me, then left me so friendless and alone that I had to wed a man thirty years my senior to give our bastard a name.'

'How strange, then, that when you were sixteen my fiancé was probably just beginning at Eton and was therefore far too young to compromise anyone, and that your stepdaughter told me just the other evening that her eldest half sister was but four years of age and her little brother a mere babe in arms. While only you can truly know their provenance, your ladyship, I doubt even you are so remarkable a freak of nature as to have endured such a remarkably long confinement it must have entered the annals of science,' Kate said coolly and stood up to withdraw to the back of the box where they would be less easily overheard, so Lady Tedinton was forced to either carry on sitting and crick her neck as well as lose much of her dignity, or stand and let Kate look down on her from an equal footing.

'I am barely four and twenty and I miscarried his brat,' the woman claimed impatiently, not even bothering to look particularly convinced by her own tall tale as she only just managed to keep her tone low and venomous. 'You're clearly besotted with the duplicitous coney catcher, which makes you even more of a fool than I thought you. If you don't believe anything else, just ask him about his little interlude with me at the Crooked Man on the road to Oxford last year and see if he doesn't give himself away for the villain he is.'

'To me Lord Shuttleworth's integrity is beyond question, madam, whilst yours is dubious to say the least. Nothing you can ever say will make me believe him the villain you're trying to paint him for some perverse reason of your own,' Kate said in so frigid a tone the others finally realised she was fighting off an enemy rather than just another veiled interrogation about her marriage plans, even if they were too far away to hear any details.

It warmed a cold place in Kate's heart when Isabella and Eiliane moved to flank her and Kit stood fluidly to emanate menace and power as effortlessly as most men breathed. Even Lady Tedinton paled under his fathomless dark stare while she did her best to look unconcerned by such a united front.

'I've been meaning to have a few quiet words with your husband, Lady Tedinton,' Kit said at last, and didn't even dignify her as a foe by pretending it was a threat rather than a promise. 'Does he escort you tonight, or are you in other company as usual?' he asked silkily.

'My lord is from home.'

'How singularly inconvenient, but I really must seek him out before I return to Derbyshire, so we can discuss certain acquaintances we have in common.'

If Lady Tedinton wasn't trembling in her satin evening slippers, then she certainly ought to be now, Kate decided, as she felt an instinctive shiver run down her back at the contained danger in Kit's dark eyes, even when it wasn't directed at her.

Yet somehow even Kit's menacing presence wasn't as chilling as Edmund's voice as he re-entered the box and saw Lady Tedinton confronting Kate. 'Ah, now I see why that supposed urgent message from Cravenhill failed to materialise. I know you like to be forward with the gossip, madam, but I'd no idea you were so desperate for it that you'd contrive a meeting with my fiancée behind my back by such devious means.'

'We have had a very interesting coze, but my patience with the infantry is limited at the best of times,' she snapped and tried to back towards the door without it seeming like a retreat.

'I hear that when it comes to actual infants it's not just limited but non-existent; your husband has my sympathy,' Edmund said, standing in her way with such a blandly social smile it only made the contempt in his eyes more telling. Surely that should kill off any lingering hope she had of engaging him in her illicit affairs?

'Neither my husband nor my children are any business of yours.'

'You consider taking too close an interest in another person's private affairs could prove dangerous to the enquirer then, do you, my lady?'

'I have no idea what you mean.'

'No, then I must be thinking of someone else likely to discover it shortly—an old friend of yours, perhaps?'

'You speak in riddles, sir.'

'Do you understand me, Carnwood?'

Kit nodded and his smile was every bit as chilling as Edmund's. 'I have the advantage over most of our kind in being brought up in a very different sphere, so I learned from a very early age to see the truth behind the false front.'

'You are fortunate in your friends, Lord Shuttleworth,' Lady Tedinton managed to reply as if she wasn't in the least bit intimidated. 'They seem to speak in the same sort of riddles as you specialise in yourself.'

'I am *very* fortunate in my friends, and even more so in my family,' Edmund said as he stepped casually past her to take Kate's cold hand in his. Just as though the vicious virago who'd just done her best to ruin that family for him was a trivial obstacle in his way to what really mattered in life.

'You two deserve each other,' she hissed venomously.

'They do,' Kit intervened before her ladyship could escape with the last word. 'Anyone foolish enough to try to come between them now they have both finally realised that very pertinent truth, Lady Tedinton, will discover how very unlucky such an intervention could be for the one who attempted it.'

'You can't touch me, you're only a counter-jumper,' she spat back, no longer looking in the least bit beautiful as her true nature glared out of narrowed eyes and a mouth suddenly hard as a steel trap.

'I'm also the Earl of Carnwood,' he replied almost mildly, 'but I'm not ashamed of what I made of myself before I became a lord. How about you, your ladyship? What had you made of yourself before your besotted lord came along, I wonder?'

'I am the daughter of a country squire,' she said like a child reciting its catechism, but Kate could see the glint of fear in her dark eyes all of a sudden and the sheen of sweat on her upper lip.

'No, you're the daughter of a country vagrant, born and raised in the workhouse. Did you think you could threaten me and mine and fear no retaliation? I make it a rule to know my enemies, Lady Tedinton. Those among them who have as much to hide as you do are reckless indeed to join their ranks in the first place.'

'You lie, and even if you didn't, you'd have to prove it.'

'My agent took copies of the parish register, descriptions of you and your mother from the superintendent and the milliner you were apprenticed to at the age of seven. You had a very hard start in life, madam, one I would never have held against you if you hadn't sought to damage my innocent sister-in-law, who also happens to be my former ward and very dear to me on both counts. I pity poor Tedinton when he finds out what you really are and had made of yourself before he wed you. How hard he fell for your charade of the genteel innocent fallen into bad company and what a triumph for you when he wed you to rescue you from them.'

'I was gently born,' she insisted lamely.

'You were the daughter of a criminal's moll and she used you as a lure to catch unwary fools, then fleece them of everything before moving on to the next. Except you tired of sharing the proceeds and informed on her and her former colleagues, so you were free to set up on your own and catch far bigger game.'

'And a fine coney I caught myself,' she admitted brazenly at last. 'My husband's a fool and deserves to pay for his endless stupidity with his life, but he'll not believe a word a shop-soiled earl like you has to say against me, especially when I tell him how sadly spiteful Miss Alstone has become towards me, and how she's even managed to turn her whole family against me, just because she heard some vicious and untrue rumours about me and her lover and is a jealous little cat intent on destroying me as a consequence.'

She rounded on Kate, who eyed the spitting fury in front of her with acute distaste. From where she stood, she could see something, or rather someone, standing half in and half out of the door, looking frozen and distraught, as if the floor had just dropped out of the world.

'Nothing to say?' the woman demanded and Kate watched her serenely for a moment.

'There's nothing I need say that you haven't just said for me,' she replied as coolly as if her fiery temper wasn't begging for release until she'd finally told the venomous creature exactly what she thought of her. No need to demean herself by falling to such a base level, at least not now.

'Indeed you have, Selene,' Lord Tedinton said wearily, as he finally opened the door he'd cracked open and discovered so much that he really didn't want to know. 'Indeed you have.'

'Tedinton, we were practising a scene from a little play we're all getting up. You know how I adore arranging evenings of dramatics for the amusement of our friends and family,' her ladyship exclaimed as if she knew she would get away with it, which was, Kate supposed, her finest weapon against her rather gullible lord.

'No, Selene, you were not. You hate them and say so every time they are suggested to alleviate your boredom with me and mine, and how odd if you suddenly acquired such distinguished friends and failed to tell everyone who would listen all about them and whatever you are planning.'

'They are *not* distinguished, they are adventurers and liars,' she said in a sudden switch from assured lady to little girlish, misunderstood victim. 'They have been plotting to bring me down and now you're letting them succeed.'

'No, I'm not. You're the one who's been plotting and

I'm the fool who stood by and let you meet your lover in dark corners to plan the downfall of an innocent young girl. I couldn't bear to believe Philippa when she came to me the night after the Wyndovers' ball and told me what she'd heard when she followed you out of the ballroom that night with your lover. I have hoped and prayed ever since that she was wrong; that she misheard and it was another man's wife who she'd heard meeting with that wastrel Bestholme and planning to kill her husband. You have no idea how fervently I've hoped and prayed for that delusion to be true ever since, Selene.'

'The little snake, I'll murder her with my bare hands!' Lady Tedinton finally betrayed herself utterly and Kate gave a horrified gasp, almost wishing she could erase the last few minutes from her memory and feel clean again.

'When Shuttleworth came to see me this afternoon and told me that he'd overheard you, too, I still didn't want to believe it, although I know him to be an honourable young man not given to making up such melodramatic tales. I badly wanted you to be vindicated, so I agreed to listen tonight, if Philippa would get you here and Shuttleworth persuade you to talk to him about his suspicions, unfounded as I thought them to be, but how very wrong I was. How could you behave so viciously towards a young woman who has never done you any harm, Selene? Miss Alstone, I really cannot apologise enough for my wife's ill-bred spite and that ridiculous pack of lies she just tried to spin you.'

'None of it was your fault, my lord,' Kate replied.

'Ah, but it was, I have been bitterly to blame in

all this,' he said sadly and she could hardly meet the sadness in his eyes as he admitted how mistaken he'd always been in his much younger wife, until tonight. 'Can I trouble you for your help, gentlemen?' he went on with resigned dignity. 'The wretched woman is too cunning for me and will escape before I can work out what must be done about her.'

'Of course,' Kit agreed with equal resignation. 'Shuttleworth?'

Edmund nodded and, with a brief smile for Kate, stepped forwards to face a task no true gentleman could ever relish.

'We will all remain here for the rest of the play,' Mrs Mausley said, stepping forwards from the shadows where she'd been standing, horrified and silenced by the whole ugly tableau even the best-mannered lady could hardly pretend not to hear when it was taking place in her own box. 'Frederick will accompany Lady Pemberley and the dear girls home at the end of it, and the rest of us will follow their carriage to make sure no harm comes to them,' she added, as if that arrangement would prove a match for a veritable army of ruffians.

'And I'll ask Pemberley to join you as soon as possible,' Edmund said shortly. Since they knew the marquis would be here as fast as his noble legs could carry him if he thought his lady was in danger, all three lords and one supposed lady left the box and trusted the remainder with the delicate task of keeping up appearances.

'Well, it's a shame her infamy is probably going to be covered up,' Eiliane said comfortably enough as she shifted her chair so as to get a better view of the stage.

'But these things have to be done,' Mrs Mausley agreed, with a significant glare at her son and daughter, who hastily nodded and looked horrified at the idea they should be the route by which such news got out. 'I suspect the woman will be found out to be mad anyway. I've thought for some time that nobody could be quite so blatantly unconcerned about her own misconduct being discovered if she wasn't unhinged, and now it seems I am proved right.'

'For the sake of her unfortunate children and poor Tedinton, I'm not quite sure if that's better or worse than her just being bad,' Eiliane put in with a sad shake of her head and Kate marvelled to see what had been a rather wary acquaintanceship between two women who had little in common becoming a firm friendship in front of her eyes.

'What will they do, then?' Kate asked.

'We must trust the gentlemen to make sure she can't do any more damage,' Eiliane said, smiling brightly at an acquaintance in a box on the opposite side of the theatre as if nothing untoward had occurred.

'One of those gentlemen married her in the first place,' Kate couldn't help muttering her dissent.

'Yes, but dear Kit and your Edmund won't allow him to ignore the way she's tried to destroy your engagement and plot to murder, however unlikely that creature she's been meeting was to bestir himself on her behalf if she did but know it. Now do be quiet, Kate dear, for Isabella and I wish to see the rest of this fine play, even if you lack the stamina for it.'

'Great ladies,' Fanny Mausley murmured as she sat down next to Kate and gave her a mischievous smile that made her realise just why Isabella liked this flighty girl so much. 'So essential to the proper regulation of society,' she parodied some former teacher mercilessly, 'but, oh, so wearying to live with,' she added in her own voice and Kate gave a splutter of laughter and earned a fine crop of glares and hushing as the curtains drew apart and Kean stepped onto the stage once more.

'Lucky it was Kean and not some lesser actor tonight, because otherwise we would have been fidgeting in those hard seats for hours wondering what their lordships were up to and not being able to leave and find out for appearances' sake. I for one am extremely grateful to him for diverting us so royally tonight,' Eiliane admitted once her own particular lord had handed them up into his fine carriage and climbed in, before ordering the door closed on the world.

'Lucky, indeed,' Kate echoed faintly and sat back in her seat to watch darkness and light flash past the windows as the coachman did as he'd been bid and got them home as quickly as possible. 'Poor little girl,' she muttered as she watched the shadows where any footpad or streetwalker or saint might walk unseen by the hurrying throng rushing home to their comfortable homes and cosy hearths after an evening of enthralling drama.

'Indeed,' Eiliane replied sadly, knowing perfectly well who Kate was talking about. 'And if she'd only behaved herself and not tried to lash out at so many others, I for one would never have begrudged her stellar rise from such appalling beginnings.'

'Don't waste your pity on her, love,' said Lord Pemberley, who had evidently been informed of what had gone on tonight by Edmund or Kit. 'It's poor old Tedinton I feel sorry for, and his unfortunate family. All he ever did was fall foolishly in love with a lovely face, and the rest of them did nothing at all to deserve a crazed harpy being thrust into the midst of their family.'

'All the same—' Eiliane began.

'No,' he stated firmly, 'I'm not having you find her some place where she can abuse the trust of those who gave it to her and worry you half to death while she does so. No, Tedinton was fool enough to marry her, he can find a way to feed, clothe and house her while somehow keeping her away from him and his at the same time. You are not getting involved with that heartless vixen in any way.'

'Very well, my love,' Eiliane said with such mild agreement Kate nearly leaned over and felt her friend's forehead to see if she was running a fever. 'I shall be very glad to get back to Pemberley after Kate's wedding,' she admitted and Kate met her sister's eyes as the coach finally pulled up outside Pemberley House and the flare of torches gave them enough light to see each other.

'Are you quite well, Eiliane dear?' she finally asked when they were all four of them inside the cosy parlour Eiliane always resorted to after a busy night to relax and reconsider the evening, and what an evening this one had been.

'Very well, Kate,' her hostess said with a dreamy smile. 'Very well, indeed.'

'Good,' she replied rather hollowly, at sea about Eiliane's distracted manner and the rather odd mix of incredulity and shock and pleasure that she seemed to be able to see in Lord Pemberley's usually humorous grey eyes even after hearing such a tale.

'I just *can't* keep it quiet, Pemberley, even if you can. Not from my own family,' Eiliane burst out at last.

His lordship looked at her, smiled and rolled his eyes to the ceiling as if consulting Jupiter, who was painted on it, even in this relatively small private room of his grand town mansion. 'Very well, love, I should have known better than to ask it of you in the first place,' he agreed at last.

'It was such a shock,' Eiliane said, blushing and looking almost girlish and confused about whatever 'it' was.

'It was that, indeed,' he replied and, distinguished peer of the realm whom the government consulted about their more insoluble problems as he was, he gave Kate an enormous schoolboy grin and laughed delightedly at some glorious joke only he and his wife were privy to at the moment.

'You know I have been out of sorts lately, Kate?'

'Yes, even I have noticed that, Eiliane,' she said solemnly, but she was beginning to add two and two and make four at last and couldn't suppress a broad smile of her own even while Izzie looked more puzzled than ever.

'Pemberley badgered me into seeing a quack as I was so tired and my stomach was uncertain and I even felt a little sad now and then, which is just not like me, as you know. I thought I needed a tonic or perhaps even a week or two in a nice quiet seaside village where I could rest and breathe in good sea air for a while, but it seems that I was wrong.'

'Oh, my!' Isabella finally burst out, eyes round and mouth half-open as she recognised those symptoms from Miranda's confinements at last. 'You're going to have a baby, Eiliane?'

'I am,' said Eiliane blissfully.

'We are,' his lordship put in, as proud as a peacock.

'I'm so pleased for you both that I don't have the words to describe it,' Kate said joyfully and hugged Eiliane gently, then threw caution to the wind and hugged his lordship as well.

'Can we be godmamas to him or her?' Isabella asked eagerly and danced up to repeat Kate's hugs with interest.

'You can, my love. Kate might be busy with her own…husband by then,' Eiliane said on a stumble that had Kate blushing nearly as much as she was herself.

Eiliane meant of course that she could be *enceinte* herself when the time came to christen my lord this or my lady that in Pember Hall's ancient chapel. The thought was so heady she could quite see why her host and hostess were acting like a pair of besotted teenagers at the prospect of becoming parents so late in life.

'I'm far too old, of course,' Eiliane claimed suddenly.

'Then what does that make me, love?' Lord Pemberley asked genially.

'Distinguished, which is most unfair of you,' his wife answered. 'I'm four and forty; that's much too ancient an age to be becoming a mother for the first time.'

'What did the doctor say about that?' he asked patiently, as if they'd already had this conversation several times already.

'That I'm healthy as a horse a good many years younger than whatever the equivalent age to me in horse years might be and that learning to sit still for a few moments a day in order to give my babe a rest would do me a world of good.'

'Sensible man,' her doting husband told her.

Kate met Isabella's eyes and they nodded to each other before leaving the room without Eiliane or her lord even knowing they'd gone.

'They're so happy,' Kate whispered when they were both in her bedroom with the door shut to keep out interested ears.

'So happy and so in love. I don't care what anyone says, Kate, even if I have to be Eiliane's age to find a man I can love like that, I'll stay single until I do.'

Kate was silent, contemplating love and good fortune and the merits and drawbacks of a civil contract of marriage.

'Anyway,' her sister said as she reviewed her declaration and evidently decided it might not be altogether tactful in present company, 'I'm going to ask Fanny's mother if I can stay with them until I come north for your

wedding, Kate. It really is high time Eiliane stopped flit-
ting about town every night as if she's got to fill every
hour she's not with his lordship with constant activity.
They need a week or two at Pember Hall together to
enjoy it and relax a little before your wedding as well
as after it. After all, dear Lord Pemberley works far too
hard as well and now at last they'll both have a reason
to look inwards instead of outwards for fulfilment.'

'Mrs Mausley will want to know why,' Kate cautioned, wondering when her sister had become so perceptive and just what she perceived about her.

'I doubt it; neither she nor Fanny is as scatterbrained
as they pretend to be.'

'I realised that tonight,' Kate said thoughtfully.
'Indeed, I realised quite a lot of things tonight.'

'High time you did, big sister,' Isabella told her with
a cheeky smile, then happily went off to plan her life for
the next few weeks and probably that of Lord and Lady
Pemberley and the entire Mausley family as well.

Chapter Fifteen

Kate sat down on her very comfortable feather bed, smoothed the delicate silk brocade of the cover and ran a hand over fine linen and lace-covered pillows almost as if apologising to them for something. Then she slipped out of her fine cream silk gown and laid it carefully aside, before divesting herself of all her evening finery. She donned a very plain dark gown, her heaviest and most concealing cloak and a dark jockey cap she sometimes wore for riding to cover her give-away hair, then sat down on the bed to wait for stillness and silence to overtake the household.

Edmund left Lord Tedinton's house in Green Street along with the Earl of Carnwood and was very glad to be doing so at last. Neither of them had a spring in their step after such an evening and Edmund shook his head wearily when Kit invited him to Alstone House for brandy and perhaps a cigar because, he informed

Edmund wryly, 'I'll get damned little sleep tonight without Miranda in my bed.' Love, Edmund thought as he bade Kit Alstone goodnight, was a hard taskmaster. It drove his friend and future brother-in-law to bark and growl at anyone who came between him and his Miranda, even when it was Kate. How would it feel to know the lady you married longed for you, waited for you so impatiently every minute you were gone, hungered for you in her bed as much as you did for her in yours until neither of you could sleep very much at all if the other wasn't there?

Like a triumph and a banquet and a victory parade all rolled into one, he decided wistfully and told himself Kate was just as unique in her own way as her passionate sister. He could hardly complain if what made her so also rendered her more aloof and in control of herself than her elder sister. It was ironic that she was the true redhead of the pair, he decided, as he let himself in through his front door with the neat key he'd had made for himself when he finally persuaded his doting staff not to wait up from cellar to attic every time he was out late at night. Miranda, Countess of Carnwood, had a thick mane of parti-coloured hair that had brown, blond and red all mixed up in it somewhere, but it was Kate who'd inherited her famously lovely mother's rich red locks. Kate, who did her best to fight the passion and intensity and sheer beauty hidden in the depths of her deep blue Alstone eyes. His Kate, who would never let her heart rule her head, or tell the world with unguarded gestures or intimate touches and gazes and stolen kisses when she didn't quite care if anyone was by or not, how very much she loved her lord.

Still, he would have her in his bed and gracing his house, or houses, and she would be the woman who birthed his heirs if they were blessed with any. Kate would be the mother of his children, the mistress of his estates and the lover of his dreams. He was a happy man, and in a few weeks' time he would be an ecstatic man with a redheaded enchantress in his bed who had no idea of her own power, or the possibilities she held once she became fully a woman and not an innocent, however she might argue with that description.

She'd walked into his heart when she'd been that unfledged beauty three years ago and now he was quite resigned to the fact that he'd never manage to remove her from it, whatever he tried. Back then, her height and those lovely bones of hers had hinted at the promise of even more startling beauty to come, even deeper enchantments to entrap the unwary. Well, he'd been unwary; he'd stumbled headlong at her feet in a tongue-tied confusion of rampant youthful lust and idealistic worship of the goddess she was too human to be. No wonder she'd looked on him so warily, as if he might embarrass them both with some public display of devotion and make them into a laughing stock; no wonder she'd refused to marry him when he'd begged her to do so as if his life depended on it. Idiot, he castigated himself as he impatiently ordered any of his staff he caught lurking in corners, just in case he needed a twenty-five-course banquet or a suit of bespoke armour in the middle of the night, he supposed whimsically, off to bed.

At last he reached his bedchamber and shut the door on the world with a heartfelt sigh, squashing the urge to indulge his household by ringing his bell and ordering someone to come and relight the candles that were usually left burning in one or two sconces ready for his homecoming, however often he told them he was quite capable of lighting them himself when he got home. After the day and night he'd just endured he felt the need for light and a fire, even if it was nearly June, and then he'd sip a leisurely glass of cognac in front of it as he tried to come to terms with all that had happened since he'd left it last.

Stretching and giving a mighty yawn, then rubbing a weary hand over his stiff shoulders and up to the rigid muscles in his neck as he felt the effects of that long and demanding ride to Derbyshire and back, he wondered about just tumbling face down onto the bed fully dressed and letting sleep and blessed forgetfulness overcome him for a few hours. He was about to force himself to reach for the tinderbox and shed some light on his undressing and ablutions when a stir of movement from the direction of the bed set his senses prickling and his thoughts racing wildly. He cautiously let them reach out, explore possibilities as he made what he could of the information available. No hairs were rising on the back of his neck, or at least if they were it was not in fear but exhilaration. His skin wasn't crawling, but an incendiary flush roared over it that he was glad only he knew about in this heavy darkness.

'What the devil are you doing here, Kate Alstone?' he demanded as he finally found that tinderbox. It only took him about half a dozen strikes of the flint with suddenly very unsteady hands to get a spark and produce flame enough to light a candle, then a spill to put to the fire they were surely going to need.

'If you need me to explain that, my lord, then we're both in trouble,' she joked sleepily as she sat up to stretch and yawn and send his heated imagination into the ether. 'You're very late in coming home, Edmund.'

'Had I known you were awaiting me, I certainly would not have been.'

'Well, that's good,' Kate replied, still feeling rather astonished that she'd fallen asleep on his very comfortable bed and trying hard to gather senses that were only concerned with his presence and all the possibilities it raised. 'You don't look terribly pleased to see me, Edmund,' she finally managed to inform him a touch inadequately.

'You really don't want to know about that,' he muttered darkly and she smiled to herself as she just caught the tail end of an even softer, really inventive series of much-tried curses.

'Oh, but I do,' she murmured in what she hoped was a sensual drawl, but feared might have come out as a doubtful whisper, not doubtful about being here, just dubious about whether he actually wanted her to be.

'Never mind me, this is about you, Kate,' he told her far too seriously.

'No, it's about us.'

'What sort of "us" had you in mind?' he asked cautiously as if he wanted her to spell it out in humiliating detail before he took up all the implications of her being here in the first place and did something about it, be it yea or nay to her implied and perfectly shameless proposition that he take her to bed and ravish her until the stars faded and she must steal home with the dawn.

Now there was enough light to see as well as sense him, she watched his face for a few clues as to how he was feeling about her intrusion and saw the strained tension about his mouth, the weariness of his shadowed eyes and wondered if she'd chosen the wrong night to come here after all. Then she called on all she knew of him and sensed the avid hunger in him, probably laid bare by that very tiredness, and saw the slight shake in his hand as he fed the fire he'd lit. No, it hadn't been wrong, she decided triumphantly, it had been perfectly right. If not, he'd have sat by it, so tired and jaded by the events of the evening that he couldn't sleep as he brooded over the whole wretched business detail by detail, just in case he could have done something differently, something that would have saved such bitterness and despair for Lord Tedinton and his unfortunate family.

'This sort of us,' she informed him huskily and she surged up off the bed and came to stand in front of him with shameless boldness, meeting his gaze with everything she'd come here to tell him tonight in her eyes.

'Stay here like this, Kate, and I won't be able to keep my hands off you for much longer,' he warned, as if that was a threat to her and not a promise and she put out a tender hand to outline his face as if still learning him in the darkness he'd just dispelled.

'I'd be highly insulted if you could,' she told him as she got to his mouth and felt it firm even more under her butterfly touch, as if that was the only way he could keep it from doing exactly what she wanted it to, which was ravishing her from her fingertips to her toes and back again—even if she was a bit foggy about the most intimate details in between.

'I can't control the need I have of you enough to be restrained and careful with you tonight. You must go, Kate, while I can still let you,' he whispered as if to speak out loud might snap his leash and let out all the pent-up desire for her that he'd subdued for so long and she'd been so afraid they'd finally killed between them.

'I don't want your control any more, Edmund,' she told him through lips that were so ready for him they'd gone full and pouting and soft and eager for the matchless taste and feel of his against hers in anticipation.

Deciding he could have all the explanations and justifications and logic his male mind needed afterwards, but not now, she impatiently breached the gap between them and let her body argue for her. At least it knew what it wanted, even if he was too much of a gentleman to do as she longed for him to and seduce her until she was mindless, beyond thought and caught up in this huge new continent of experiences she and her lover had what felt like for ever to explore.

'I just want you, my love, so please will you seduce me before dawn breaks and this all gets a lot more complicated and public?'

'Even more complicated than it already is?' he said

would-be coolly, but she felt the shock jar through him at those two words, the sudden change from that weary edge in his husky voice to an energised, utterly present lover without a tired bone in his body. At least that eagerness soothed her jumping nerves at making that bold statement of fact. *'My love?'* he echoed as if unable to quite believe his ears.

'Yes! Now will you just kiss me and get on with making me and you into that "us" we just talked about? We only have a week for our clandestine affair, because if you think we'll have any chance of loving in every sense of the word under Kit's roof once he gets me back to Wychwood, then you have far too sanguine a nature, Edmund Worth.'

'I have a very hopeful temperament,' he told her with the hint of a laugh back in his voice. 'Heaven knows, I've needed it badly enough these last three years.'

'Edmund!' she protested and glared up at him with demand and need and just that slight edge of temper in her eyes.

'Kate,' he breathed her name as if it was a promise; 'Kate,' he repeated as he brought his lips so close she actually heard herself keen an inarticulate invitation. 'My lovely Kate.'

Impatient for now of the reverence in his voice, even while she took it in and stored it up to gloat over later, she licked her lips and slyly brushed his with her tongue as she did so. Instantly she was engulfed in fire and need and joy as he took her mouth in a kiss that abolished thought for both of them.

She had those transforming, sensually matchless

kisses from the night of the Wyndovers' ball to warn her, and entice her, of what a difference making love with Edmund might make to the very essence of her life, but that night she'd still been unaware of so much. Now she felt the heat of him, the hardness of him and wanted everything, all of him, all over her. She stretched against him, blissfully butting curves and long, lushly sleek limbs against the dense-packed muscle he somehow managed to fit on to his deceptively lean frame. With nothing held back, she had the sheer luxury of being able to explore him boldly. Running her hands over his powerful shoulders, she felt those muscles loosen and unknot under her hands, then change again and flex as he shifted to hold her even closer and smoothed his own exploring hands over her eager body.

He melded her even more intimately to him by widening his stance, bringing one leg round to draw her explicitly against the hard maleness he made no effort to disguise from her. Wriggling wantonly against him, she gasped an inarticulate, greedy moan against his plundering mouth and let her hands wander lower, over the cleanly streamlined narrowness of his waist to appreciate the tight male buttocks that were braced with the weight of both of them as he curved her even more closely, yet more intimately together. Even this wasn't enough, this wasn't someone else's book room or a terrace where other lovers might be too close by; this was my lord's bedchamber where nobody would interrupt them until morning, and probably not even then. The presence of that wide feather bed lured and promised and intrigued her more than any other bed ever had in her life. There they could explore, discover and experience so much more that she almost wished he'd stop kissing her and learning her inch by tantalising inch long enough to get them there without any further ceremony.

'Hmm,' she managed inarticulately when he raised his mouth from hers long enough to gasp in an unsteady breath.

Feeling his lips curve against hers, she wondered what the infuriating man could find at all funny about a perfectly sensible comment. She frowned, then pouted, then paid the price by having her lower lip oh, so gently nipped, then soothed with his tongue and explored until that inarticulate murmur turned into a long feminine moan of pleading she'd never even thought could leave her own mouth before she realised she was all his and he was hers.

'I can just about stop now, if I have to, Kate,' he told her huskily, even as his lips seemed unable to put more than a half-an-inch gap between his and her mouth to say it. 'I've waited so long for you, I could still just about wait another month until we're married,' he told her and the words sounded as if he had to think about shaping every one with truly Edmund-like determination, because any words but love words and lovers' murmurs had no real meaning between them in his half-lit bedchamber in the still watches of the night.

'You might be able to manage that titan feat of self-control, my lord, but I can't,' she told him, her turn to feel the foreignness of everyday language on her tongue as she wriggled against him as seductively as she could with only instinct to go on, her hands busy again all the while as her fingers tugged incompetently at buttons as if they'd never felt or heard of them before. 'Ham-fisted,' she scolded herself grumpily.

'Just as well if you never seek employment as a valet, then,' he joked distractedly, but seemed to abandon his over-gallant attempts to save her from herself as he used the gap created by her attack on his waistcoat to palm her firm, high breasts and light another level of conflagration within her.

Through the workaday cambric of a dark morning gown she had no idea why either she or her maid had packed at the time, she felt her breasts seem to rise and swell under his fascinated hands. Nipples already peaked and tingling seemed to heat and pebble even more under his sensitive touch and all she wanted was to feel his skin on hers, his hands hardened and calloused from the reins as he rode these last few days for her, for her hand, for her promises, for her as his wife. But tonight, this was for her as his lover, his woman, his blatant, burning desire for her and hers for him and that had nothing to do with all the pomp and panoply of aristocratic alliances and settlements and contracts and stern-eyed trustees.

At last she fumbled enough buttons free and triumphantly shucked the two halves apart, even making the sacrifice of losing his wicked exploration and the awesome stimulation of his spread palms, and the delicious almost pressure of his fingers padding against her nipples until the quicksilver heat deep inside her was becoming almost an unbearable pleasure pain.

She would have twisted her body and pressed her legs together in an attempt to appease it, if his very obvious arousal hadn't been too temptingly already there and hard against for her to relinquish. So instead she moaned again and her shallow pants of breath made a light descant against the urgency of his deeper breathing as he searched for control of himself and her wriggling and shifting against him in protest made that arousal even mightier.

His turn to forget what buttons and buttonholes did as he fought the wretched things into submission where they ran down her back. Luckily she'd had to helpfully leave some undone when she'd put the dress on, since she couldn't reach so high up her own back, so at least it didn't take his fingers as long to learn how to undo the rest again as it had hers. But she was making up for it by divesting him of most of the buttons his shirt had ever rejoiced in before tugging it from his evening breeches and forcing him to stop his attentions to the rest of her wretched gown in order to shrug out of the fine lawn and draw it over his head to throw it somewhere it certainly deserved to be sent for coming between Kate Alstone and her compelling lover's intriguing torso.

Content to explore the delicious novelty of satin-smooth skin over iron-hard muscle, and play with the light dusting of golden-brown hair that adorned parts of his torso in such an interesting way as she'd never even let herself dream of, she felt him push, persuade and tug her gown off her shoulder, then slide it off her fingertips until even the sleeves finally gave in to his touch and fell away. With the gown a heap of soft fabric at her feet, it took him mere seconds to shuck her out of the flimsy chemise that was all she'd thought necessary for this particular nocturnal visit.

All but naked, she stood a little apart from him to let them both appreciate the fact. Shockingly, she didn't feel in the least bit shy to have his hungry eyes devour every detail of her as if he couldn't learn her fast enough or comprehensively enough for his taste. His hands were on her even as her arousal and the burning, wet heat between her legs protested that, whilst she was naked all but for a pair of soft-soled slippers, he was still an impeccably dressed, if very obviously aroused, gentleman from the waist downwards. Then the feel of his roughened palms on her bare skin spun all thought of anything else but the pleasure of his touch away.

The pad of his strong fingers now tantalised her narrow waist, then moved up to rest just below the swell of her breasts and he must be able to feel the shallow breathing the sweet tension of waiting for more provoked in her, because his hands were suddenly warm on her rib cage, almost as if he'd share the very process of breathing itself with her. At last he moved and those tantalising forefingers of his outlined the curve of her lower breast against that rib cage and then went up around to test the rich swell of them without allowing them the luxury of touching her nipples, until she thought she might burst into flame if he didn't put his hands to work on them at last. Then he was there, still exploring delicately, still with one finger, to outline an amber areola as if describing female perfection, if the awed wonder in his willow-green eyes was anything to go by.

He flicked a fingertip across her pebble-hard nipple and she gasped and lost the use of her legs. Luckily he knew, knew what he was doing, what he'd just done and plucked her out of her fallen skirts and her satin slippers and into his arms, against that delightfully hair-roughened chest, so this time it was her turn to feel his breath stutter and then hurry under her skin, except her skin was not an interrogating, arousing, tantalising digit; it was a peaked and already overheated breast and the vulnerable indentation of her waist and she couldn't even think to where the curve of her bottom was brushing against him, inviting and anticipating so much more.

'Stop wriggling, woman,' he demanded in a voice so husky she hardly recognised it, and promptly wriggled a whole lot more in the hope of hearing it rasped and hoarse with need of her once again.

'I like it,' she told him, casting him a look of heavy-eyed invitation she really hoped he couldn't refuse.

'Maybe you do, but there's a time and a place for everything,' he husked and the sound sent shivers down her exposed spine and made her snuggle against him even more determinedly. 'And this is it,' he told her as he set her on the bed and stood a little back to watch her with such a blaze of need and fierce joy in his eyes that she felt any last maidenly qualms melt away unmourned.

'Oh, it is, it is indeed, love,' she said softly.

'Love indeed,' he echoed and finally shrugged out

of his breeches and stripped off his fine evening stockings and kicked his elegant evening shoes into some corner his valet would doubtless tick and tut about in the morning.

Chapter Sixteen

If the sight of her had made him gasp, her first sight of a naked man, a living, breathing naked man who, unlike the famous classical marbles at Wychwood, was very obviously and very fully aroused, should at least have made her blush, she supposed, in a brief nod to her otherwise very proper upbringing. He stood, all narrow hips, long strong limbs, leanly muscular torso and wide shoulders, his muscles taut and golden-brown skin stretched smooth and warm over them, and looked at her with eyes that asked her not to find him alien or impossible now they were so far along their road that turning back would probably leave him racked with pain and frustration, as well as doubting them as lovers and unsure of her all over again.

A rush of love hit her and something much more earthy and passionate, and perhaps yes, that was part of love as well, she decided as it scorched through her and she let her awed, delighted eyes meet his and describe it all for her. She met his gaze with all the feminine pleasure she felt in rousing him so emphatically absolutely on display; the urge to move under his gaze like a blatantly sensual wanton shook her for a moment and she considered the more modest alternative before dismissing it and writhing against the silky velvet under her sensitised skin, as if the feel of it might compensate her just a little for the lack of him there instead. She raised a hand to caress the long line of her own waist, leg and hip and heard a feral growl as he sank down beside her, face savage with need and dominant with denial that anyone should pleasure her tonight but him, even if the one doing it was herself.

She gave him a smug smile and a look she hoped said, 'Well, and what *are* you waiting for then?' and withstood the answering storm with a delighted welcome. Now his fingers were intent on stoking her arousal as high and hard as his own was obviously driving him, for they didn't play and tease so much as rouse and imprint her with his touch, his longing, his possession and she revelled in it all. His mouth was ravenous on hers, as if he'd somehow manage to quench years of longing for her into one storm of wanting, for now. She met it, set her tongue to dance and flirt with his, spared a hand from learning his broad back to stroke it down the side of his face as they kissed as if they couldn't bear to stop.

She knew his face so well, had thought she had his features off by heart, and yet learning them with her fingers was so much more intimate, so much more than just looking. He watched her eyes with his as their mouths melded and moved. She felt the way his taut skin stretched over high cheekbones and lean cheeks, traced his determined jaw as he flexed it to take their kiss even deeper, to tangle up her senses in him even more potently. Willing and active in her own seduction, she raised that finger to trace the edge of one eyebrow, the silky tips of his unfairly lush eyelashes, and her insides melted at the intimacy of it, the power of it. She loved him, and at last she knew it, so she let it show as openly as she could, along with the heat and wanting, the delicious burn of arousal and the thrill of sensual curiosity. Seeing the way his irises contracted, then expanded again as he blinked in the face of her unguarded gaze, she wasn't at all surprised to feel him shift her against him as if he couldn't wait any longer, had lost the ability to be infinitely patient with such a wanton virgin when she clearly didn't want him to be patient any longer.

He lowered his head to trace open-mouthed kisses over her jaw and down the slim throat that stretched and luxuriated in every touch; meanwhile he slid one hand down her waist and spread it over the springy curls at the vee of her thighs, sending a confident finger to explore the hot wetness between her legs, the intimate ache he knew would lie at the heart of her. That touch suddenly seemed a delight and a torture as he stroked and thrust and her body took up a rhythm she hadn't even known it knew by instinct alone. She writhed against the silky bedcover, tried to lock her legs together to hold back the tearing heat within, but he raised his head from sucking on her mercilessly aroused nipple and his eyes asked for her to trust him, even if he seemed as beyond words as she was.

Reminding herself that she would very likely follow him into hell itself if she had to, she relaxed her muscles, let his wickedly knowing hand work its magic and her head fell back as a melting rush threatened to overwhelm her, even while his fingers drove her even further along an urgent, sense-stealing journey to something beyond any words she had to describe it. Striving against it even as she wanted to plunge straight into that hot compulsion for more, she mewled in protest so he seized her mouth again and echoed the driving rhythm of his fingers against her most secret core and she shattered. Her body plunged and bucked under his touch and her heart pumped and sang as she shot into a new world of shattering pleasure, but she came back from it feeling oddly lonely, fulfilled yet not quite full of joy.

'Now,' he promised hoarsely as he positioned her pleasure-soaked body to accept as much of the weight of his as he'd let her, whilst he leaned most of it on his arms and used his knees to centre his rigid arousal at her heated, still-throbbing core.

Nodding frantically as she felt the weight and the potential and the potency of him, she let him raise her knees slightly and splay them to make her even more open for him, then she ran her hands over his striving body as he thrust into her and felt him shudder with delight and relief as she managed to take him, open to him even as the strangeness of being so full, so stretched made her marvel and exult in every extra iota he inched into her. He came up against the barrier he'd been testing for so carefully at last and she waited, trusting him with the taking of her virginity, waiting for it, longing for the loss of it even as she knew it would hurt. Using internal muscles she hadn't even known she had, she flexed about the fact of his starkly aroused shaft within her and heard him give a great gasp of half protest and half elation as he breached her maidenhead and buried himself in an intimate joining that took the jagged pain away in the sheer marvel of it. Cautiously she learned the full fact of his penetration and the potency of him so hard and deep and broad inside her, and then she met his eyes with wonder in her own and smiled a full, womanly, rather smug smile at him.

'Witch,' he told her with love and tenderness in his eyes, as well as what she now recognised as rampant lust, and he withdrew most of his length from her with a teasing look as she gasped reproachfully, then he gave her a wolfish, triumphant smile as he sank into her again and went even deeper this time, until she felt utterly possessed and filled and on fire for more, even while she wondered incredulously how there could be anything more than this.

Which he proved to her there definitely was, with as little treading on eggshells while he did so as she wanted of him. He thrust into her in a surging driving rhythm she learnt and matched and travelled with him as they strove for that beckoning fulfilment he'd taught her already, but this time it would be everything she'd felt wistful for not having the whole of last time, for this time he would be there, too. Kate felt her body begin that spasming of her inner muscles again that this time she knew indicated she was nearly at the peak of all this glory, but now she had his wondrous silky hardness fully engaged inside her to make them complete, drive them on together. He thrust more deeply as the beat of their bodies changed and went deeper and even more driven, until she cried out in desperation before finally, richly, witlessly she tumbled into deeply satisfied glory as he arched over her in an ecstasy that shook through them both with its fierce intensity.

Still taken to that somewhere wonderful he'd taught her was theirs by aftershocks of exquisite feeling, racked with delight such as she'd never dared consider possible even in her wildest dreams, Kate came back to herself with her lover slack muscled, love-shot and gloriously heavy against her tingling breasts as he laboured to catch his breath in her arms and reassemble himself somehow. She felt the delicious weight of him, still passion-dazed as he rested far too briefly on her satiated body and reviewed the last half hour with smug appreciation. Her love, her lover and her future husband stirred in her arms and shifted so he took his weight off her delight-fully stretched torso, despite her incoherent murmur of protest. He raised himself from her and tried to disen-gage fully, until she locked her legs about his waist and refused to part with this new and astounding connection to him, although he was now but half-aroused within her and inclined to be far too gallant to do anything to remedy the matter.

'I'm too big for you, you'll already be sore in the morning, my love.'

'Maybe, but now I want you inside me, and I never want to let you go,' she told him seriously. 'We belong,' she managed to explain herself rather inadequately in her own eyes, but it seemed that he understood her as he flipped her over. She lay splayed over him, still locked together and content to just be so for a while, to feel and preen a little at their own extraordinary cleverness in finally finding each other, then wonder at what they'd just done so thoroughly and so very well every pore and sinew still sang with remembering such an exquisite shock of pleasure.

It didn't last above ten minutes, that state of half-spent contentment as she rapidly proved how right she was not to heed his warnings while she experimented with that novel position he'd put her in and found it was excellent for rousing half-exhausted lovers into reinvigorated, rampant and demanding ones. Lazily Edmund ran his hands over her hips and cupped her buttocks until he could push her forwards a little, bowed over him until he could recline against the pillows and plunder her breasts like some luxuriating potentate being fed exotic fruit by a doe-eyed houri, or so she informed him when she could find enough breath from panting at the new bloom of hot need his very skilled attentions were rousing in her all over again.

'Can you ride astride?' he asked wickedly and she flexed her lithe legs and arched her supple back to show them both that she could indeed.

It proved to be the most exciting and mutually satisfying form of exercise she had ever discovered. They were both far more breathless at the inevitable lovely end of it than she'd ever been from such a wholesome, almost innocently illicit pleasure as riding astride over the peaks and moors, when she was told she was far too

old to run wild over her grandfather's estates in such a
hoydenish fashion. Now she reflected, as she finally felt
him disengage from her, then felt him tuck her slack and
utterly relaxed body against him with a contented sigh,
she knew that had been her way of keeping wild Kate
Alstone alive until she could safely be herself again in
her lover's arms. With a richly satiated murmur of assent
she felt those arms close about her, as if he couldn't bear
the thought of parting from her any more than she could
of leaving him, as she surely must now the dawn was
already lightening the sky.

'Why, my Kate?' Edmund asked her at last.

'Because there wasn't another way to let you know
how I feel and have you believe me body and soul,
Edmund,' she told him as she thought back to the very
moment last night when she'd known she had to go to
him. She'd had to prove that she now loved him absolutely, passionately and with every wild impulse and
wayward emotion she'd smothered and denied for so
long.

'I might have taken your word for it,' he told her as
he ran his silver-green gaze over her as if he couldn't
help looking and looking again, just to make sure she
wasn't a very fevered fantasy, or a delicious, desperately
dear dream who might still desert him.

'But one day you might have doubted us; you could
have stood apart from our so-convenient marriage and
your wildly passionate wife on that day and wondered
what if? What if you hadn't been such a gallant fool and
rescued me from my folly and loneliness that night, what
if it was just as convenient for me to say "I love you" to

my husband when we were bound together for life as it was to adore what we did together in our marriage bed? After I got past that awful thought and knew I loved you body and soul, Edmund, I had to find a way to let you know beyond any doubt that it's you I want and need and that I'll only ever be a shadow of a woman without you. I woke up to what we are to each other at last and how could I not come to you when you're everything to me?'

'Oh, Kate my love, you humble me. I had so many words stored up for you against the one-day fantasy I spun about you from the first moment I set eyes on you. You made the rest of that ballroom look like an etching in black and white compared with the full glorious life of you and I wanted you so much it hurt.'

'I know, I'm such an *idiot*,' she chided herself.

'You're my idiot,' he told her with an insufferable smile.

'I most certainly am,' she informed him just as smugly, 'and you're mine.'

'I'm yours, full stop, or your personal idiot?'

'Both,' she told him mock resentfully as he tipped her off the bed and stood up himself, knowing day was all but here and they had to part.

'I don't want to leave you, Edmund,' she told him with her feelings for him naked in her eyes, her body so changed by the love they'd shared that she felt every inch a mature and beloved woman as she stretched and yawned and met his eyes with her own full of sleepy sensuality.

'You have to. I don't know how I'm going to smuggle

you out of here without anyone knowing you've been here in the depths of the night as it is,' he told her and aimed a mock slap at her buttocks as she wiggled them as provocatively as she could while reluctantly retrieving her filmy chemise and donning it with a sensuous shiver as the fine silk caressed much-loved curves and whispered over sensitised breasts and hid her reverently manhandled body from his hungry gaze.

'Too late,' she told him without noticeable shame. 'I didn't sneak in here when nobody was looking and hide in corners to get here last night, Edmund. I walked through the front door and your butler and I had a very interesting conversation about interior decoration and future domestic arrangements while he conducted me impassively upstairs and informed me solemnly that all the staff would be retiring early and rising late.'

'The old rogue,' Edmund said, seeming quite torn between awe and indignation that the stately Lawson could be quite so devious, quite so complicit in such scandalous behaviour on the part of a single lady and his unsuspecting, if deeply delighted, master. 'I ought to pension him off.'

'That man is not going anywhere until he wants to. He's nearly as big a fraud as our Coppice under that chilly manner he cultivates so carefully and I like him extremely for it.'

'Not too extremely, I hope,' he joked and her heart danced that he could do so easily with her at last. 'Ah, well,' he went on, 'at least we'll still have him to help us out when we have to cook our own dinners and sweep our own floors, because the rest of my staff have discovered what a scandalous household they're going to be living in from now on and have left for more respectable quarters,' he said cheerfully.

'I'm never going to be able to go back to being coldly polite and proper with you, Edmund, even for the sake of your household and our personal comfort, so please don't ask it of me.'

'Of course not, how could I expect or want you to be anything other than who and what you are, my Kate? But I won't let you come to me like this again, love, for I care about your reputation even if you don't. I nearly cost another lady her good name and her prospect of a good marriage once because of a few indiscreet rumours and a careless act or two and I vowed never to do so again. Certainly not with the female who matters to me more than the rest of womankind put together.'

'She was the one Lady Tedinton pretended to be for some twisted reason of her own, I suppose?' she asked as coolly as she had it in her to risk questioning him in order to find out something she didn't want to know.

'Yes, and only for you would I risk telling a soul about it after that. Word somehow got about that I had been indulging in a liaison with a lady possessed of a Frenchified name and Selene Tedinton decided that I added to her standing in society as a lover very nicely, I suppose, and hinted that the lady was her. In reality I wouldn't touch her with a ten-foot pole, but Therese is a true lady and I couldn't refute Lady Tedinton's ridiculous posturing without revealing my one-time lover's true identity, especially now that Therese is very happily wed to another man.'

'Did you love her?' Kate had to ask, even if it might cost her more than she dared contemplate to hear an affirmative.

'Never. I still hurt so badly after making myself see I had not only lost you, but never had you to lose in the first place that I was incapable of loving another woman, then or now. But Therese was a widow and understood loss even better than I did at the time. We made the blankness easier for each for a while, that's all. I'm not proud of using another woman to block out my need of you, Kate, but you were very much unavailable on every level there can be between a man and a woman at the time.'

'I didn't trust what I had begun to feel for you then, Edmund, and it frightened me so badly that I managed to convince myself love didn't exist for me and that I would never let myself indulge in passion and its fell consequences as my sister had so disastrously. I suppose I needed to grow up and three years on, maybe I've managed to do enough of it to realise life is a gamble and, if you are to be my reward for taking a risk or two, then you're more than worth it.'

'Then you're willing to forgive me an *affaire* that was over two years ago, I hope, my love?'

'Only if you promise me solemnly never to look at another woman in that way so long as we both live on this good earth of ours and have each other to love,' she returned implacably, knowing she could trust him now as she should have then, but feeling that he needed her to be territorial and witchy about it all just the same.

'I'll promise never to do *more* than look if you like,

for I am a man, lovely Kate, and therefore fallible and foolish. But why would I risk doing more than feeling a brief moment of fleeting admiration for a lovely face or form as a wonder of nature, when I'll have the beautiful, passionate woman I've dreamt of in my wildest fantasies ever since I first set eyes on her in my bed every night for the rest of our lives?'

'I really couldn't say,' she managed demurely enough, but the look she slanted him beneath her eyelashes was pure invitation to take her to his bed once more and prove it to her very thoroughly.

'Stop it, witch. As it is, we can't risk any more daylight than this in case some fool coming home with the dawn sees me escort you back to the bed you should have been sleeping innocently in many hours ago.'

'I dare say I shouldn't have come,' she said, suddenly vulnerable and unsure of herself and him once more.

Kate wondered if she had shocked him by coming here, offering herself to him so blatantly that he could hardly refuse her brazen attentions without hurting her pride and her heart far more than he was capable of doing. He seemed suddenly able to read all her feelings and her fears though, for despite his stern resolution to get her home before daylight found them out, he strode over and took her in his arms to give her a reverent kiss full of promise as chaste as if they were both fully dressed and had a pack of interfering relatives waiting in the next room.

'Never say so, love, for I can't even begin to tell you how happy a man you made me by doing so, in defiance of all the conventions and your upbringing and

that cautious heart you once insisted on keeping as close
guarded as a miser would his gold. We'll find ways to
be together again before we're wed somehow, without
endangering your good name. I love you, Kate, with all
of me. Don't you ever doubt it or forget it,' he vowed
when he raised his head and watched her so seriously
that she felt tears sting and threaten.

'And I love you, Edmund. Most of me has done so
since we first set eyes on each other, but it took until
tonight for it to let the last little bit know about it.'

'Then that's all that matters,' he said with a boyish,
purely Edmund Worth smile she treasured and took with
her to gloat over as they stole downstairs.

He urged her out through the garden door into the
side streets and she fought the ridiculous urge to giggle
all the time they flitted hand-locked and still dreamy
and heavy limbed with such powerful loving, she covered with her cloak from head to toe like an illicitly
escaping princess, as she whispered in his ear when they
paused in a shadowy doorway to let a tradesman's cart
go past. They reached Pemberley House by a route she
doubted she could remember again if she tried, but as
he urged her silently to the garden door she had stolen
out of last night, she shivered and hated the very idea
of parting from him now the time had come.

'I'll come to see you as soon as I have snatched an
hour or two of sleep, then bathed and shaved, my lovely
Kate,' he murmured as if he could hardly bear to part
from her, either, and she leaned up to snatch a kiss that
he gave her back with interest. 'Go, before I undo all
the good we just did your previously pristine reputation

by coming back here so early in the day by being discovered making love to you in the shrubbery by one of Lord Pemberley's astonished gardeners,' he urged her with a mischievous grin that made her heart turn over with love for him.

'Goodnight, Edmund,' she murmured with a fatuous smile.

'And a very good morning to you, Kate,' he replied with a wolfish look.

'Oh, go away, you wicked man,' she chided obligingly and flitted through the door and shut it behind her.

Chapter Seventeen

Now she had just had the wedding she'd once secretly dreamed of, before Miranda's elopement put her off the idea of marriage altogether for far too long, and it had been every bit as wonderful as she'd believed it would be in her childish fantasies and so much more besides. Kate walked down the aisle of Wychwood Church on her newly made husband's arm and marvelled how the rituals and heady frivolity of the joyous family wedding she'd thought she would never have until a few weeks ago had meant so much to her. At last she was very much married to the potent gentleman strolling at her side like a sleek-limbed predator, agreeing to be tame only in so far as he chose to be. The feel of Edmund's firmly muscled arm under her fingers reminded her that, in marrying him and agreeing to all this, she'd given all she was and could become into his keeping, and what a powerful and passionate lover she was getting in return, she recalled with a delighted shiver that had nothing at all to do with wedding-night nerves or being cold.

'Don't worry, Kate,' Edmund reassured her with a wry smile. 'You're not as easy to read as you seem to think, so I dare say almost half the congregation don't yet know you're wishing them at the devil so we can be rid of them all the sooner and be alone once more.'

'I'm not that transparent,' she told him with a fine imitation of her old vexed frown. 'I'm not really, am I, Edmund?' she added, hating the idea of hurting her nearest and dearest, even if she did want to be alone with her new husband rather badly after three whole weeks of not being lovers in aught but her memory.

'No, love, you're managing to disguise it very well from most of them.'

'Kit knows, even if he's said nothing to either of us. I swear he knew what I was about from the very instant I set out to compromise you beyond all hope that night I came to your house and lay in wait for you like an overeager houri.'

'You looked more like a scandalously ardent lady, recklessly in love and totally unashamed to admit it to me,' he chided proudly as they paused on the threshold of the church by mutual consent. 'And I was never more pleased to see anyone in my entire life,' he added wolfishly.

'Luckily I'd never have wed you if I wanted a tame husband,' she joked back, but there was too much reality in her words and she wished she'd learn to stop her hasty tongue with him of all people. Now he'd finally freed her from even wanting to be the once cool and detached Miss Alstone, who thought all she deserved from life was an arranged marriage and a complacent husband, her impulsive nature seemed poised to get her into trouble at almost every turn.

'I don't think, oh, dear wild wife of mine, that you would have wed anyone else when it actually came down to saying your yea or nay,' he murmured and lowered his head to kiss her and halt the eager throng behind them with a sentimental 'ooh!' that Kate was far too preoccupied to hear for eagerly kissing him back.

Far from blushing and becoming pricklingly conscious of so many eyes riveted on them from within and without Wychwood Church, she rose on tiptoes to meet him mouth for mouth, lip to lip, and press herself so close that they were body to body as well. He was quite correct, of course, and had been all along; she would never have wed anyone but Edmund George Francis St Erith Standon-Worth, Viscount Shuttleworth, when it came to the stark fact of actually having to do so.

'Maybe you're right,' she conceded as he reluctantly raised his head. She noted with distracted surprise that she'd so far forgotten herself as to raise hands covered in fine white kid gloves embroidered with silver to muss his immaculately cut and ruthlessly smoothed hair into the curling pelt she loved so much, making him look very different from the grave young lord who presented a composed public face to the world. She was beginning to realise how wildly that image flew in the face of his truly passionate and headstrong nature, but not as wildly as hers once had in the face of one equally wayward and just as wild.

'Don't expect me to meekly agree with you all the time, though, from now on, will you, Edmund?' she warned him unnecessarily.

'Now, where would be the fun in that?' he asked with his face alight with anticipation, as if he could already taste the joy of making up after the fiery quarrels they'd surely have.

'There wouldn't be any, not without you, my love,' she told him happily.

'Are you two going to stand there blocking the door-way all day?' her chief bridesmaid interrupted impatiently and Kate turned to give her little sister a smug look, for she was so full of insufferable pride in her own achievement after finally netting the love of her life and the most eligible ex-bachelor of the *ton* that she didn't mind who knew it today.

'Just you wait until it's your turn, Isabella Penelope Alstone,' she warned. 'Then perhaps you'll know why we're doing it.'

'I shall certainly manage the whole business far more handily than you two have done and not take three years to get myself to the altar,' her sister told her briskly. 'Now, are you finally going to move out of the way before I get crushed from the back by this charge of well-wishers behind me?'

'Aye,' said Edmund, just as smugly, towing his bride out of the church door and into the warmth of the glorious June day before she and her sister could start pulling caps and then standing with her to proudly show the world what a fine and fair viscountess he'd caught on his wedding day.

Laughing as he answered the cheers and frankly expressed encouragement of the wedding guests and the many spectators who'd turned out to wish Kate and her groom well, he bowed to his newly made wife and smoothed his own dishevelled locks, before solemnly resuming his fine top hat at a rakish angle. Then he seized her hand again and placed it in the crook of his elbow as if he had no intention of letting it go for a very long time.

After a rush of delighted kisses for her and congratulatory pats on the back that he weathered manfully, Edmund stood ready to hand Kate up into the open carriage the estate workers had decorated with hoops of lush flowers and ribbons and the odd wedding favour that should have made her blush, but didn't. Who would have thought when she went about her reluctant husband hunt at the beginning of this Season that she'd come home with the love of her life instead? Not her, she realised with a wry smile of self-knowledge, as she watched his eyes go silver-green with the very sight of her so frankly besotted with her newly wed lord.

'You really are a very *convenient* husband, Edmund,' she told him wickedly.

'Climb into this carriage and stop tantalising me and I'll show you just how wrong you are about that epithet, darling Kate,' he offered with a lecherous leer that made her laugh like a schoolgirl.

'I do love you, you know?' she told him very seriously as she moved her hand in his so he could help her up at last.

'Yes, I do know that at last, and rather better than

you did yourself at times, if I remember rightly. Now be quiet, woman, and hurry up and throw that infernal bouquet at someone so I can kiss you properly.'

'Your wish is my command, husband,' she told him with mock humility and hurled the lovely thing with apparent carelessness straight at Amelia Transome, her second adult bridesmaid, who blushed and tried her best not to look at Edmund's best man, even as Mr Cromer managed to look conscious and proud and resigned to the direction his future happiness was to take all at the same time.

'Why not Isabella?' Edmund asked with only vague interest as the carriage pulled away and they waved to their many well-wishers.

'Because she can look after herself from now on. If she wants to marry, I dare say she'll do as she says and go about it in her own way, and if she doesn't, then she'll manage that just as she pleases as well. She asked me when she came to town to leave her to live her own life now and just get on with mine, Edmund, so I'm going to take her at her word and do just that from now on.'

'You did a very fine job of guarding her from harm when she needed you to, Kate. You were painfully young when you were left to protect and bring up your little sister virtually alone by those who should have looked after you instead, but she's a wonderful, bright and happy young woman now and that's mainly thanks to you. So here's hoping we make half as fine a fist of raising our own daughters when the time comes.'

'I like the sound of them, Edmund, so long as you give me a son or two to spoil and chide and love as well,' she murmured and felt her heart sing at all the lovely possibilities in front of her and her new husband as they finally drew away from the village and could concentrate on kissing each other at last.

'How long will it be before they all go home, do you think?' he asked huskily as they emerged from that protracted and passionate interlude to find they were already at the Court and the horses were still and the coachman impassive, as if they'd all been waiting some time for the bride and groom to come to their senses.

'Well, they probably mean to stay for several days and celebrate the birth of Kit and Miranda's son and heir in proper style, now they're all assembled and more than ready for a family party,' Kate replied with an affectionate glance behind her at the laughing, joyously smiling guests piling out of their carriages behind them.

He groaned and looked hunted at the very idea of being called upon to forsake their marriage bed so often, or even put off getting into it in the first place for what seemed likely to be far too many hours. 'I love your family, Kate, I adore both your sisters and esteem Ben and Charlotte Shaw as if they were your true family as well, and that's not to forget Eiliane and her marquis also, of course, but when can we finally quit them all for the time being and go home, my love?'

'In about three hours, Miranda and I thought,' she said, taking pity on him and herself, for it sounded more like three days to her as well just now when she wanted her husband nearly as urgently as he obviously desired his wife.

'Thank heavens for that, then,' he answered brusquely

and Kate loved him even more when he was being such a man and refusing to admit how much having all this fuss and family around them while they made the most important promises of their lives had meant to him.

'I might need to change out of all this finery after an hour or so, though,' she offered with not very believable innocence, because three hours sounded far too long after three interminable weeks of abstinence to her as well.

'And I'm working on my skills as a ladies' maid, so I might even manage to master that row of hooks I can feel running down the back of this infernally proper creation if you keep still long enough.'

'Later, my love, and my very impatient lover,' she chided softly, then squeaked with surprise as he seized her and ran up the steps with her as if she weighed far less than she knew she really did. 'Put me down, Edmund, it isn't even our threshold,' she protested.

Edmund grinned and continued to cradle his new wife in his arms while he got his breath back, then turned to watch his host with a laughing challenge written all over his face.

'Feel free,' Kit told him equably from where he stood with his arm about his own wife, who looked about as joyful as a woman could be without actually weeping for it, and Edmund for one was profoundly glad she'd refrained from doing that. 'She's all yours, Shuttleworth,' Kit told his new brother-in-law with a wave at the flushed, distracted, lovelorn Kate Worth who was trying not to laugh as she squirmed in her husband's strong arms until he bent his head to snatch a quick kiss and she stilled to kiss him back with a passionate concentration he very obviously appreciated.

'At long last!' Edmund shouted back. 'At very long last, my love,' he murmured far more softly in Kate's ear and carried her over the threshold to pause once more and kiss her very thoroughly indeed with a silent promise never to let her out of his arms for long, ever again.

* * * * *